One Lucky Summer

Summer

Jenny Oliver

ONE PLACE. MANY STORIES

HQ
An imprint of HarperCollins*Publishers* Ltd
1 London Bridge Street
London SE1 9GF

www.harpercollins.co.uk

HarperCollins*Publishers*
1st Floor, Watermarque Building, Ringsend Road
Dublin 4, Ireland

This paperback edition 2021

1
First published in Great Britain by
HQ, an imprint of HarperCollins*Publishers* Ltd 2021

Copyright © Jenny Oliver 2021

Jenny Oliver asserts the moral right to be
identified as the author of this work.
A catalogue record for this book is
available from the British Library.

ISBN: 9780008297572

MIX
Paper from
responsible sources
FSC™ C007454

FSC
www.fsc.org

This book is produced from independently certified FSC™ paper to ensure responsible forest management.

For more information visit: www.harpercollins.co.uk/green

This book is set in 10.6/15.5 pt. Sabon

Printed and Bound in the UK using 100% Renewable Electricity at
CPI Group (UK) Ltd, Croydon, CR0 4YY

For my sisters,

Leanne and Emma

CHAPTER ONE

Returning to Willoughby Park had never been at the top of Ruben de Lacy's to-do list. Now he was there, he recognised why. The rooms were as cold and dark as they always had been. Littered with ostentatious antiques and dustsheet-clad furniture. So far, Ruben had confined himself to just two rooms. A plain guest bedroom formerly known as the blue room for obvious reasons, and the kitchen, which had been rarely occupied by his parents when they had been alive; meals were always cooked by lovely Geraldine, a matronly figure who smelt of washing powder and sometimes onions.

From the cupboard under the stairs, Ruben had dug out his old wellington boots and Barbour and whiled away five minutes yesterday taking photos of himself by the giant stone lions out the front for Instagram, captioning the best: *Lord of the Manor?* It was amazing what boredom and being completely ill at ease in a place could bring out in a person.

Now he was sitting on the back terrace, soaking up some sun, waiting for the estate agent to get back to him, which was an ongoing battle due to the lack of phone reception. He was also struggling with a humongous black cat who seemed to have some wily point of entry into the house that Ruben hadn't yet discovered. To his horror, he'd found it asleep on his bed that morning. Oh well, it'd be someone else's problem soon enough.

The doorbell rang. Ruben sighed. Who was it? Someone to offer their condolences maybe? No, he couldn't imagine anyone in the village sad to have seen his father, Lord de Lacy, go.

Ruben yawned, stretched in the warm sunlight, then got up to open the front door. On seeing who was standing there, all he could say was, 'Oh, Jesus Christ. I completely forgot.'

'Yes, you did,' replied the woman on his doorstep, thin lips and beautifully coiffed blonde hair. 'Hello, Ruben.'

'Hello, Penny,' he managed.

Standing awkwardly next to his ex-girlfriend, feet turned out like a duck, eyes as saucepan-wide as they'd ever been, stood his eleven, no, twelve-year-old daughter.

'Hey, Zadie,' Ruben said with a lame half-wave that he regretted as soon as he'd done it.

'Hi, Ruben,' said the girl, smiling shyly.

Ruben looked back up at the ferocious blonde. 'I'm really sorry. It totally slipped my mind.' He winced as he said it, aware that one wasn't meant to say they had forgotten about looking after their daughter, in front of said daughter, who was sucking up every detail like an overzealous Dyson. 'Why didn't you ring me?'

'I did ring you but it went straight to answerphone. And I emailed,' Penny said, eyes narrowed, expression challenging.

As he had discovered trying to finalise things with the estate agent, the signal at the house was terrible. And Ruben doubted he'd updated Penny with his new email address.

'How did you know I was here?'

'Instagram, Ruben. Where does anyone look to find the vain?'

Ruben could feel himself blush as he remembered posing in front of the Georgian entrance columns in his flat cap and Barbour, and suddenly felt like a bit of a tool.

'When I didn't hear from you I was going to ask my mother, but she's taken a fall – she's OK, don't worry, not that you would. And as you know, but you've probably forgotten, I'm going on my honeymoon tomorrow – yes, I did get married, it was wonderful, thanks for asking.' Ruben had the inappropriate recollection that Penny hadn't paused for breath the one time they'd slept together either. 'And Zadie was insistent she stayed with you.'

They turned to look at Zadie, who was beaming up at Ruben, her sequinned rucksack glinting in the sun, her heart-shaped sunglasses perched on her head.

He tried to remember the last time he'd seen her. There was that dreadful time he took her to the Royal Academy of Arts champagne reception and she set the alarms off reaching for a Damien Hirst. Or was it when he'd lost her at the London Aquarium, which, while very stressful, had actually led to a pretty good date with the mother-of-two who'd found her.

The giant black cat appeared from the bushes and wound its way through Zadie's legs, making her giggle. Distracted from the current predicament, Ruben tried to unsuccessfully block its entrance into the house with his foot but the cat went in regardless. Zadie followed, delighted. Any further attempts Ruben might have made to evict the mangy animal were paused by Penny's authoritative beckoning for him to move out of Zadie's earshot.

Ruben frowned, one eye still on the enemy cat as he followed Penny down a couple of steps.

'I can't believe you forgot, you complete moron,' Penny hissed, dragging him further away by the sleeve. 'You'd better treat her right or I will kill you. And I mean it. Actually murder you.'

Ruben reared back, unused to people taking such a tone with him. 'All right, steady on.'

'If it was up to me, I'd have told her exactly what a loafing good-for-nothing you are, but that is not the kind of parent I am,' she snapped.

'I'm not a loafing good-for—'

She cut him off. 'I'm not interested, Ruben. Do you know how often she goes on and on about spending time with her *real* dad? Not that Barry isn't like a real dad to her, but there you go. You have two weeks, don't mess it up!'

Ruben looked from Penny's murderous ire back to Zadie lying on the floor with the cat on her belly. The sight of both causing him a great deal of discomfort. 'I'm not actually planning to stay here that long.'

'I don't care where you go, Ruben, as long as you take her with you, you can go to the bloody Bahamas if you want. Just stay away from St Tropez because that's where I'll be.'

'Nice choice.' Ruben loved St Tropez.

'Please focus on the task in hand,' Penny sighed. 'Here's her suitcase.' She hoisted a pink Hello Kitty suitcase up the front steps and plonked it down next to Ruben. 'She's a vegetarian now ...'

Ruben rolled his eyes.

Penny ignored him. 'If the worst comes to it just give her cereal, she loves cereal.'

4

'I love cereal,' Ruben said, pleasantly surprised.

'Well, there you go, perfect for each other,' Penny said curtly, and without pausing for breath turned towards Zadie and said sweetly, 'Darling, Mummy has to go now. You'll be good, yes? Anything you need, you call me.'

'OK,' Zadie said brightly, scooping up the cat and coming over to give her mum a kiss goodbye.

'Erm, hang on a tick—' Ruben tried to interject.

'You'll be all right, yes?' Penny bent down so she was level with her daughter.

Zadie nodded.

'It's only two weeks,' Penny said, seeming to reassure herself more than anyone. Then she glanced uncertainly from Zadie to Ruben and added, 'It's not too late to change your mind, honey.'

'Absolutely, it's not too late,' Ruben agreed.

But Zadie went to stand by Ruben's side, still clutching the fat flea-ridden cat. 'I'll be fine. *We'll* be fine! We'll have a great time,' she added, placing her soft hand in his.

Ruben held it awkwardly.

Penny pursed her lips. 'Mmm.'

Zadie laughed. 'Honestly, it'll be fine.'

Ruben felt his face get warm. 'Penny, listen, I think we should …'

But Penny ignored him and gave her daughter a giant hug, the cat squashed between them, determined not to give up his new-found ally.

'Penny, really …' Ruben said a little more urgent now.

'Like I said, I'll kill you,' Penny hissed.

'OK, OK,' Ruben held up a hand to ward her off.

Penny blew Zadie lots of kisses and called, 'Bye, honey. I love you,' while beeping open her BMW.

'Have a good honeymoon,' Ruben shouted with saccharine insincerity.

'I will,' Penny called back, her tone equally false. 'Look after her,' Penny ordered as she got in the car.

Ruben did a bored nod as if he'd got the message.

Penny was looking worriedly at Zadie, who called, 'I'll be fine here with Dad.'

'Ruben,' Ruben corrected.

'Ruben,' Zadie giggled like it was a joke.

Penny shook her head like he'd failed at the first hurdle.

Twenty-four hours in, Ruben had failed at the second, third and fourth hurdles too.

All he wanted was a second on his own. Half an hour tops and he'd be happy. He had wondered more than once if it was possible to take the batteries out of a person. When he'd gone to bed he'd been so exhausted he'd fallen straight to sleep only to be woken up at seven o'clock sharp with her standing over him, dressed in a multicoloured unicorn onesie saying, 'Me, my mum and Barry all read together in the morning. Barry gets up and makes us both a cup of tea, like every day, without fail.'

'That's nice,' Ruben had replied, bleary-eyed. 'I don't drink tea.'

'You don't drink tea?' And she was off. By the time he'd managed to locate his dressing gown and fumble himself to a sitting position, he'd found out that Aunty Janice drank seventeen cups of tea a day and Uncle Peter couldn't understand the obsession with high-street coffee when you could have a cup of PG Tips for relatively free. Who were these people, Ruben wondered, and why hadn't they taken Zadie for two weeks? As if on cue, 'They now live in Australia. Barry was really sad to see them go. He cried.'

'Did he?' said Ruben, trying to sound engaged. Ruben usually enjoyed a leisurely wake-up that involved a good stretch while Amazon's lovely Alexa brought him up to date with the news and what weather to expect.

'Barry says that real men aren't afraid to cry. Do you cry, Ruben?' Zadie was sitting on her knees on the bed.

'When was the last time I cried?' Ruben rubbed his forehead. He couldn't remember. By all accounts it should have been when he'd got the call to say his dad had died, but he knew for certain that there had been no tears.

The rest of the day with Zadie had carried on in much the same fashion. Question after question. Ruben longed for a glass of '52 Latour in his pants on the balcony of his London flat smoking a Cuban and indulging in some Radio Four quietly so the attractive Gen Z on the floor below didn't hear. Instead, it was Little Mix and Stormzy. Ruben had actually bought a pair of Stormzy tickets recently to impress a Tinder date but the affair had come to an end before said concert had taken place.

Outside it had started to rain. Huge great globs of water keeping them inside. The black cat sat forlornly soaked on the windowsill. Ruben didn't want to be confined indoors with his ever-present daughter following him round as he hauled open drapes in the various bedrooms just to get some light into the place.

'Ooh, this is nice, that's nice,' she said, picking things up, putting them down. She opened things and shut things, she dropped things. She broke things. 'Sorry, sorry!'

'It's fine, it's fine,' he heard himself say, growing increasingly tight-lipped while trying his hardest to remain relaxed. He caught his facial expression in one of the giant gilt mirrors and saw a flicker of his father in his agitated expression. Internally imagining, while a candlestick toppled as Zadie reached for a porcelain figurine, what his dad would have said had he done the same.

And if he heard another word about bloody perfect stepdad, Barry ... Barry who cried but also Barry who fixed things. Barry who was great at washing-up and could kick a football like a pro. Barry who built their extension single-handed and had the neighbours queuing up for one of his unique garden water features.

And she was always hungry. Ruben thought he was hungry a lot of the time, but this was another level. When the incessant moaning got too much, he drove to the Co-op at the petrol station, wound her up and let her go. Hence why, by dinnertime, they were eating Sugar Puffs standing up in the kitchen. 'My mum says we have to have dinner at the table, it's proper family time.' Ruben was too exhausted to listen. He closed his eyes and dreamed of his noise-cancelling headphones lying casually on his desk at his London flat. For a little calming self-indulgence, he furtively checked his Tinder, Instagram, Twitter and weather apps. 'Barry says we're not allowed phones while we eat.' Suddenly a drop of rain landed on his nose and Zadie said, 'Oh, you've got a leak.'

Ruben looked up to see a large grey damp patch on the flat-roofed kitchen ceiling spreading above them. 'Shit.'

'Shall we call Barry?' Zadie asked. 'He'd know what to do.'

The cat, who Zadie had brought in dripping and refused to

let Ruben evict, was asleep on a kitchen chair. It opened one pitying, disdainful eye, exacerbating in that look everything Ruben was feeling.

'Shoo!' he said to the cat, clapping his hands.

'Don't!' Zadie stepped between them but it made no difference, the cat wasn't going anywhere, it just curled back up in a different position.

The rain dripped from the ceiling to the tiled floor.

'I'll call someone,' said Ruben, getting his phone out and finding there was only one bar of reception. He had to go right up to the top floor to get anything resembling a signal. Zadie trotted after him. When he turned to question her shadowing, she said, 'It's scary down there on my own.'

Ruben remembered being terrified of the house at night. The creaking of the stairs. The hoot of the owl. His father's irate bark, *'For Christ's sake, leave him. Let him cry. No son of mine is a coward.'*

He called the emergency roofer. 'I'm sorry, sir, I can't really hear you. Tonight? Oh no. No one available tonight. We can be there first thing tomorrow.'

'Fine.' Ruben would just put a bucket under the leak for now.

They headed back to the kitchen, Zadie so close she was almost wrapped round his waist, followed by the thump of the cat. She caught him checking his reflection in the hallway mirror, an ingrained habit, and pulled his hand to make him pause.

'Do you think we look alike?' she asked, a little shy as she stood next to him. Her wide eyes and black-framed glasses. Plump, pink puppy-fat cheeks. Expression so open it was almost painful. In contrast, Ruben looked old. The other day he'd discovered his first grey hairs. His cleaner, Hildegard, had recommended a spray that women use to cover it up. There was nothing, he discovered, like spray-on hair colour to make you feel old. Standing beside Zadie he looked ancient.

'Maybe,' he said, non-committal, turning away before he could even consider resemblances. His body starting to envelop itself in a protective force field.

Zadie shrugged. 'I think we do.' Nothing was able to dent her limpet enthusiasm.

In the kitchen, the patch on the ceiling was getting exponentially bigger. The bowl he'd put on the floor was already full.

Zadie stared up at it, hands on her hips. Now she looked like her mother. 'It's got much worse.'

'Yes, I can see that, thank you.' Curse his life.

'Barry would know what to do.'

'I'm sure he would,' said Ruben, bashing about in the cupboard under the sink for a bucket.

'That'll fill up really quickly,' Zadie commented when he appeared with an old red one.

'Yes,' he muttered in agreement.

Then after a few seconds. 'I think the bucket has a hole in it.'

'Bollocks.'

'That's a pound in the swear jar.'

'A pound! Are you kidding me?'

'Some words are worse than others.'

Ruben could think of a million words he'd like to say but he couldn't afford it.

'When we had a leak once, Barry fixed it himself. He went out the skylight on to the roof. It was really exciting.'

'I'm sure it was.' Ruben replaced the broken bucket with the bowl and searched the kitchen for something more substantial.

The cat stretched and yawned, mocking Ruben's inadequacy. The rain splashed on another area of the floor.

'There's another leak!' Zadie was hopping.

'For Christ's sake!' As soon as he said it, Ruben flinched and stopped. He had his hands on his hips, his brow furrowed. If he looked in the mirror now he'd be the spitting image of his father. He took a deep breath, exhaled slowly like his yoga teacher had taught him. He could do this.

'Shall I call Barry—'

'No,' Ruben held up a hand. 'No, I'll do it myself.'

Zadie's eyes lit up.

Ruben yanked on his old Barbour and pushed his feet into his wellingtons, while Zadie slipped on her Converse. He was outside in the garden shed before he really stopped to consider what he was doing, pushing spiderwebs and plant pots out of the way to get to the ladder on the far wall. Something fluttered in the darkness, Ruben yelped as a bat flew out, making him jump, and Zadie laugh. He searched the shelves for a tarpaulin and something to hold it down with, finding a rusty staple gun in a box of old tools. Zadie held onto the bundle of plastic and the staple gun as Ruben swept away more cobwebs to haul the ladder out and up the path. The rain had slicked back their hair, soaking through his coat, getting in his eyes.

As soon as he'd stepped outside the house he'd realised it was a mistake. He wanted to go back inside. If Zadie wasn't there he'd have left the leaking bucket where it was and ignored the whole fiasco till a professional could fix it in the morning. He'd have just thrown money at the situation. But the deadly combination of her heroically capable stepdad and the memory of his own authoritarian father had propelled him into this ridiculous no-man's land as he tried to out-do one and banish the other, succeeding only in making a mockery of himself.

The ladder tipped and swayed as he extended it to its full height, hands slippery with rain, and propped it up against the side of the house, pushing the leaves of a buddleia out of the way and securing the base against a particularly vile faux wishing well, another of the garden ornaments for which his father had such a penchant.

'Shall I hold it?' Zadie asked, face soaked.

'Definitely,' said Ruben, as he tested the slippery ladder rungs, more reluctant now than ever to head up to the kitchen roof. Nothing but pride spurring him on. His wellingtons slid as he started to climb. The whole endeavour was foolish. But Zadie seemed to be enjoying herself. 'This is exciting, isn't it?' she grinned, little wet hands holding tight to the ladder.

Rain slicked his hair to his forehead. The staple gun weighed down his coat pocket. He had a folded tarpaulin under his arm. It was dark, the noise of the rain was deafening. He could see the dreaded black cat smugly stretched out along the kitchen radiator, not out in the pissing rain with a pointless point to prove. 'This is ridiculous,' he muttered.

'You can do it, Ruben!' Zadie urged him on.

He exhaled, slow and resigned. His wellie slipped as it caught on the rung and made him wobble. When he got to the roof, he held onto the gutter with one hand and leant forward to examine the felting. He should have brought a torch. What kind of idiot goes up on the roof in the dark and doesn't bring a torch?

Annoyed with himself, he looked down. It was quite a long way. Instead, he focused on where the hole might be by following the line up from the red bucket he could see through the almost ceiling-high windows, and started to staple the tarpaulin at random over the approximate area.

It was an ill-conceived plan and he knew it, but he couldn't back out now.

'Barry would be SO impressed. I'm not sure even he would go out in the rain.'

Ruben swiped the water from his eyes. 'You said—' but then he stopped himself, it was too petty. He imagined Penny catching sight of him in horror – he'd been tasked with being a responsible adult and looking after his daughter and he was precariously up a ladder in—

'Is that thunder?'

'Fuck.'

'That's five pounds!'

The tarpaulin was too big, buckling where he'd stapled it in crumpled lumps. He imagined his father watching with a sneer – *'de Lacys never show weakness, boy!'* Even more frustrated now, Ruben tried to flatten the tarpaulin, steadying himself on the gutter, stapling great pockets of the woven plastic. He stapled through his index finger at the same time as the cheap guttering snapped.

'Argh!' he cried, yanking his stapled hand back in shock. The plastic beneath his other hand shearing, his foot losing purchase and suddenly he was falling, sliding down the ladder, his hands grappling for hold, ungainly in his tragedy. Zadie's little face gasped in horror. Fear infused every pore of his being as his body whacked and thumped against the ladder.

The buddleia softened his fall. But it was the crumbling wishing well that took the brunt of the impact, smashed first by the ladder and then further destroyed by the weight of Ruben's body.

He felt a moment of triumph considering his father's passion for ornamental garden statues, but the triumph was short-lived as the bruising pain from the fall kicked in. Zadie was peering over him with a look of sheer and utter panic that he was dead.

'It's OK, I'm OK.' He sat up. His head throbbed. His back ached. Rain pelted his skin.

Zadie fussed around him. But Ruben just sat for a moment, staring at the broken old stones between his legs, thankful that the wishing well wasn't real otherwise he'd have plummeted metres underground, thinking enough was enough. He would leave for London in the morning. He'd get his cleaner Hildegard to babysit.

But then something among the rubble caught his eye. His brain was a little slower to compute as his hand reached to pick it up.

Zadie stopped fretting and asked, 'What's that?'

It was a little blue plastic box. Ruben hadn't seen one for years. It immediately brought back memories of unconcealed excitement. Of unfolding a square of paper. The staccato hand-writing in black biro. He remembered school holidays racing through the woods. Light flickering through canopies of leaves. The thrill of the chase. The crackle of bonfires. Waves crashing on the beach. The dart of something in the undergrowth. The goading, the fun, the triumph. The dares to reach out for antlers soft as velvet. The warmth of a darkened room. The flicker of a TV. Hot coffee. Illicit cigarette smoke. The throatiness of her laugh. The shocking green of her eyes. The scent of her skin. The humour of her gently mocking gaze.

My God, he must have had a knock to the head.

'What is it?' Zadie asked again.

Ruben's hand rested on the lid of the box, reluctant to open it as a strange mix of warmth and trepidation infused him. 'It's a clue,' he said, 'for a treasure hunt.'

'Ooh! Can we do it?' she asked, voice squeaky with excitement.

Ruben didn't reply straight away. Instead, he turned the box over in his hands, mulling over the possibilities and found himself suddenly less inclined to dash back to London. He looked across at his overeager daughter. 'The thing is,' he said, forehead creasing, 'it's not really our treasure hunt to do.'

CHAPTER TWO

'Don't look at me like that, Olive.'

Olive didn't think she was looking at Mark in any particular way. If anything, it was her complete lack of personal expression that she found perplexing.

'You know as well as I do it hasn't been working for a while.'

Olive was stumped. There was Mark, her partner of eight solid years, standing by the front door all packed and ready to go. If she hadn't come home from work early she'd have – she presumed – been notified via email. Mark didn't like to talk on the phone.

'Can you say something?' Mark said, hovering by the front door in a blue and white striped shirt that Olive didn't recognise.

'You're wearing a new shirt,' she said because Mark didn't buy new things. He wore the same jumpers he'd had in college. When she bought a new bed he didn't understand what was wrong with the one they'd inherited from his parents. Sweet, kind, ordinary Mark who made a lasagne at the beginning of the month and cut it into squares for the freezer. Mark who sat behind his desk in the spare room, head obscured by the piles of paper. Glasses falling down his nose as he peered into his microscope. Dishevelled, familiar. Too busy saving nature to care about his appearance. When he'd finally look up and realise she was in the room, he'd grin and say something like, 'Mitochondria, Olive. Gotta love mitochondria.'

Not now, however, now he was itching to get away, hair more coiffed than normal, wearing his new shirt, with his belongings stuffed into an assortment of Sainsbury's Bags for Life.

'Look, I'd better go,' said Mark, reaching for his bags.

'You can't leave.' Finally, she found her voice. One tinged with an edge of desperation.

'Olive,' he said, 'I think even if I asked you, you wouldn't be able to look me in the eye and declare your undying love.'

Olive opened her mouth but her voice was gone again. She frowned. Then she said, 'It's not about undying love, Mark, it's about what works. This. Us. We work.' When had the man who was the poster boy for honest, predictable dependability cared about down on the knee declarations of love? 'I do love you,' she said.

'No, you don't.'

'I do.'

But Mark shook his head. 'It's not enough, I'm afraid.'

Not enough? Olive thought of all the things they'd done together. The comfortable, reassuring routine of their lives. The way he folded his clothes before he got into bed. The smell of his deodorant. The mug he liked his tea in. Those things couldn't just disappear without consultation. The worst of it was, she thought with a flash of guilt, that if anyone in the partnership was going to leave, she'd always assumed it would be her. That she quite firmly held the strings.

A car horn beeped outside. Mark looked sheepish. 'I've got to go.'

17

Olive was still catching up. 'Who's that?'

'Just a friend,' said Mark, unable to meet her eye. 'Barbara.'

'Who the hell's Barbara?'

'Just someone I met.'

'Where?'

'Nowhere.' He twitched awkwardly. 'She's awakened something in me, Olive. Something I didn't know I had.'

Olive paused, looking at him questioningly, then went to peer out of the window of their ground-floor flat. A silver Mercedes was parked over the drive, at the wheel was a mousy-haired woman in a blue polka-dot top Olive recognised from a Marks and Spencer's advert. Not a boyfriend-stealing Jezebel but a perfectly ordinary citizen.

Olive didn't know what to do. She refused to cry although she felt more desperate than she'd have imagined. There was no paperwork to divvy up – they weren't married, the flat was rented, they had two months' rent put away for exactly such circumstances. She would give notice. The car was in her name because Mark rarely drove. It was all very simple. *'You're such a practical couple,'* people would say at parties and only now did it seem like an insult.

Swallowing down a wave of emotion, a sudden sadness that tonight he wouldn't be sitting on the sofa to watch Netflix with, she did the only thing she could think of, she opened the front door for him.

Mark looked at her. 'I'm sorry, Olive,' he said, eyes beseeching, before, head down, he dashed out to where Barbara was waiting in her Mercedes.

Olive leant against the wall. She had a vision of the sad squares of lasagne for one in the freezer. It was not, she said to herself, how this was meant to go.

The phone rang as Olive stood at the door to Mark's office in the spare room. Her vision tunnelling as she took in the sight – piles of stuff on every surface, papers lining every shelf, a cheap office chair that he'd wheeled from the university when they were updating and giving the old ones away free. That was the Mark she knew. The one who this room smelt of.

The landline handset was under those papers somewhere, she could hear it. She didn't try to look for it because it was always someone trying to sell her something.

The answerphone clicked in. Olive stared at the overgrown houseplants on the shelves. The chipped mug still with half a cup of tea in it. The old microscope slides with toxic green mould all over them. The plastic pencil pot. The chewed biros. All the things she had found so endearingly simple. Now she just felt the emptiness of the flat. The cheap desk clock ticking the seconds.

'Oh hi. Hi,' said the voice on the answerphone, cut glass and a little awkward. 'This is a message for Olive King. Ruben de Lacy here.'

Olive froze.

'Long time no see, eh?' he laughed.

And suddenly Olive was frantically searching for the phone. Lifting papers, the movement causing a ripple effect, like the two-pence machines at amusement arcades. Piles of paraphernalia slid to the floor to reveal the phone on the edge of Mark's desk.

'Hello, Ruben?' she said, breathless, heart beating overly fast. 'How did you get my number?'

'Olive! You're there. I got it off your Aunt Marge. She's the only one of you with a listed number,' Ruben replied, his voice catapulting Olive back to a time and a place that didn't exist for her any more.

'Anyway, you'll never guess what ...' he was saying, an excitable girl's voice in the background shouting, 'Is that her? Have you got through? Tell her, tell her!' And Ruben, slightly irritable, 'All right, all right!'

The signal was terrible. Olive felt like perhaps this whole thing was a dream. That'd be a relief. Wake up, Olive. But Ruben carried on, 'I'm back at Willoughby Hall, Olive, and guess what I've found—'

'What?' Olive asked, brain torn between trying to catch up and simultaneously forget.

'The first clue, Olive,' Ruben's voice was tinged with amusement. 'For the treasure hunt. For your dad's treasure hunt.'

Olive almost dropped the phone. Ruben's line cut out. She sat on the edge of the desk trying to let her brain catch up with what was happening. She saw her family's little cottage on the Willoughby Park estate. Her dad beaming that he'd hit the jackpot. His explorer hat hung on the peg now for good. The adventures were over. He'd found his treasure. He was home.

Looking around Mark's shambolic office, Olive wondered what her dad would think of her now.

The phone rang again. 'Sorry about that, signal's bloody awful. So do you fancy coming down here? Do the treasure hunt?'

Olive didn't know what to say, everything going far too quickly for her liking. She could barely believe she was talking to Ruben de Lacy. 'I'm not sure,' she said, buying herself some time. The whole idea was madness. She couldn't possibly go on a treasure hunt.

'Come on, Olive.' Ruben laughed. 'It'll be fun. I can't do it without you.'

At the sound of his laugh, memories, supersonic like rainbows, sped past her, too fast to catch hold of. Too bright. A door very firmly closed.

He started telling how her he'd found the clue in a wishing well. As he talked, she got her mobile out and typed Ruben de Lacy's name into Instagram, curious about who he'd become. There he was, bold as brass. With a page open to anyone. The first shot was of him dressed in a Barbour and boots posing in front of Willoughby Hall, captioned, *Lord of the Manor?* Olive cringed; who was this guy? All floppy hair and cheesy grin. She could certainly handle seeing him if this was what he'd become.

She skimmed some more photos: keys to a new Austin Martin, selfie with a brunette in sunglasses on a Caribbean beach, cocktails with other equally floppy-haired friends, a box-fresh Peloton bike set up on a penthouse balcony.

Oh Ruben, she thought with a twinge of disappointment. Despite everything, he had lived up to the cliché of his parents' expectations after all.

It made her think again about her own dad. What *would* he think if he could see her now? Safe, predictable, no sense of adventure. *'You want something in life, Olive, you have to go looking for it. There's no such thing as X marks the spot.'* She imagined him looking down at her current existence with such dismay she felt her stomach curl in on itself.

On the other end of the phone, Ruben said, 'So what do you think, Olive? Want to find some treasure?'

And with the exquisite shame of her dad's disappointment so clear in her mind, Olive found herself replying, 'OK,' before her rational brain could stop her.

CHAPTER THREE

'OK, let's call for backup.' Fox Mason went to swap his binoculars for his police radio.

'Are you fucking kidding me?' In the darkness of the unmarked car, Dolly King's hair shone silver as she swung round to face him. 'If we wait for backup he'll be gone. I've waited six months for this moment.'

Fox lowered the radio. 'So what are you going to do? Storm the place on your own?' He huffed a laugh. 'You don't know how many people are in there. You don't know if he's carrying a weapon. You don't know—'

'You don't know, you don't know, blah blah blah,' Dolly cut him off. 'I know the little shit isn't carrying a weapon because he hasn't carried one for the last six months. He's too much of a wimp.'

Fox let her annoyance hang in the air. The words left like a large puff of smoke to float in the confines of the car specifically to embarrass her. They were sitting in a black Audi down a Lambeth side street where pigeons pecked chicken bones on the pavement.

'Dolly, he's not worth the breach of protocol. Believe me.'

In her head Dolly was repeating the words 'believe me'

in a babyish imitation of Fox's voice. He was so annoying. This was their first week on the job together and everything he did put her back up. Just the way he held the radio pissed her off, bringing it to the opposite side of his mouth than the hand holding it, the same way drama students used to smoke cigarettes at college.

Dolly was itching to get out of the car.

'You're not going into that flat alone,' he said, like he could read her mind.

She glanced out at the net-curtained window of the second-floor flat they were watching. 'Are you forbidding me?' Dolly ran her tongue along her lip, watching Fox all calmly amused, feeling her blood surge.

The streetlamp above them kept flickering. In the black sky the moon was just a fingernail sliver.

'Yes, I'm forbidding you,' Fox said, raising the radio to his mouth again. Big arm muscles bulging under his black T-shirt. 'You go in there alone, you risk the entire investigation.'

Dolly watched as he started to speak into the radio. He made her skin bristle. All pumped like he spent every second grunting over free weights but kept his voice permanently calm. Before that moment there was no way she would have actually gone into that house alone, she knew the risks, but something about his disallowing her pushed her over the edge. 'He's not stupid enough to hang around. He'll be out and gone before you're finished radioing it through. And then the entire investigation is shot anyway,' she said, pulling on her cap. 'You forbid me? Just watch me, asshole.' A second later Dolly was out of the car and in a crouched run across the street.

'Dolly, get back here!' Fox whisper-shouted. 'Jesus Fucking

Christ.' He was out of the car and behind the bonnet. 'I am *not* coming in with you!'

She was hidden behind a big black rubbish bin that reeked of fish. Something spilt on the floor made her trainers stick to the pavement. 'Fine,' she hissed back. 'Get back in the damn car and wait.'

Fox swore under his breath.

Dolly watched the window on the second floor. The net curtain twitched. The little shitbag was on edge. It was his grandmother's flat. It was her birthday. She'd bought him up. Dexter Smith had dropped off the radar for the last couple of weeks, just when they had enough evidence to arrest him, but Dolly's instinct told her that he wouldn't miss Granny's big day. She wondered if whatever rubbish present he'd nicked for her was worth it.

'Dolly, you are not going into that flat alone!' Fox was running across the road in her direction.

'Fine,' she called back, heading for the double entrance doors. She knew the lock had been broken for months. 'Come with me then.'

She could feel Fox behind her. 'You're going to get us both suspended.'

'Don't be such a pussy.'

'That's the most pathetic comeback.'

Their whole interaction was in hushed whispers. Dolly sniggered. She was enjoying herself. Enjoying seeing him riled. She had visions of herself snapping the cuffs on Dexter's skinny wrists, all smug as she paraded him past a fuming Fox.

She sprinted up the stairs.

'Dolly, stop!' Fox ordered. 'Do not go in that door.'

Technically, he was her superior. But the job had been as good as hers before they brought him into the team. The official line was that he was the best and they couldn't pass up the opportunity to have Fox Mason in their squad. The real reason was that Dolly's boss thought she still had some growing up to do. Which was bullshit. She'd worked her ass off for that job.

'Dolly!' Fox hissed, creeping up the concrete staircase behind her. Layers of thick cream paint on the walls and a million health and safety signs.

But Dolly was in front of the door with the polished knocker shouting, 'Police!' before Fox could stop her.

She knew it was a mistake the second she kicked the door in. There was Dexter's granny pointing a WWI twin-shot musket at her while Dexter himself leapt out of the kitchen window.

'Hold it right there!' Dolly shouted at Dexter, just as Grandma loaded the barrel of the musket, threatening, 'I'm not afraid to shoot!'

Dolly was pretty certain the grandmother *was* afraid to shoot, but Dexter was already gone. Jumped two storeys down onto hard concrete.

Dolly turned smack into Fox. 'Go!' she shouted. 'Go, he's jumped!'

'For Christ's sake!' snapped Fox, and both of them legged it down the stairs.

'You leave my boy alone!' the grandmother shouted behind them.

'I'll be back for you for possession of a firearm,' Dolly shouted as they slammed through the front doors and sprinted round to where the kitchen window dropped down to the back yard.

Dexter was getting into an ancient brown Ford Fiesta that obviously belonged to his granny. He'd hurt his arm from the fall and was reversing at haphazard speed out of the space while clutching his arm to his chest.

'Get in the car!' Fox shouted.

'I'm getting in the car!' Dolly hollered as she threw herself into the passenger seat.

'You're a liability,' he said as he sped deftly out of their spot after the Fiesta, blue lights flashing, while radioing for backup. 'Christ.'

Dolly sat next to him, fuming.

He drove really well. Much better than her, which was even more annoying. Almost robotically focused.

Dolly's skin was tight. She leant forward. 'He's cutting down Winsmore Avenue.'

'I can see,' Fox said, all calm authority.

Dolly tapped the dashboard. 'Shit,' she muttered. Replaying the events in her head. Seriously, what had she expected?

Fox stared straight ahead, zeroing in on the erratic Fiesta.

Dolly wanted him to shout at her. Wanted some kind of reprimand so she could shout back in her defence.

But he just drove down the starkly lit back streets, staring straight ahead, refusing to engage.

Ahead of them, the Fiesta suddenly swerved sharply round an intersection by the town hall and doubled back so he was now heading away from them.

Dolly had to grip her seat as Fox followed suit, turning hard and fast with a screech of tyres on warm tarmac, siren blaring, just as a group of teenagers pouring out of a club thought it would be funny to intercept the chase. They staggered into the road yelling and shouting. 'He didn't do it!' one of them called, top off, shirt tied round his waist, laughing as he stood on the middle white line, waving his arms.

'Watch out!' Dolly shouted.

But Fox had already seen him and turned the wheel hard right to avoid slamming into the kid. The force of the turn at full speed smashed Dolly's head against the window. Then the whole car flipped one-eighty and they careered down a side street on the roof for fifty metres until they crashed into the wire fence of a twenty-four-hour parking lot.

Dolly was still in a daze, hanging upside down, when Fox reached forward and turned the ignition off. 'Happy?' he said.

Her shoulder felt like someone had swung an axe through it. 'Ecstatic,' she replied.

DCI Brogden had skin that turned mottled purple when he was angry. Today, even the top of his bald head was a blotchy mauve.

As he listed all of her offences, Dolly wondered if he knew he turned that colour. Had he ever looked at himself in the mirror when he was furious?

'And not least the car, which is going to cost us God knows how much. You're a bloody liability, King. I've said it before and I'll say it again. A liability!'

Dolly found it really annoying when people said things like: 'I've said it before and I'll say it again.' Why say it again? She heard it the first time. And don't get her started on 'To be fair' or 'One hundred and ten per cent.'

'Are you even listening to me?' Brogden snapped, right close up to her face. Dolly could smell the Nescafé Gold Blend on his breath.

'Yes, sir,' she said, fighting the urge to turn away.

'For crying out loud, you're lucky you're both not standing here dead. But to be fair,' Brogden paused, 'I'm not sure I care about losing you any more, King. Fox on the other hand …'

Dolly glanced across at where Fox was standing tall and pumped next to her, face impassive. He had a giant black bruise down the side of his face with a cut that ran from eyebrow to jaw and a big dressing on the inside of his wrist to patch up the gash he'd got freeing Dolly from the car.

Fox had wrenched her jammed door open to haul her out, petrol dripping onto the road, people filming on their phones, Dolly's dislocated arm hanging from its socket.

'You want to pop it back in or shall I?' Fox had asked, as Dolly stumbled delirious from the pain.

'I'll do it,' she said stubbornly, hardly able to stand.

Fox said, 'OK,' then grabbed her tight and clicked it in anyway.

'Jesus mother of God!' Dolly screamed, clutching her shoulder like someone had just chain-sawed it off.

Fox said, 'All done.'

Dolly vomited all over the pavement.

At the station, Brogden was still sounding off. Ranting and raving. Dolly's throbbing shoulder made her woozy, but there was no way she was going to give him the satisfaction of asking to sit down. Fox did an excellent impression of looking like he was listening. Maybe he was.

'I've warned you before, King, that you need to grow up,' Brogden was behind his desk again, voice now one of resigned disappointment, 'but you never listen. I don't know what else I can do for you.' He shuffled some papers, no longer looking at her. The batteries on the wall clock had died and Dolly watched as the minute hand kept trying to move beyond the number six but dropped back every attempt. She could empathise.

'Fox,' he said, glancing up, 'I'm sorry you're even involved in this, but I'm afraid my hands are tied. Both of you are suspended from duty until further notice.'

'What?' Dolly gasped. 'You can't—' She wanted to point out that backup had arrested Dexter Smith two hundred yards up the road when the Fiesta had run out of petrol outside Iceland. That wouldn't have happened had Dolly not kick-started events.

Brogden held up a hand to silence her. 'I can and I will. Someone has to teach you a hard lesson.'

Dolly was about to argue again but he shook his head. 'I don't want to hear it. Dolly, get the hell out of my sight. Fox, I want a word.'

Dolly blew out a breath, incensed. 'Yes, sir,' she said with curt annoyance before stalking out the room past Fox, who remained focused straight ahead.

But she didn't go far. Instead, she paused and leant against the wall outside Brogden's office to listen to what else he had to say.

'Take a seat, Fox.'

'I actually prefer to stand,' Fox replied. 'It helps me think.'

Dolly rolled her eyes.

Brogden said, 'Suit yourself.' Dolly imagined him having to stand up and go round to talk to Fox. He'd feel weird addressing him from the chair. Face to face, Fox was a good head taller. It was a clever tactic for alpha-ing the chat.

'I didn't want to have to suspend you for this but my hands are tied.'

'As you said,' Fox replied.

'Yes. You're one of the best we have and I will do everything I can to make sure this doesn't affect your record.'

'Please don't grant me any special favours, sir. I'm happy to take full responsibility for my mistakes.'

Behind the wall, Dolly made a face. He was so smug.

Brogden went on, wrong-footed by Fox's self-possession. 'Good, fine. OK. Well I er …' He paused, Dolly could hear him pacing. 'I put the two of you together because I thought you might be able to knock a bit of sense into her, given your record.'

Dolly bristled. She fought the urge to march back in but she knew her position was precarious enough.

'I can see it was a waste of time,' Brogden said. 'A mistake *I* can take full responsibility for.'

Fox didn't reply.

Dolly was tempted to peer round the doorframe to catch his expression. What was he thinking?

Brogden lowered his voice a touch, still trying to lure Fox firmly onto his side of the fence. 'What I will say is serve the suspension, just get it done, and when you're back we'll fix you up with someone new. Steer well clear of Dolly King. Yes?'

There was a pause.

Dolly found she was holding her breath.

Then Fox said, 'Yes, sir.'

And Dolly shook her head, thinking how they were all the same, but unsure what else she'd been expecting.

*

The sun was blinding as Dolly walked down the front steps of the station, her arm throbbing as the painkillers wore off. Her hair was in a weird side-ponytail, unable to tie it up one-handed. She had trouble getting her sunglasses on, eventually undoing one of the folded arms with her teeth. She had a Sunkist from the vending machine. She hated Sunkist but it was the only drink in a can and she couldn't undo the top of a bottle. The last thing she needed right now was to walk into the rec room and have to ask the likes of Mungo or Rogers to unscrew her cap. Especially as news of her suspension would have filtered giddily down ranks, they'd love it.

She took a seat on a brick wall that surrounded an old chestnut tree, the bark scratched with initials, and a bike chain that had been there so long the trunk had grown round it like an overspilling belly.

In her pocket, her phone buzzed with a message. It had been buzzing the past couple of days but as always, she never had the time to answer it. Now she had all the time in the world.

She'd been suspended. She couldn't believe it. She tipped her head back against the tree but realised it hurt her shoulder, so sat up straight again. What had she been thinking?

She struggled to pull her phone out of her pocket. The screen was a stream of unanswered messages. WhatsApp groups that rolled on without her. Text messages lost in the abyss. Voice notes that seemed to have come into fashion without her even knowing about them.

She listened to her messages. All very boring. She drank her Sunkist. Far too sweet with a nasty aftertaste. She watched an old woman haul her shopping trolley onto the bus as no one else in the queue offered to help.

'Hi there, this is a message for Dolly King, it's Ruben de Lacy here.' For a moment, Dolly couldn't breathe. 'You may remember me, from Willoughby Hall? I got your number from your Aunt Marge – who incidentally has asked me to tell you to call her back.' He laughed, low and rumbling.

Dolly stopped listening. She was engulfed by the sudden memory of perfect white teeth and dappled sunlight on beautiful tanned skin. Brown hair, just slightly too long so it curled back off his face. Sharp straight nose. Mouth that tipped up in the kind of smile that knew all your secrets. Thick dark lashes and hooded lids over eyes so dazzling they used to keep her awake at night, pained by their beauty. She wept once out of the pure desperation of wanting him to touch her. To pull her so close that she would be engulfed by the scent of the expensive washing powder Geraldine the housekeeper used on his clothes, and the aftershave he'd nicked from Harvey Nichols on a shopping trip with his mum just for something to do. He told them stories like that as if they were nothing, when to Dolly they were the whole world. She would write them down then rip the page out of her notebook and post it into the money box she had that couldn't be opened unless smashed. Like she was storing a secret version of him that one day might come true.

'Dolly, I'm calling because I've found a box in the garden of Willoughby Hall with the first clue of your dad's treasure hunt. The one he ... you know? Anyway,' Ruben coughed, 'I've spoken to your sister ...'

Dolly winced. The bubbles of the Sunkist gave her a pain in her chest. She had visions of soft winter sunlight patterning through snow-laden branches and little boxes hidden in tree hollows. Long grass crisp with frost, robins and red berries, deer antlers strewn with bracken. She saw her sister, Olive, with her long streaming hair, red lips and big clumpy boots up ahead with Ruben, running faster than Dolly could catch up. The pair of them tearing open a clue while Dolly wailed and her mother stroked her unruly hair and told Olive to wait for her sister next time.

Sitting by the chestnut tree, outside the police station, Dolly felt her cheeks get hot at the exquisite sharpness of the memory.

'Dolly?' a voice said behind her, and she swung round to see Fox. The movement made her wince again in pain.

'Don't get up,' he said.

'I wasn't going to,' she replied, touching her cheeks, hoping they weren't red, not wanting him to see her caught off-guard.

Fox chuckled as he took a seat next to her on the wall.

'How's your shoulder?' he asked.

'Hurts like hell,' she replied, finishing off her drink and chucking the can into the rubbish bin three paving stones away diagonally.

'Nice shot.'

Dolly said, 'How's your wrist?'

Fox leant forward, elbows rested on his knees, and examined the dressing on his wrist. 'Bit sore,' he said, then he glanced her way and added, 'Brogden's going to do everything he can to get rid of you.'

'I know,' Dolly replied.

Fox contemplated for a second then said, 'I'd like to help you.'

Dolly scoffed, edging away from him with a look of disdain. 'I don't want you to help me.'

Fox smiled as if this were the answer he'd been expecting. 'Dolly, this is what I'm good at, it's what I'm trained in. Helping people.'

Dolly was perplexed. 'I don't want anyone to help me. There's nothing wrong with me. If anything, you're part of the problem.'

Fox shook his head, calm and unaffected. 'I'm not part of the problem.' He leant back, stretched his arms up, then clasped his hands behind his head. 'Dolly, anyone could sense the disquiet inside you.'

Dolly shook her head in disbelief. 'If you say so, oh wise one.' She stood up to leave.

'Seriously, Dolly,' Fox looked up at her, moved his hands so they were resting open in his lap, a move to show magnanimity that he'd probably learnt on some online life-coaching course, 'I'm probably the only person who can save your job for you right now.'

It took everything she had not to mimic the sentence back at him like a child. 'Well maybe I don't want to save my job,' she replied pettily, looking away at the sun reflecting off the peeling foiled windows of the police station.

It was Fox's turn to laugh. 'Please. You live for that job.'

Dolly couldn't think of a smart reply quick enough. The truth as stark as it was depressing. She did live for that job. This guy had been there all of a fortnight and he could see that. She knew the curve of the station door handles better than she knew the front door of her flat. She knew the stains on the stairs, the chips on the staff kitchen counter, the mug she liked best and hid at the back of the cupboard, the sound her locker made when she swung it shut, the irritated silence when she nailed someone like Mungo with a perfectly timed put-down, the warm pints at the Lion and Leopard in the sunshine, the morning briefings, the keys to the car, the feel of her badge in her pocket. Holy shit. Her heart rate was through the roof. She could not lose this job.

Fox sensed the moment of weakness and stood up himself, towering at least a head taller than her. 'Let me help you,' he said, expression coaxing like she was a fish on the cusp of the bait.

Dolly stared straight at him – the faux sincerity on his face, the perfected patience. 'No,' she said defiantly.

'Why not?' he asked.

'Because I don't like you,' she replied tartly, and picking up her bag started off up the street.

She'd thought that would be the end of it. With any normal person that would be the end of it. But not Fox, clearly. She could hear his big steps bounding up the road after her. She could hear the laugh on his breath.

'I'll have you arrested for stalking,' she said as he fell into step next to her.

'No officer in this jurisdiction would arrest me,' he replied, all cocky grin as he flipped on his sunglasses against the glare. 'So why don't you like me?'

'I don't want to hurt your feelings by telling you,' she said, looking straight ahead as she walked on.

He laughed again. 'I like you.'

'Good for you,' she said, annoyed that she got a kick out of hearing that about herself. 'I like me, too.'

Fox's lips twitched in amusement. He dodged an electric scooter coming towards him. 'Get off the pavement, mate,' he shouted after the rider. The guy gave him the finger. Fox sighed.

Dolly kept walking in the direction of the Tube.

'So what are you going to do for your probation?' Fox asked. 'Sit around sulking?'

'How well you know me,' she said, one brow arched.

He smiled. 'I think I've got you pretty well sussed.'

Dolly searched for a response that would wipe the smug smile off his face and found herself saying, all cool and aloof, 'If you must know, I'm actually going on a treasure hunt.'

'Are you?'

Was she?

'Yes,' she retorted as Ruben de Lacy's face flashed up in her mind, making her swallow down a shuddering wave of trepidation. The piercing blue gaze that looked at you and you alone. The easy smile. The affable flirtation. She felt a wave of nausea. No. There was no way she was going to do that. The only reason she might go on that bloody treasure hunt would be to show Ruben de Lacy who she had become. That would give her some satisfaction. But it wouldn't be enough of a reason to go back there. Not by a long shot.

Dolly looked directly at Fox, challenging him to call her a liar while his expression searched for cracks in her story, ways for him to wiggle himself in and take his do-gooding hold. She knew his aim, it was all so he could saunter back to the station and say, 'Guys, I did it. I broke in Dolly King. She's as sweet as a kitten now.'

'Yes, Fox, that's what I'm doing,' she said, nose in the air, defiant. 'Not that it has anything to do with you.' Then she spun round, weird side-ponytail swishing against her face, and marched off towards the Tube station.

'I get it,' he called after her, hands on his hips. 'Running away. Nice. Good tactic.' As she got to the entrance, she heard him shout, 'You can only run for so long, Dolly!'

Before going through the ticket barrier, Dolly turned and shouted back, 'Your pop-psychology won't work with me, Fox.'

The echo of his laugh followed her all the way down the escalator.

CHAPTER FOUR

The sound of Ruben's voice and the mention of her dad had sparked something inside Olive – an excitement, a desire – that she hadn't felt for years. Perhaps what mousy Barbara had sparked in Mark.

She passed the familiar sights of her childhood the further west she went along the A303, the battered sign to Wookey Hole Caves, Exeter Airport, Dartmoor National Park. Excitement fighting with apprehension in her belly. Four hours of podcasts and she was down to one about sparking joy by finding different ways of looking at life. Out of the window she noted that the Little Chef they always stopped at whenever they were going up to London was now a Starbucks. Where was the joy in that? No toasted teacakes and Coke floats, just corporate globalisation. Except, if she were forced to find a bright side, she did quite like the Starbucks logo and her dad always said the Little Chef's attempt at an espresso wouldn't even be recognisable as coffee when compared to the stuff he drank in Istanbul or the rainforests of Brazil.

Maybe she could find similar joy in her current state of unexpected singledom. Maybe it was a blessing – a light shining on the life she'd been living and finding it wanting. Maybe it was time to admit she'd been doing it wrong all these years. That made her think of Ruben, which she didn't want to do. She cancelled that by remembering his tacky Lord of the Manor pose on Instagram.

Olive pulled in at the Starbucks. The queue was really long and the espresso was horrible. Maybe finding joy wasn't so easy.

Her phone rang. Olive had to stifle a sigh; it was Aunt Marge.

'So you're on your way to Willoughby Hall? How exciting. Is Dolly going?' Aunt Marge was Olive's dad's sister. They'd lived with her in London as teenagers. She spoke as fast as she lived her life. No time to waste. Her jewel-encrusted hands always gesticulating wildly, her bright red talons tapping on the table, her skin sunbed mahogany.

Olive chucked her cup in the bin. 'I don't know.'

'Have you spoken to her?'

'She doesn't answer her phone.'

'Why doesn't she answer her phone?'

Olive yanked open the Starbucks door and headed back to the car. 'I don't know, Marge, why does Dolly do anything?' She stopped herself adding, *I'm not her babysitter.*

'True, true. OK, I'll give her another ring. Maybe pop round. You have fun.'

Olive got to her car, feeling her anxiety levels rise at the mention of her sister. 'I'm not sure it's going to be that fun, Marge.'

'You might be surprised.'

Olive had learnt over the years that there was no point arguing with Aunt Marge. Their chats were always perfunctory. She got in the car. 'I've got to go, I'm driving.'

'OK, ta-ta, love.'

It was the final leg of the journey and the road ahead seemed endless. A hawk on a telegraph pole. A tractor in a field. The sun was sharp and bright through the windscreen. It was warmer than it had been all summer. The verges were lush with wild-flowers after the almost non-stop spring rain. Then suddenly there was a sign for Willoughby Park. The paintwork worn and chipped, the word CLOSED stamped across it.

Olive sat up straighter at the wheel, her heart beating like crazy. She pulled her sunglasses off as she took the familiar turn up the main path on instinct, the big metal gates propped open, she presumed for her. It was so weird being back. Everything identical yet nothing the same. She slowed, almost to a crawl as she saw the great sprawling parklands that swept over hills and down valleys as far as the eye could see. The famous four-hundred-year-old oaks, the grazing deer, the Jurassic ferns skimming the surface of the black water lake. And in the distance, the Big House – Ruben's house – all cream and Georgian with its sweeping front steps and high polished windows, big stone lions and manicured garden with a flopping white magnolia that bloomed for a fortnight then morphed into a monster of rotting brown flowers.

How perfectly it all fit with her memory. She drove on slowly, winding her window down, hit by the smell of fresh-cut grass and salty air. It was like jumping into a photograph. She could see ghosts of people who weren't there, hear their voices, hear her own voice. Adrenaline tickled over her skin.

In the distance she could see the sea and felt an expected jolt of sadness. She could picture vividly her family's cottage down there by the rocks. She was prepared but – as her dad used to say – you can never be one hundred per cent prepared for anything.

The sight of Ruben de Lacy and a small girl racing down the path was enough to snap her back into the present.

It was definitely his daughter. They looked identical, except the girl was a lot less self-aware. Ruben was exactly like his Instagram. All swagger and cool. Slicked back hair, achingly on-trend sunglasses, wearing a black shirt and a pair of lime-green shorts that should have been a fashion disaster but which somehow he managed to pull off.

He directed her to a space outside the house and then came and stood by the window of her car, whipping off his super-cool sunglasses, grinning. 'You made it!'

He had the same bashful smile and radiating ease, but with more lines round his eyes, Olive noted as she climbed out of the car. It was strange who people became – in retrospect all the signs were pointing to this smoothly self-assured adult version of him, but it was still unexpected.

The little girl was hopping with excitement next to him. 'I'm Zadie,' she said, and thrust out her hand.

Ruben did a quick, 'Olive, this is Zadie, my daughter. Zadie, Olive – who as I've explained used to live down at the cottage by the sea and is the owner of the treasure hunt box.'

Olive was still trying to process the fact that Ruben de Lacy had a daughter. Not only did he have bachelor written all over him but if Ruben had children she'd have presumed they'd be the type who wore tiny Ralph Lauren trainers as babies and had their own YouTube channel as teens. This girl was all puppy fat and saucepan-wide eyes with a very eclectic taste in fashion.

'Hi,' said Olive, arm outstretched as she shook the clammy little palm. 'Nice to meet you.'

'You too.' Zadie clutched her hand firmly. 'I don't see my dad that often, just so you know, this is all kind of new. My mum's just got married, in case you were wondering. Ruben's not like with her any more. Not that they were ever married. You're really pretty.'

Olive and Ruben seemed to be equally dumbstruck by the download of information. Ruben however, clearly more used to it than Olive, was the first to recover his composure. 'Well, there you go,' he said. 'Everything you needed in a nutshell. And more.'

Olive suppressed a smile. 'Fascinating,' she said, and Ruben raised his brows to convey a shared astonishment.

It was such a tiny gesture but it made Olive blush. Oh my God, she hadn't blushed in years. She couldn't believe it. She looked away, walked round to the boot of the car to get her bag.

'Do you have children, Olive?' Zadie asked, immune to any undercurrents.

'No,' said Olive, a little bamboozled by the directness of the question.

'Zadie, you're not really meant to—' Ruben tried to keep her in check, but Zadie was having none of it. 'Are you married?'

Olive held in a smile. 'No.'

Zadie trotted along next to her as she went to grab her handbag from the front seat. 'Boyfriend?'

Olive shook her head. For the first time in eight years she said, 'No.' How strange it was to be back to square one. Like a prop was missing. Things she hadn't really thought about, like how driving five hours on her own was exhausting when there was no one to share it with.

'Girlfriend?' Zadie questioned, hands clasped behind her back.

'No.' It was Ruben who answered for her. 'Unless …'

Olive shook her head.

Zadie glanced between them. 'Ooh, did you two used to be a couple?'

'Blimey, Zadie, that's enough! Be quiet.' It was less jokey, more scolding from Ruben.

Zadie looked abashed.

Olive noted the tension between Ruben and his child.

Ruben, however, glossed over it by clasping Olive by the shoulders and giving her a kiss on the cheek that smelt of toothpaste and Hugo Boss. 'Great to see you, Olive. You look amazing.' He raised a brow in appraisal. 'Very sophisticated.'

Olive was suddenly very conscious of her clothing – her black cigarette pants, her white trainers, her gold wishbone necklace, and her white shirt, still fairly crisp after the five-hour drive because it was a staple of the collection of technical luxury fabrics she designed and created. The company took high-quality natural fabrics – cotton, silk, linen, wool, cashmere – and blended them with more versatile fibres, making them more suitable for everyday but without any synthetic feel. Wool that didn't shrink. Silk and linen that didn't crease. Cashmere that didn't need to be dry cleaned. Or as the company's copywriters put it: *Because you deserve luxury, every day.*

She had come up with the idea sitting at the kitchen table of Mark's flat as she watched him eat Bran Flakes in a bobbly old woollen jumper that looked like it had once belonged to his father, and a shirt underneath that he was in the endearing habit of only ironing the bits that poked out. Back when they had had long discussions into the night about politics and science. When his dishevelled scientist persona was a refreshing contrast to her fractious city life. When the fact he batch-cooked lasagne was novel rather than expected. When she'd proposed her idea to him, he'd mulled it over and said the science was possible, in fact, it was the first time he'd been actively engaged in anything she was working on. All the other times he'd looked on a bit bemused and said, 'Fashion is just beyond me!' This time, however, he'd sat with her for hours as they went deep into the technical construction of the new fabrics. It was nothing like the crazy, avant-garde stuff Olive had worked on at art college, nor was it like the couture fashion job she had at the time, but there was something warming and addictive in the interest it provoked in Mark, she had enjoyed working with him on a project. They had been good times, sitting at the small kitchen table surrounded by ideas and papers and endless cups of coffee, both of them a little high on the obvious commerciality of the project. The end result was clever and unique enough, when paired with her focused, clean-lined designs, to catch the eye of a luxury fashion conglomerate who bought the idea and the brand, and where she now worked as one of the creative directors and had worked for the last six years. Mark, who always erred on the side of caution, had encouraged her to take the money and the job offer. Olive had been on the fence. There was no guarantee, had she not sold the idea, that she'd have been able to make it anywhere near as successful – in fact it was highly unlikely – but some days she'd stare at the glossy ad campaigns and the revenue spreadsheets and think how once it had been just hers.

She enjoyed her job. The clothes *were* demure and sophisti-cated. Just as Ruben had said. But somehow, right now, being back at Willoughby Park, standing in front of Ruben in his bright green shorts and Zadie in her rainbow colours, it didn't feel like a compliment. It felt more like a disappointment. Like she was a walking embodiment of the safe, sensible life she had chosen for herself.

Olive could feel Ruben watching her; she'd forgotten his

knack for reading her every expression. Right now she couldn't look at him. 'Well, it's just erm ...' she didn't finish. Instead, she turned to Zadie in her tie-at-the-front blue hounds' tooth shirt, pink neckscarf and tomato-red mini-skirt and said, 'You look fabulous. I'm very jealous of that skirt.'

Zadie beamed. 'It's great, isn't it!' Linking her arm through Olive's and leading her into the house. 'I'll show you to your room because Ruben really needs to start cooking. It's like nearly dinnertime. Did you know, Olive, I'm a vegetarian and my stepdad Barry works in plant-based meat substitutes, and Ruben didn't even know what those were! Can you believe it?'

Olive said, 'No, I can't believe that,' to Zadie's wide-eyed incredulity, hyper-aware of Ruben behind her and his scrutiny of her every move. His presence was very disconcerting. He was the same but not the same. Less showy than the Instagram pics suggested. In certain lights and angles she could see the old him. But it was more in the mannerisms, the way he stood, walked, carried himself, even the way he tipped his head when he was listening. Oh God, she'd just have to try not to look at him.

Right now though, as she was dragged through the austere furnishings of the de Lacy residence – a place she'd only glimpsed through the windows or open front door – and engulfed by the musty scent of dust and sun-warmed polish, it all reminded her of voices she didn't want to hear and views that made her want to simultaneously stare and avert her eyes. She had never been more grateful for the inane verbal diarrhoea of Ruben de Lacy's estranged daughter.

CHAPTER FIVE

Dolly King spent most of the little spare time she had exercising or at home. Her flat was like a little haven. A microcosm of the Amazon rainforest, plants everywhere, hanging from the ceiling, in pots up the stairs, trailing along shelves and cupboards and down over the kitchen table. Her cat, Tabitha, appeared occasionally because she wasn't actually Dolly's cat, she was her elderly neighbour's, but her neighbour had five cats and Tabitha seemed to appreciate her own space. Dolly's bed was always made with fresh linen and her washing put away the minute it was dry because the flat was too small to have anything hanging around. Her clothes were just an endless cycle of police uniform and gym kit. She'd done triathlon for a couple of years before it got trendy and all the competitors became really annoying with their slick next-gen suits hunched over iPads obsessing over biofeedback that told them nothing more than that they simply didn't have enough grit.

Nowadays, Dolly preferred to train at Roy's boxing gym down the road where the idea of recording your data on an iPad would have you laughed out of the dirty, sweaty ring. Roy was about a hundred and four, was missing one of his front teeth, and sat on a folding chair hollering obscenities at anyone who wasn't puking with exhaustion by the end of a session.

Even a dislocated shoulder injury was no match for Roy, who stood her in front of a wooden bench and gave her sets of repetitive leg exercises that left her muscles trembling with lactate and exhaustion.

That was how Fox Mason found her. Sweaty and shattered.

'Oh, you have got to be kidding me!' Dolly shook her head in disbelief when she saw him striding up in black tracksuit bottoms and a threadbare white sweatshirt. She stood up from her scratched plastic chair, sweat streaming down her temples, hair slicked back damp. 'Seriously, you can't follow me places. We are not on duty. We aren't partners at the moment.'

Fox held his hands up like he was innocent. 'I'm just here to train.'

Dolly towelled her face dry. 'Yeah right!' she said, and then with faux surprise added, 'I just came to train at the exact same gym as the woman I'm stalking.' She rolled her eyes.

Fox shrugged, hands in his pockets, wearing his normal deliberately unthreatening half-smile. 'Coincidence is a funny thing.'

'Don't even try it.' Dolly couldn't believe he'd followed her there. 'Look,' she said, chucking the towel on the chair and smoothing her hair into place. 'I know you seem to have this knight in shining armour thing going on. And I know you want to prove to Brogden that you're some kind of hero, but you are not going to use me to get there. OK? So just back off. Go and do your weights at whatever swanky gym you usually go to and leave me the hell alone.'

She was just turning to get her water when Roy creaked to his feet and shouted, 'Fox! You old dog, get over here!' It was the first time she'd ever seen Roy crack a toothless smile.

Dolly's face fell.

Fox grinned at her. 'Sorry, what was that you were saying?'

Dolly knew she was blushing a shade of scarlet that no amount of sweaty exhaustion could hide. 'I, er …' She was so embarrassed, she didn't know what to say. 'I didn't know you trained here.'

'Likewise,' he said, yanking his sweatshirt over his head as he strode straight past her in the direction of Roy and the sparring partner he was lining up.

Dolly looked down at the scuffed black floor, mortified as she replayed everything she'd accused him of in her head. Her heart thumping in her ears.

'Get on with it, Dolly, stop wasting my time!' Roy hollered.

Dolly jumped to attention, catching the wry smile on Fox's face as he started to warm up.

The gym was dark and dirty. Spiderwebs swung in the corners of the roof as the kicks and punches vibrated through the air. It was all grunts and groans. Droplets of blood and sweat on the floor. A kettle with a bunch of dirty mugs and a table with a couple of folders made up Roy's desk, along with a shelf of garish gold trophies from his younger days. There were black-and-white photos of various boxers who he'd trained, and a signed photo of Muhammad Ali that he'd bought from the side of the road in Vegas but claimed was a bona fide gift from The Greatest.

Fox was in the ring.

Dolly did her step-ups with gusto, trying not to notice. He was in a black vest and shorts and old red gloves that were faded almost to pink. He was fighting Bruno, Roy's brightest young star. A few people in the gym had paused what they were doing to watch. Dolly carried on with her routine. But as the fight got going and more people ventured ringside, she found herself pausing, unable not to look.

Bruno always drew a crowd but in this instance, she hated to admit it, Fox was equally mesmerising. By the ropes, old Roy couldn't keep the grin off his face. He was loving it.

Dolly forced herself to focus on her squats and lunges, up and down, over and over again, stubbornly determined to keep her eyes off the ring.

There was an 'oooh' from the crowd and she glanced over to see Bruno was down. Pride stopped her from looking at Fox and she found herself annoyed that she wondered if he was looking at her.

Her legs were like jelly by the time she finished. The match was six rounds down. The cut on Fox's cheek had opened up and blood was dripping down his neck, shoulder and onto his arm. There she noticed a tattoo of a fox's face, staring beadily at her. Dolly had to roll her eyes. Typical.

Chucking her towel over her shoulder, she headed over to the changing rooms. When she'd joined, despite there being at least a handful of women who trained at the gym, there hadn't been female changing rooms, and when Dolly had complained, Roy had cleared out a store cupboard and drawn a stick figure of a girl in a dress on the front of the door. Some hilarious joker had added massive boobs. Dolly had pulled her police card and told Roy she'd report him to Trading Standards, after which he reluctantly expanded the store cupboard, added a shower and bought a cheap sticky sign from Homebase that read 'Ladies'. He'd blanked Dolly for three weeks and then put her in the ring with one of his toughest, up-and-coming seventeen-year-olds and watched as she'd beaten Dolly to a pulp. But it had been worth it for the shower afterwards.

Now, washed and changed into canary-yellow tracksuit bottoms and a black T-shirt, Dolly hoisted her bag over her good shoulder and left the gym deliberately not turning round to see what had happened in the ring but she could hear a lot of laughter, heavy panting and congratulations. That type of stir round the gym would only have been caused by Fox beating Bruno, which made Dolly even more determined not to look.

Outside the sun was piercing compared to the dungeon darkness of Roy's. She slipped on her sunglasses one-handed as she let the door slam behind her.

When it didn't slam with its normal heavy thump, she glanced over her shoulder and saw a sweaty, bleeding Fox propping it open. 'What's the rush?' he asked.

'What do you think?' Dolly replied, starting to walk away.

To her annoyance, Fox laughed and jogged after her. His white sweater was slung over one shoulder and a towel was over the other, which he used to stem the bleeding on his face. 'Don't you want to know who won?' he asked as they walked side by side.

'Not particularly,' she said. 'But I'm assuming you'll tell me.'

'Not at all,' he said, and carried on in silence.

Dolly now wanted to know but wasn't going to ask.

As if Fox could tell, he chuckled.

Dolly was determined never to know.

'So what happened to your treasure hunt?' he asked.

'Nothing,' she said and caught him smirk.

'What?' she asked, stopping as he paused at an ice-cream van to buy a bottle of water but the guy didn't have any, so Fox ordered a 99.

'You want anything?' he asked.

'No,' she said. 'Thank you. Why were you just laughing?'

'I wasn't laughing.'

'OK, smirking.'

'I never smirk.'

'You smirk,' she said, watching the ice-cream guy hand over a really tempting-looking 99 with a Flake. 'And I'll have a Calippo, actually.'

Fox sucked in a breath. 'Well, seeing as you asked so nicely, one Calippo,' he said to the vendor.

Dolly took the orange lolly. 'Thanks,' she said.

'You're more than welcome,' he replied.

After a couple of seconds, Dolly said, 'Did you know I was going to be at the gym?'

Fox bit the Flake in half, seemingly buying time, before glancing across at Dolly a little guiltily and saying, 'I had an inkling.'

'I knew it!' she said, the dripping Calippo in her hand somehow making her victory have less impact. 'I can't believe you followed me to Roy's.'

'I didn't really follow you,' Fox countered. 'I've known Roy for years, I was meant to pop in sometime soon. I just made it sooner rather than later.'

'Why won't you leave me alone?' Dolly asked. They'd arrived at her flat. It was the basement of an old Victorian house just around the corner from a giant car wash.

Fox crunched the last of the 99 cone and said, 'You got me suspended yesterday. I want some good to come out of it.'

'Well, learn to cook or something,' Dolly said, stopping, still slurping the Calippo.

'I can cook,' Fox replied, propping himself up on a street sign.

'Seriously, you don't have anything better to do?'

'No. As you're well aware, I'm serving suspension, because of you. And like you, I live for my job. Why have we stopped?' he asked. 'Do you live here? I really need a glass of water.'

Dolly huffed as she walked round the corner and down her basement stairs, past her mishmash of terracotta pots filled with ferns and geraniums and one lone Stargazer lily. Fox's presence behind her was unnerving. No one came to her flat.

She unlocked the door and went straight to the kitchen where she poured him a glass of water then thrust it into his hand, hoping he'd drink it and go.

But Fox's attention was elsewhere. He was walking round slowly admiring the artwork, pausing before a painting of a vase of peonies. 'This is good,' he said.

Dolly nodded. To any normal person she'd have said that her mother painted it.

Fox carried on. He perused the books on her bookshelf. Nodded. Carried on. Glanced down at the rug her sister, Olive, had brought her back from a work trip to Bangladesh. Ran his hand over a patchwork throw on the sofa. Dolly crossed her good arm over her bad. She waited. Fox sipped the water. 'Nice place,' he said.

'It's OK,' she replied.

He looked up, eyes vaguely amused. 'I pictured you living somewhere different.'

Dolly walked away into the kitchen, she'd had enough of his analysis. 'I don't want to know how you pictured me,' she called, getting her own glass of water; the Calippo had made her thirsty.

The doorbell rang as she was gulping down tap water. 'Hang on a minute,' Dolly shouted, putting the glass down and jogging through to the lounge, but Fox had already answered the door.

'Ooh, well who are you?' Dolly's Aunt Marge was standing in the doorway, dressed in polka dots and a Gucci bumbag, giving Fox a very appreciative once up and down. She was tiny, in her late sixties with sinewy arms and hair so red it almost glowed.

'Fox Mason, madam. Colleague of Dolly's.' Fox thrust out a hand to shake.

'Marjorie King. Aunt of Dolly's,' Marge drawled with a coquettish moue. 'I hope you don't mind being sized up by a woman twice your age?'

'I'll take it where I can get it,' Fox replied, and Marge cackled appreciatively. Then she saw Dolly. 'Oh, hello darling, how are you? What's happened to your arm?'

'Nothing,' said Dolly warily. Her aunt never just dropped round unannounced. Her social calendar was busier than anyone Dolly knew. 'What's happened? Why are you here?'

Marge scoffed. 'Can I not just see my favourite youngest niece?'

Dolly narrowed her eyes with suspicion. 'No.'

'OK, very well,' said Marge, making her way into the lounge. 'I can't actually stop for long because I'll be late for aqua aerobics, but I'm here because no one can get hold of you and' – she started absently flumping Dolly's cushions and rearranging objects on the coffee table – 'I think it's really important that you go back to Willoughby Park for your dad's treasure hunt. You are my responsibility and I think it would be good for you.'

Dolly could almost see Fox's ears prick up with interest.

'Aunt Marge, I'm a grown woman,' said Dolly, slightly exasperated that this was happening. 'I'm not your responsibility any more.'

Marge's phone buzzed with a message that she read immediately with a wry smile, then glancing up occasionally as she tapped out a reply, said to Dolly, 'You'll always be my responsibility. And I think your dad would have wanted you to do it.' She put her phone in her bag, arms now folded across her chest. 'When you were children, it was his favourite thing to watch you lot hunting down his clues.'

Dolly hadn't thought of it for years. The times when her dad would arrive, always unexpected and unannounced from whatever exotic trip he'd been on, in his khaki shorts and beaten-up backpack, to squeals of delight. The hero's return. He'd make them all wait in the house, baying like dogs to be set free as he laid clues all round the grounds, then he'd sit back, his tanned arms wrapped possessively around their adoring mother, as they bounded off with wild excitement. Her overriding memory after that was of always being the one at the rear, struggling to catch up with Olive and Ruben.

'And as far as I know,' Marge added, bracelets clacking as she refolded the quilt over the back of Dolly's sofa, 'it's gold at the end.'

'Are you serious?'

'As I've ever been,' said Marge, eyes wide and knowing. 'My brother had finally struck it lucky, apparently. I remember him telling me, crystal clear.'

'I don't think it's gold,' said Dolly, unconvinced.

'Suit yourself.' Marge shrugged. 'See it as a last hurrah then, darling. When I spoke to Ruben, he said he's planning to sell the place. I think you need to see it, don't you? Think of all those memories.'

Those memories were exactly what Dolly was trying *not* to think about, furiously trying to stop any emotions playing out on her face. Just the mention of Ruben de Lacy and she saw herself, all frizzy-haired and puppy-fat non-boobs, in dreadful flowery dungarees her mum had made her that she thought were the coolest things ever, swinging in and out of trees like a little monkey, perching on the high brick wall watching as Ruben lay in the sunshine like a bronzed Adonis, trying to get him to notice her by doing the coquettish big eyes she'd seen on *Dawson's Creek* but failing miserably. That scrap of memory alone was enough to make her whole body inwardly flinch, her insides bunching up with a shiver of pinpricks. She had learnt over time and with a great deal of self-discipline to avoid the sensation of vulnerability. Puberty, for Dolly, had felt like one of the crabs they found at the beach, cowering under a rock waiting for its new soft shell to harden. Unknowing. Nervous. A wobbling jelly of exposed emotion just waiting to be trodden on. The feeling, in retrospect, was as unpleasant now as it was then.

She remembered one time as a kid, sitting on the old living room rug, her head resting against her mum's knees, cheeks wet from crying about something – probably the hated sounds of the shots from the annual deer cull in the park or just simply having to go upstairs on her own for fear of what lurked in the wardrobe in her room. Her mum had stroked her hair by the warmth of the fire, musing, *'You're just like me, Dol, you feel things more than other people.'* Dolly had stared into the flickering flames, the soft touch of her mum's hand on her head, the smell of her perfume, the cotton of her dress beneath her cheek, cocooned, momentarily safe from the world. *'Like most special things in life, it's a blessing and a curse.'*

Dolly found herself feeling suddenly claustrophobic and overcrowded in her flat. Aunt Marge had turned to Fox and was saying, 'I think it would help her very much to go. It was a funny time for them all back then—'

'Marge!' Dolly cut her off.

'Sorry, darling.' Again Marge turned to Fox, who was watching with bemused enjoyment, and said, 'She's always like this. Very snappy, but it's just her way. Very soft underneath. That's why I—'

'Stop it!'

'Sorry, sorry!' Marge slapped herself on the wrist. 'Bad Marge.'

'Look, Marge, thanks for coming by but,' Dolly steered her towards the door, 'I don't think I'm going to go.'

'Why not?' Marge frowned, face powdery with make-up.

'Yeah, why not, Dolly?' Fox interjected with an expression of mock-confusion. 'You said yesterday that you absolutely *were* going.'

Dolly wanted to kill him. Fox's eyes sparkled.

'I'm sure they'd give you the time off work,' Marge pushed, to which Fox started to reply – most likely to tell her that Dolly had been suspended – but before he could get any further, Dolly clamped her hands onto Marge's shoulders and bustled her out the front door. 'It was lovely to see you, but I don't want you to be late for aqua aerobics.' Once outside, Dolly added, almost pleading, 'Marge, I just don't want to go to Willoughby Park. OK?'

Marge looked her in the eye for a moment and then smiled

softly. 'I know you don't,' she said. Then she reached up and touched Dolly's cheek with her cool, slim hand. 'But you should go, darling. I want you to see it, to see Olive. She's already there.' Dolly didn't want to see Olive. Marge said, 'It'd be good for you.'

Dolly focused on the cracked concrete tiles at her feet.

Marge moved her hand to smooth Dolly's hair back from her face, tucking it behind her ear. 'Can you go just for me? So I feel like I've succeeded in some respect as a stand-in parent.'

Dolly snorted down at the floor. 'I think that's emotional blackmail.'

Marge nodded. 'Yes, I think it is.'

Dolly looked up. 'I'll think about it.'

Marge gave her a kiss on the cheek. 'You do that, darling. Now let me say goodbye to that hunk indoors before I go.' She brushed past Dolly to give Fox a proper farewell. 'It's been a delight to meet you,' she said, clasping his hand tight in hers, to which Fox replied, 'You too, Ms King.' Marge grinned lasciviously, 'I'll see you soon, I hope.'

Once Dolly had safely removed her aunt from the vicinity, she walked into the flat, flicking her hair casually as if nothing of interest had occurred. Fox's head inclined, eyes quietly assessing. When he looked at her like that she felt like a skinned rabbit.

'Gold, eh?' he said.

'I highly doubt it,' Dolly replied, staring straight at him, face shuttered, refusing to further indulge.

He said, 'I'm assuming this Willoughby Park is somewhere far away.'

'It's in Cornwall,' Dolly said flatly, trying not to picture their old cottage at Willoughby Park. Just doing so did something to her insides. Gave her the sensation of butterflies. She could smell it. She could hear the sound of the key in the front door lock and the sound of the waves out of the window that was so familiar it faded in and out of the air, appearing only when she really listened.

Fox said, 'So are you going to go?'

'Looks like I'm going to have to,' she replied tartly, knowing in her heart that she couldn't deny Aunt Marge, not after everything she'd done for Dolly. She'd just have to rock up, wow Ruben, not get riled by Olive, be completely detached and blonde and brilliant. Dolly blew out a breath, pumped. Then, catching Fox's all-knowing eye, she moved to stand by her open front door, ushering him out by implication.

Fox took the hint, walking round the sofa to the coffee table to put his glass down. 'Well, thanks for the water,' he said, all polite smile. 'I'd better be going.'

He hung his head slightly as he walked past her, the blood on his cheek dried in a thin felt-tip pen line. Lashes lowered. She would have felt victorious were it not for the vague twitch to his lips. She watched him pause on the bottom step, look up at the blue sky, lick his lips then turn and say, 'Have a good time.'

'I will.' She did her best fake smile.

He nodded. 'Good luck getting there, with your arm and everything.'

Dolly suddenly remembered her sling. The shocking pain in her shoulder when the painkillers wore off.

'I take it you were thinking of driving,' he added, now seemingly making himself comfortable on her doorstep, eyeing her geraniums with fascination, even leaning forward and dead-heading one of her variegated pink ones.

She pictured Willoughby Park, the winding beach path down to the cottage, miles away from anyone, deep in the Cornish countryside. An oasis of lush green grass and trees so high they touched the clouds. Deer roaming the grounds. Cool winding streams and giant fallen trunks decaying into the land. This wasn't somewhere you got to by train. Nor bus. She needed a car.

'I mean …' Fox was examining the jasmine she had trailing up to the railings. 'This smells nice,' he said of the plant before carrying on. 'If you were looking for someone to give you a lift, I have nothing to do for the foreseeable future.' He bent to give one of her freesias a sniff. 'This is nice too.' He inhaled again then stood up straight and turned to look at Dolly. 'But I do get the impression you would be less than enamoured by my presence on your journey.'

Dolly was frantically running through every possible driving option in her head. She could get an Uber but that would cost a fortune down to Cornwall, if Uber even drove all that way. She could ask a friend but they were all working and had their own lives going on, she couldn't ask someone to drop everything, especially as she'd been out of the loop for ages. She gave her arm a little test to see if she could hold a steering wheel and the shot of agony made the decision for her. She looked up to see Fox watching her. With a smile he said, 'OK, well I'll be going,' and trotted off up the stairs, surprisingly agile for the size of him.

Damn you, she wanted to shout. Instead, she took a deep breath, steeled herself and said, 'Wait.'

Fox paused. 'Are you talking to me?'

Dolly sucked on her cheek. 'You know I'm talking to you.'

Fox looked innocently down at her over the railing.

'Why are you doing this?'

'I like a challenge.'

Dolly looked heavenward, up to the ice-blue sky, then back at Fox's annoyingly condescending face. 'This is all because Brogden said they thought you could sort me out, isn't it? You want to prove that you can.'

Fox thought for a second, the muscles in his arms flexing as he did, like he couldn't help himself. 'What's wrong with that?'

'What's wrong with that?' Dolly raised one perfectly arched brow. 'You've been feeding me all this altruistic rubbish.'

Fox frowned, put out. 'No I haven't.'

'You said you wanted to help me.'

'I do.'

'But for your own ego.'

Fox looked straight at her, amusement flickering in the corners of his big brown eyes. 'Does that make it easier for you to accept my help?'

Dolly scowled. She hated this. Fox was waiting, leaning all relaxed on the railing.

'OK,' she said.

He feigned misunderstanding. 'OK, what?'

'OK, you can drive me.'

Fox grinned. 'Oh no, Dolly, you're going to have to ask much nicer than that.'

Dolly felt her body get hot with annoyance. She swallowed. She took a deep calming breath. All the while, Fox hung over the railing, smiling down at her.

'Please, Fox, could you drive me to where I need to go?'

Fox's eyes lit up. 'That's more like it.'

Dolly glared at him.

He laughed this time, really guffawed at her expression. 'Nothing, Dolly, would give me greater pleasure.'

CHAPTER SIX

Ruben never got up early until Zadie had come to stay. 'Morning!' she hollered at his door, dressed in whatever bonkers outfit she'd picked for the day.

Last night, Ruben had sat up drinking whisky alone as Olive had slipped off to bed early claiming tiredness after her long journey – and no doubt Zadie's non-stop questioning. 'I like your hair, Olive. Have you read Harry Potter, Olive? Have you seen that Ruben's hair is going grey at the side bits, Olive?' Now though, he was determined to take charge. Get to know who Olive had become himself rather than be constantly interrupted by his child. Find out what had happened to her after all these years.

But as he rocked up to breakfast, praising himself for his early-bird timing, he was confronted by Olive and Zadie already up and dressed, pondering the clue.

'Is it weird seeing your dad's handwriting?' Zadie was asking. 'If he's, you know, dead.'

Olive nodded. 'Yes, it is. Very much so.'

Zadie frowned, staring at the clue in Olive's hand. 'I just think it would be really weird. Like if I saw Barry's handwriting after he died.' She shuddered. 'Spooky.'

The mention of stepdad Barry in this context didn't sit as comfortably as it should have with Ruben. What about his own handwriting? Would Zadie miss that? Did she even know what it looked like? Why did he care? 'Toast, anyone?' he asked, all chipper.

'We've already had breakfast,' Zadie said without looking up. She was studying Olive's profile with more fascination than the clue, which had them all as stumped today as it did last night. Her hero-worship growing by the second, as Olive read it out in a low concentrated voice: '*Cold as ice, little mice. Dark as night, what a fright. In the corner? Getting warmer …*'

Ruben had no idea what it meant. Instead, he followed Zadie's lead and took the opportunity to study Olive, but a little more covertly than his daughter. She had the profile of a Roman statue. Serene. Poised. Hair tied perfectly. Clothes like a uniform. She was still stunning, but in a more muted, understated fashion. There was nothing, if you really studied her, that told you anything about her. Except the telltale bags under her eyes which suggested she hadn't slept well. Was it still there though? he wondered. Underneath it all. The girl who had dazzled him so completely. Who wore slogan T-shirts and ra-ra skirts made out of her old Paddington Bear curtains? The person whose single-mindedness and courage had been the backbone to which he'd based so many decisions in his life. Just the idea in his mind of having Olive's eyes watching and judging had led him to take paths in his life he never would have taken had he been left alone. Signposts towards 'the easy route' had been swerved simply because he'd wondered: what would Olive think?

Suddenly Olive sat up, eyes blazing with a familiar fire. 'It's the cellar at the cottage!' she exclaimed. 'We would dare each other to go down there. The mice are because they lived behind the coal chute, which is right in the corner. And it was always freezing because it was always flooding.'

Ruben grinned. 'Yes! Well done.'

Olive beamed like she had forgotten her demure persona for a moment and allowed her face to be as wide and open as it once was.

Zadie clapped. 'Let's go!'

And just as quickly, Olive's face closed. 'What about Dolly?'

Ruben crossed his arms. 'What about Dolly?' They'd been through this already. No one had got through to Dolly. She didn't answer any calls. Waiting for Dolly would be like waiting for the wind to change. 'She's probably working. Aren't people in the police always working – married to the job and all that.'

'Maybe she's on a top-secret mission,' Zadie chimed in. 'My friend's dad is one of the policemen at Buckingham Palace. He's met the queen. Do you think Dolly's met the queen? I'd *love* to meet the queen.'

As Zadie talked, Ruben mused over the idea of wild little Dolly as a member of the police, arresting people. The image was incongruous. When he'd last seen her she ran with her legs sticking out.

'Come on,' he said to Olive. 'Unless you're stalling.'

'Why would I be stalling?'

'Maybe worried I'll find the clue first?' If there was one thing Ruben knew about Olive King, it was that she could never resist a good challenge.

'Oh please,' Olive scoffed.

Ruben shrugged. 'I was always the better clue finder.'

'You were not!' Olive laughed at the idea.

'I think you'll find I was.'

'When?'

Ruben shrugged. 'Always.'

'That is just such rubbish. I found all the clues.'

It was Ruben's turn to scoff at the audacity. 'I think not, Ms King.'

'Oh I think so, Mr de Lacy.'

He stood back. 'After you, then.'

Zadie whooped.

They walked out into the sunshine, the black cat watching them from the steps as they crunched down the drive, Zadie running then walking slightly ahead. 'Which way?' she called.

Ruben pointed straight ahead to a path that ran through the manicured park to a copse of trees and eventually down to the beach.

'It's been well looked after,' said Olive, surveying the grounds, her expression masked by sunglasses.

'Terence has been here all along. Kept the gardens up – they were still open to the public until recently. And he made sure the house wasn't falling to bits.'

Olive glanced over her shoulder at the big house behind them. 'But no one's lived here?'

Ruben shook his head. 'Nope, no one's lived here.' No one had even visited as far as he knew. He was curious as to whether any of her family had been. 'Have you ever been back to the cottage?'

Olive shook her head, 'No, never.' She really did look tired. More so than just a bad night's sleep. He was itching to ask her more. Most of all, he wanted to know why she was single, but just up ahead Zadie had paused to wait for them.

'Where do you live, Zadie?' Olive asked as they caught up with her, which Ruben saw as a deliberate tactic to change the subject.

'In Hove, down by the coast,' Zadie replied.

Ruben frowned, 'Do you?'

Olive looked at him perplexed, astounded that he didn't know this simple information about his daughter.

'I knew she lived by the coast, but I thought it was …' Where had he thought it was? He hadn't really thought about it. He had just transferred money if and when Penny asked for it and presumed they were getting on quite happily without him. Which they were, which was why Zadie would be upset if her stepdad died and she saw his handwriting rather than Ruben's.

Zadie was saying, 'Yeah, I love it. We have a little house by the beach and a sausage dog called Yap—'

'Didn't your parents used to have sausage dogs?' Olive asked as if the vague memory was returning.

'Unfortunately, yes.' Ruben made a face. Sausage dogs were one of his pet hates. His parents had two that they'd treated like babies. They were the most loved things in the house. When they took them for walks their legs were so short they could never keep up, so his mum and dad would end up carrying one each, letting them lick their faces in adoration. He'd never seen his parents kiss each other in his life, and the only kiss they offered him was a peck on the cheek as they dropped him off at school for the term, but dog saliva they'd had no problem with.

'Oh, don't look like that. They're lovely. You'd love Yap,' Zadie declared.

Ruben relented with a 'Maybe,' mainly to win over Olive, who was clearly unimpressed at his lack of knowledge about Zadie's home location and love of Dachshunds.

They kept walking. The sun warming their backs. Olive had to take off her sweater, and Ruben's eyes were drawn to the strip of pale white skin revealed as she did. He looked away and saw Zadie watching, her expression both admonishing and intrigued.

The path forked at the base of the hill.

Ruben said, 'Up there, isn't it?' trying to divert Zadie's watchful attention.

Olive nodded.

Zadie kicked some leaves and mused, 'So was this park like your garden? Did you hang out together?' Ruben could sense she was fishing for information.

Olive said, 'I wasn't really allowed in here. We were never meant to go beyond our wall.' She glanced at Ruben; it was hard to tell what she was thinking. She'd got much better at disguising her emotions.

'Why?' Zadie looked perplexed.

Olive turned the question over to Ruben, who said, 'Because my dad didn't want riff-raff on the estate.'

Olive shook her head, the frustration at his dad's opinions still clearly cut sharp.

Ruben could hear with crystal clarity his father's tirades having caught *'The bloody King children'* trespassing. He'd had a habit of inspecting the grounds purely, it seemed, to exercise his authority were he to see anything amiss. He'd march down to the cottage to issue his reprimands to Olive's father – 'Fallen on damn deaf ears! He just bloody laughed. Let the children roam. The man's an idiot. Roam! It's *my* land!' – that would then lead to an evening of rage and fury at the de Lacy house. But then as quickly as he'd leapt on a problem,

Ruben's dad would retreat again, distracted by a champagne reception or a trip to the House of Lords, and they were all free again. Much like his treatment of his son, complete disinterest until he sensed a problem.

As they strode in the direction of the cottage, Ruben pointed out the giant boughs of the old oaks. The grazing deer and the darkened depths of the woods where storm-fallen tree trunks became lurking crocodiles they used to climb on. When they went a bit further and he saw the ancient targets he built for his air rifle, he paused in surprise. 'I can't believe these are still here.'

Even Olive seemed momentarily taken aback. Wistfully surprised as her hand traced the bulls'-eyes she'd painted.

Ruben remembered the smell of her hair as he showed her how to aim. A way of getting close that he'd learnt from films. Wrapping his arms round her to line up the shot. Olive turning her head a fraction and whispering, 'I know how to shoot, Ruben.' The smile on his lips as he said, 'I know you do.' Dolly behind them, oblivious, waiting impatiently for her turn.

The thought of him, Olive and Dolly together, taking it in turns to fire at the crudely drawn targets felt like a whole other lifetime. The nostalgia intensified when he saw the bench by the old willow tree and added, 'Oh wow, do you remember this? This is where I slept when I failed my GCSEs. My dad was so angry he locked me out of the house.'

Zadie looked shocked. 'He did what?'

Olive said, 'God, I remember that.' She narrowed her eyes as it came back to her. 'My dad found you and brought you to ours for breakfast. You were frozen and all wet from dew, do you remember?'

'Was I?' Ruben had obviously wiped that part from his memory.

'That's awful,' muttered Zadie, pity in her eyes, which Ruben waved away.

'Oh, it was fine. Nothing serious,' he laughed. 'He did it all the time after that. God knows where he thought I went because I wasn't allowed at yours,' he said to Olive, 'but I did go to Olive's,' he clarified for Zadie. 'Slept on the sofa with that terrifying dog.'

Olive looked wistful again, 'Oh, Everest. He was lovely.'

'Don't *Oh Everest* me, he was a beast.'

Olive laughed. Ruben immediately remembered that he liked making her laugh.

Zadie had gone very quiet. 'I think it's just really sad. What you're saying.'

Ruben's brow creased, unable to fathom that she was upset about something that had happened to him. 'Don't worry about it, kid,' he said, strangely warmed by her emotion. 'I was all right.'

They had reached the denser woodland. Moving into single file on a narrow path through the ivy-covered uneven ground. All around them hidden animals and birds made the leaves rustle, squirrels darted up the trees. Leaves crunched under their feet.

'Here,' Ruben said, picking up a long stick to use as a walking staff and handing it to Zadie. Then he got one for himself. 'It's like we're in *Lord of the Rings*. "You shall not pass!"'

Zadie took the stick with another of her expertly pitying expressions. 'I have no idea what you're talking about.' Then she found one for Olive and said, 'You've got to be part of the stick gang.'

Olive was a little reluctant at first, but when she took it she said, 'It's actually quite helpful on this uphill bit.' Then she added, 'God, we used to race up this thing.'

Ruben blew out a breath, already feeling over the hill from his misunderstood *Lord of the Rings* reference and refusing to cow to any age-related weakness stated boldly, 'I could still race up it.'

Olive laughed. 'Go on then.'

So he did, picking up his pace and marching past her. Next to him Zadie nipped along like a puppy. Ruben could feel his heart rate start to increase but he was blowed if he was going to slow down. Zadie chattered away, completely unaffected by the steepening gradient.

'You don't have to prove anything to me, Ruben,' he heard Olive call behind him as his legs started to burn.

'Proving it to myself, Olive!' he huffed, forcing his pace up till he made it to the top. Zadie skipping and twirling beside him.

It only took Olive a minute to catch up. 'Feel better?'

'Well, I've proved I'm not old and unfit,' he said, trying to surreptitiously catch his breath and wipe the sweat from his brow.

Zadie looked confused. 'Are you saying Olive's old and unfit? I don't think Olive's old and unfit.'

'I'm not suggesting that,' Ruben scoffed, infuriated by the constant voice at his side throwing a spanner in the works. 'I'm just, you know, saying I don't want to be trapped in the clichés of middle age. Before you know it you're watching *Antiques Roadshow* and *Gardeners' World*,' he laughed.

Olive raised a brow. 'I quite like *Antiques Roadshow*.'

Ruben felt himself backed into a corner. He too didn't

mind a bit of Sunday night *Antiques Roadshow* but it wasn't something he admitted to women. Usually when he said something like that it was met with humorous nods of agreement. 'You know what I mean.'

'Not really,' Olive replied, staring straight at him with mild amusement. He was reminded again of the effect she had, keeping him always on his toes.

Zadie said, 'What do you watch, Ruben?'

Weighing up the current situation and playing for a laugh he said, 'Never missed an episode of *Love Island*.'

Olive snorted.

Ruben grinned. It felt like a win. 'And I am a big fan of *Gogglebox*.'

Zadie gasped, 'Oh my God, we *love Gogglebox*! My mum says watching TV with me is like *being* on *Gogglebox*! What music do you like?'

'Well,' Ruben started proudly, drawing up the collar on his shirt to emphasise how young, cool and hip he was, 'I actually have a couple of Stormzy tickets for later in the year.'

Olive rolled her eyes again, but this time he saw her deliberate refusal to smile even though he could tell she wanted to. He enjoyed having a Stormzy concert to pull out the bag to show a certain disregard for the conventions of adulthood, ignoring the fact he'd bought them to impress a Gen Z Tinder date who'd blown him out, deeming him too conventional, in favour of a more open relationship with a free-climbing hipster barista.

Then Zadie said, 'Maybe I could come with you to see Stormzy?'

Caught off-guard, too busy congratulating himself, Ruben

found himself pausing for too long before answering. He wondered if the horror at the suggestion was as visible on his face as it felt inside. He didn't want to waste the Stormzy tickets on Zadie. They'd cost him a fortune. They were date-worthy. Zadie he could take to McDonald's or the aquarium again.

Ruben had actually given absolutely zero thought to what would happen after these two weeks were up. His main focus was just getting through the fortnight. After which, he'd assumed they'd all return to normal. She'd head to Brighton or Hove or wherever it was she lived. And he'd cruise on back to London town, happily unencumbered. But no, from the expectant look on her face, a real father would think further ahead. 'Maybe,' he said, but he had taken too long to answer and Zadie said, 'It's OK, you don't have to.'

He saw Olive wince.

Before he could say anything else, Zadie cut him off by pointing ahead and saying cheerfully, 'There's the sea. And the cottage ...'

Ruben turned too, glad for the distraction, 'Ah, yes, there it is.' But all the while he could sense Olive's judgement. The cool, dark gaze that kept him on high alert. She was seemingly immune to his charm. Even when he gave her a nudge on the shoulder and said, 'So how do you feel about going back?'

She answered simply, 'Fine,' without hesitation.

Their feet skidded as they came out of the forest onto the shingly path that led to the beach. All of them stopping still when they saw the cottage, the rocks jutting out beneath it, the waves lapping gently on the thick dark seaweed.

'Oh my God,' breathed Olive.

72

Ruben swallowed.

Where once had been the picturesque little cottage of yellow Cornish stone and grey slate tiles, a garden of tumbling scarlet roses and unkempt lavender flooded with bees, was now a derelict wreck, boarded up and fenced with metal. 'Danger! Keep Out!' signs plastered all over its graffitied walls. A swing seat in the garden hung snapped off its hinge. Drainpipes jutted from the gutters like broken limbs. Squirrels nested in the roof. The chimney leant precariously to the right.

Olive started to walk towards it, slow like it was an animal she might scare away.

Zadie glanced at Ruben for a cue. 'Was that Olive's home?'

He nodded. 'Yeah,' he said, surprised by the lump in his throat as they followed behind, 'yeah it was.'

He could remember the smell when he stepped inside of wet dog and brewing coffee, and soft, warm chocolate cake. He had only remembered the smell of his own house when he'd walked back in last week, it was never a scent he could conjure up, more a reminder to lock down his emotions and take his shoes off.

He could remember the King cottage like favourite snapshots in a photograph album. The feel of the big heavy knocker on the front door, stolen now by the looks of it. The flush on their old Victorian toilet that you pulled like a lever. The gaudy Christmas tree that touched the ceiling. The chaos and the madness where everyone was doing something but no one knew what the other was doing. Open a door and Mr King would be sitting asleep, desert boots discarded on the floor and his beloved lurcher at his ankles. Behind another, Mrs King would be repainting the sitting room – 'I like pink in the springtime.'

Open another and Dolly would be lying on her back staring up at the ceiling – 'What are you doing?' 'Seeing what I can see in the wallpaper.' And Ruben would lose ten minutes lying on an ancient Persian rug trying to see the castle and horses that Dolly could make out in the old woodchip Anaglypta. What would Olive be doing? He always knew where to find her – in her room sewing something, cutting something up. Or urgently poring through magazines and newspapers and books as if searching for an answer that, once found, might finally let her know what question she was asking. He could picture her now, frowning, flicking through pages, annoyed with the world, plagued by dissatisfaction, barely glancing up when he came into the room. Never saying hello, only what was on her mind at that present moment. 'Ruben, I hate my hair. I think it's holding me back.'

He turned now to glance at Olive as she yanked open a gap between two wire metal hoardings, her hair knotted neatly in a tortoiseshell clip. 'Do you remember that time you asked me to cut your hair?'

'Sorry, what?' Olive asked, not really paying attention, squeezing through the gap, the sharp metal catching the edge of her T-shirt.

'When I cut your hair, in the upstairs bathroom?' Ruben repeated, hauling the metal fence out further so they could all get in easier.

'You didn't listen to any of the instructions and just sliced a massive chunk out of it,' Olive replied drily, kicking fallen tiles off the path.

'True,' he said, ushering Zadie through the gap and letting it clang shut behind him, 'but you rescued it.' He remembered her snatching the scissors off him and setting to work giving herself a choppy new cut that stuck out at all angles but made her look edgy and dishevelled, like she didn't give a shit about the world. 'I remember your mum crying when we came down the stairs.'

Olive paused with her hand on the front door. 'Yeah.'

As she tried the latch to no avail, Ruben could see Olive as she was then, leaning against one of the old oaks sheltering from the pouring rain, smoking a fag she'd pinched from him, wearing one of her dad's camouflage shirts buttoned to the neck and a pair of lopped-off jeans, only disdain for her mother's howling distress that her daughter's luscious long locks were now stuffed in the bathroom pedal bin.

Olive said, 'It's locked.'

Ruben said, 'Stand aside.' And lifting his foot, kicked the door hard. Nothing happened. Except his leg hurt. Olive sniggered. He gave her a look. 'Sorry,' she said. He inhaled through his nose, made a show of beefing himself up, which made both Olive and Zadie smile. Then he kicked again. This time the door crashed open, bashing against the wall, then swinging shut again with force.

'Well done,' said Olive, impressed.

Ruben tipped his head like it was nothing.

She put her hand on the door and pushed it open more gently. Inside it was dark and bare, a few discarded bits of furniture were upended. More graffiti on the walls. Olive rolled her lips together, steeling herself. Ruben stood next to her. Zadie to his right.

Olive glanced across at him. 'How do *you* feel about going back?' she asked, clearly hesitant.

Ruben was close enough to be able to smell her skin. He could still remember the feel of her hair between his fingers as he held it between the scissors. The stutter in his voice as he started to cut. The secret, deliberate movement of picking up a curl between his fingers and stuffing it into his pocket. It was derailing. If he wasn't already outside, he'd have thought he needed some fresh air.

Olive was waiting. Watching.

'Oh, totally fine,' he said, striding forward with a grin.

CHAPTER SEVEN

The London sky was so blue it looked unreal, like a child's drawing. The air was summer warm and smelt of last night's rain, uncollected rubbish and the sticky sap from the lime trees that lined the road.

Fox Mason had just roared up outside Dolly King's flat on a gigantic Kawasaki motorbike, yellow and black like a wasp. Kitted out in full leather, he pulled off a black helmet embossed with the same fox as was tattooed on his arm.

Dolly stood on the pavement aghast, rucksack by her feet, unable to believe what she was seeing. 'You said you had a car!'

Fox was doing an amazing job of keeping a straight face. 'I didn't say I had a car.'

'You did!' Dolly wanted to stamp her foot but wouldn't give him the satisfaction.

'I said, I could give you a lift,' Fox replied, patting the pillion seat on the beast of a bike. It wasn't brand new, it looked like it had done some miles but it had been beautifully cared for. He chucked Dolly a leather jacket and laughed, deep and rumbling, the movement ricocheting through his He-Man-sized biceps and washboard abs.

She stood speechless, holding the jacket with her good hand.

Birds twittered in the spindly pavement trees. A sparrow wrestled with a crisp from a dropped packet in the gutter. A thousand expletives ran through her mind. She'd been expecting him to drive up in a battered Jeep or suchlike. Not this thing.

If there was one thing Dolly hated, it was motorbikes.

'Do you need a hand with the jacket?' Fox asked.

'No, thank you,' Dolly replied stubbornly, holding the collar between her teeth as she shoved one arm into the sleeve, the weight of the leather immediately hot under the blistering sun.

Fox watched her struggle for a while, trying to catch hold of the other sleeve over her shoulder before she gave up and stood staring at him.

He looked at her like he didn't understand.

She huffed. 'Can you help me?'

'Certainly.' He got off the bike and walked round to help her hitch the jacket up over her shoulder, bringing it round the front and zipping it up with her arm cradled inside, no attempt to hide his smug satisfaction that she needed his assistance. 'All right?' he asked.

She nodded, not meeting his eye. There was actually one thing Dolly hated more than motorbikes and that was having to ask for help. She hadn't asked anyone for help for years. She'd bought her flat on her own. She'd plumbed her own bathroom. She'd driven herself to hospital once when she thought she was having a heart attack, which actually wasn't something to be proud of and, having done it, wouldn't do it again. It transpired she hadn't been dying, just experiencing a severe panic attack, which in itself infuriated her and led to many an aborted attempt to take up meditation but ended with Roy from the gym's advice to just 'kick the shit out of it'.

'Hand,' Fox said, holding out one of a pair of leather gloves to push onto the fingers of her good hand.

Seeing that they were trembling slightly, Dolly tensed and flexed her fingers. The gloves were too big. It was all too big. These weren't the spares of an ex-girlfriend. Nor, she concluded, were they the spares of an ex-boyfriend either because they all smelt of Fox.

'Don't look so terrified,' he laughed.

'I don't look terrified,' she countered.

'I hate to break it to you, but you're not half as poker-faced as you think you are.'

Dolly scowled. 'I just don't like bikes.'

'No?' he asked, black eyes intrigued as he looked down at her.

'No,' she replied, ignoring his inquisition, tugging the glove down further with her teeth.

'Any reason why not?' he asked, picking up her bag.

'Just bad experiences as a teenager,' she replied.

Fox took the spare helmet off the back of the bike and replaced it with her luggage, lashing it into place. 'Overzealous ex-boyfriend?' he said without looking up, either a mind-reader or just fully aware of the bad-boy bike-riding clichés.

'Something like that,' Dolly said, slightly annoyed she fit the mould so obviously, reaching forward to take the helmet from him. He went to help and she said, 'I can do it.'

Fox looked down to hide a smile. How did it happen that he seemed to be constantly mocking her? To always have the upper hand? Dolly huffed into her helmet. The only good thing that could come from the motorbike was that they wouldn't have to make small talk for the next four hours.

But then Fox put his own helmet on and suddenly his voice resounded through her head. 'I'm a good driver, I promise. There's nothing to worry about.'

Dolly flinched, startled. The microphone was crystal clear. Fox's eyes crinkled in a grin. 'So we can keep in contact,' he said, tapping the side of the helmet, gesturing to the headset.

All Dolly seemed to do when she was with him was roll her eyes. 'Great.'

'I can hear you, you know?' he said, swinging his leg over the bike.

'I know,' she replied, climbing on behind him. It was all coming back, the feel of the bike between her legs, the clutch of the jacket in front. The press of the two of them together and then the roar as he threw the bike into gear.

But it wasn't completely the same, because Dolly was a grown-up now. She wasn't the angry, naïve, displaced teenager. And Fox's leather jacket didn't smell of damp like her ex-boyfriend's – a guy called Jake who never washed his hair and referred to himself in the third person as The Great Destructor. Nor did she feel so lowly and confused about herself, she would never dream now of clinging onto Jake's crappy bike while his gang drove like maniacs and threw eggs at politicians and bricks through the windows of big corporations. She wouldn't sit and absorb a spouted agenda of chaos nor would she give him her mobile phone to check all her calls nor think it was her fault when he clamped his hands tight about her throat in placid fury.

But still, just being on a bike again brought back enough memories of that time to make her sit rigidly unrelaxed.

Fox's leather jacket didn't smell of damp. It smelt a little bit of bonfire. He drove the bike how she'd imagined he would, with the same calm precision with which he policed. As they cruised up the main road she tried to make herself relax. Did some deep breathing to settle her nerves. She realised he was probably taking it super slow for her and felt herself begrudgingly thankful. Gradually she shifted position, didn't clutch quite so tight, dipped a fraction into turns and even glanced to the side to see the buildings zoom past.

'We join the motorway up ahead, OK. So the speed will increase,' she heard Fox's voice over the headphones.

'OK,' she said back.

'You all right?' he asked.

'Yes,' she said. 'Thank you.'

Pressed up close, Dolly realised quite how huge Fox was. It was like sitting behind a statue of granite.

'This speed OK?' he checked, like she was at the hairdressers constantly being asked if the water was the right temperature.

'Yes, it's fine.'

'Sure?'

She laughed, 'Yes, I'm sure.'

She knew he was smiling through the movement of his shoulders.

She found herself smiling too, relaxing. 'You don't have to keep checking, honestly.'

'OK,' he said, keeping his distance from traffic that she knew he would usually weave between.

'You can go a bit faster if you want,' she said, more because she felt guilty that he was taking it slow for her rather than through any desire to speed up.

'No, it's fine,' he said, shaking his head.

She didn't push it. Just looked to the side at the passengers in the cars they passed. He was too big to look over his shoulder. She could rest her head on the huge expanse of his back if she'd wanted, but she didn't. Instead, she held on with one hand and cushioned her dislocated arm in a cocoon against him. It was weird to be so close against a man that she had no intention of having sex with, especially a big man like Fox. Dolly went for tall, sinewy types. In fact, she could barely remember when she'd been so close to anyone. Anyone she wasn't arresting or defeating or being defeated by in the boxing ring. She hadn't seen her friends for months because of work. She hadn't seen her family. Not that Aunt Marge – nor Olive for that matter – were massive huggers. Her mum had been a hugger – squishing her in tight, her hair falling round Dolly's face, the pause as she smelt Dolly's skin. Always that slight squeeze at the end that made you feel like you were breaking out of her arms too early.

As she stared at the traffic, Dolly wondered what Olive and Ruben were doing right now. She could imagine them reminiscing. Rolling over old times. Would they be laughing at her, Dolly wondered, cringing suddenly at the memory of herself – hair in wild frizzy corkscrews, gappy teeth in braces, a million freckles and a nose too big for her face. And those effing dungarees. How had her mother allowed her to wear them? Or worse, perhaps they weren't thinking about her at all. So easily forgettable. There was a family joke about a hide-and-seek spot that Dolly had found in an old tree hollow, so good that no one found her for an hour. Initially Dolly luxuriated in the praise, it only occurred to her later that Olive and Ruben had simply stopped looking for her.

'So what's the deal with this Ruben de Lacy guy?' Fox asked.

Dolly frowned. *Could* he somehow tell what she was thinking? 'What do you mean?' she asked, defensive.

'Your aunt. She said he was going to sell the place.'

'Oh,' Dolly breathed a sigh of relief. Then she added a dismissive, 'Nothing. He was just our neighbour. His family owned the land. He's nobody,' she added and realised in that one word she'd said too much.

'*Really?*' said Fox, suddenly interested. She could detect his disbelief at her dismissiveness.

'Yes, really,' she replied curtly, her body tensing again, pulling away from where she rested against his back.

The sound of Fox's laugh reverberated round her helmet. 'Dolly, man, you are so easy to wind up.'

She seethed at his amusement. 'Whatever.'

'It was only a question, don't get so defensive.'

'I wasn't,' she snapped.

'You were!'

She didn't reply. She could feel him clocking up information on her. Noting it all down in his internal filing cabinet. A child in the car next to them was having a screaming tantrum. Dolly could happily pound her fists in irritation.

She remembered the day Fox had walked into the station. Brogden practically bouncing off the walls with pride that they had been the team selected for his transfer. The great Fox Mason. Ex-Marine. Holder of the Conspicuous Gallantry Cross medal for bravery. Spent time in the Gulf. Renowned hostage negotiator. Then, when he joined the force, he policed the meanest streets of London, was down with all the gang leaders, infamously kept the respect of those he'd banged up. Dolly had zoned out during Brogden's waffling speech.

Even Mungo and Rogers had nudged her with a snigger at the dramatic build-up. And then Fox had walked in with his understated swagger and, refusing the stage, had chosen to talk to the team individually, suggested everyone have a cuppa so they could just chat informally. Totally against Brogden's carefully orchestrated welcome ceremony. He'd had Mungo and Rogers onside before you could say Nescafé Gold Blend. Then he took them all to the pub after work, bought the first two rounds. Transfixed them with tales of covert operations and feats of endurance. Made Mungo spit out his pint as Fox talked of chopping his own toe off with a Swiss Army knife on one particular mission to stop the gangrene spreading. Dolly had sat back and watched with a mix of suspicion and jealousy. It had taken her years to get those same guys on side. Fox's routine seemed like well-practised manipulation to her.

'So, go on then,' Fox said as they cruised along a wide empty stretch of motorway, the sun warm on their backs, a couple of dead badgers at the side of the road being pecked at by crows. Wind turbines stationary in the still air. 'What's the story?'

'There is no story,' Dolly replied.

'You really are very defensive, Dolly.' Fox overtook a giant milk tanker. The size of it next to them made Dolly feel especially vulnerable.

'No, I'm not,' she could feel the edge in her voice.

'Your aunt said it was a funny time back then. Like funny haha?' Fox mused, trying to stumble on the answer. No reply. He thought for a second. 'Not funny, haha?' He paused. 'Is it not good with your sister? With this Ruben character?'

Dolly had stayed silent when she should have spoken.

Ruben went, 'Mmm, interesting,' with the smug deduction

of a TV detective. 'See, this is why I'm so good at my job,' he laughed.

'What? Arrogance?' she replied tartly.

'You're so funny, Dolly,' he said drily. Then carried on as if she hadn't spoken, 'So … I'm sensing some complex family history here.'

Dolly stiffened. 'There's no family history.' She had a sudden flash of Willoughby Park, reaching up on her tiptoes and her lips touching Ruben's, the coolness of his mouth, the smell of Marlboro Lights on his breath. The horror on his face.

'Every family has history, Dolly,' Fox replied, lifting his hand to wipe something off his visor, a squashed fly probably.

Dolly squeezed her eyes shut to make her mind go black. 'Not mine.'

They drove on for a minute or so in silence, Dolly presuming that was the end of the discussion. Then Fox said, 'Do you know, according to the Dalai Lama, the more honest and open you are the less fear you'll have, because you won't have the anxiety about being exposed to others. Don't you think that's interesting?'

Dolly couldn't believe what she was hearing. 'According to the Dalai Lama?' she scoffed. 'Is that from your Quote of the Day calendar?'

'No, Dolly,' Fox replied, carefully moving round a caravan that suddenly pulled out into the middle lane without indicating. 'I learnt it from a Tibetan monk.'

Dolly snorted a laugh.

'You don't believe me?' asked Fox.

The sun was getting hotter, the parched ground was dotted with mirages of puddles up ahead. Brambles and blackthorn bushes tangled at the roadside like snakes.

'Actually, I do believe you. I can totally imagine it,' said Dolly, rolling her eyes at the very idea. 'I just think it's ridiculous. Where was this Tibetan monk?'

'Tibet,' Fox replied, deadpan. 'His name was Ngawang.'

'I'm sure it was,' she replied, not quite sure whether she believed him or not. 'What other gems did he teach you?'

'Well, my favourite is "Recognise, overcome, then transcend."'

Dolly had never heard anything more ludicrous. 'Do you have them filed on index cards?'

'Some of them,' Fox replied, glossing over her mockery.

Dolly sighed. 'So go on then, why were you with a monk in Tibet?' she asked, waiting for some epic tale of heroism and bravery.

'Because when I had a breakdown and left the military,' he said, matter-of-fact, 'a monastery in the Himalayas seemed like a good place to go.'

That shut her up.

'Anything else you want to know?' he asked, as if any aspect of his life were there for the taking.

So much! Dolly's brain screamed. Instead, she said, 'No,' as if she wasn't curious at all and they drove on in silence.

Dolly gazed at clouds closing in on the fading blue sky and wondered why Fox had had a breakdown. The thought of it didn't align with his macho bravado. Or maybe it did. Maybe it aligned exactly. She wondered what it would be like to be so honest. If she'd actually listened to his Dalai Lama quote then perhaps she would know. Dolly didn't tell anyone about herself. Only the neighbour's cat and it would walk off halfway through. It was weird to imagine just saying the truth when asked. The thought of it almost made her laugh.

The air was still clammy and warm but up ahead the sky had gone from picture-perfect to ominously black, grey pastel lines sheeting the horizon. Just looking at it made Dolly think of thunder.

They approached signs to a service station and Fox indicated. 'I just want to grab something to eat. You want anything?'

'No, thanks.' Dolly wasn't hungry. Fox ate all the time. She knew that from their stakeouts. Him always stopping for a Snickers or something. For someone so Zen he ate like shit.

'I'll wait here. But can you take my helmet off before you go?' Dolly asked as they pulled up in the car park.

Fox obliged with, 'The great Dolly King asks for help,' and a grating chuckle.

Dolly folded her arms and waited staunchly by the bike. She stood, watching people coming and going with their Burger Kings, wondering again what Olive and Ruben were doing. Knowing them, they'd probably already finished the treasure hunt. So aligned in their innate competitiveness, it was pointless even trying to compare. As children, Dolly would still be reading the clue as Olive or Ruben hollered the answer and the other set off in hot pursuit. She remembered one Christmas, her mother mortgaged up to the hilt in Monopoly, shaking her head at Olive and Ruben and saying, 'You two should go into business together. You'd rule the world!' Even then Dolly had felt the red-hot stab of jealousy. Why couldn't they rule the world as a three?

Dolly checked her phone: nothing. She ran through her head what she would say when she saw Ruben, considered his appraisal of her. She wasn't stupid, she knew she looked different. She was honed and toned and her hair was the colour of gold. She'd grown into her features. Her nose was less obvious, her big eyes had stayed the same. She didn't have the time or inclination for much make-up, but her one indulgence was her hair salon bills. The tree-climbing, frizzy-haired tomboy was a thing of the past. She allowed her imagination to run away with itself, to conjure up what Ruben's face might look like when he saw her. She wouldn't admit it to a soul but she was wistful for a double-take. Maybe even a low whistle. That was the fantasy. The idea of it made her bite down on an embarrassed wince. Admitting it even to herself made her blush.

'Hello gorgeous,' a voice said next to her. 'Waiting for me?'

Dolly's head shot up.

She was surrounded by four guys in black leather. Younger than her but taller. Big lads munching on Burger King Whoppers. The one talking to her had a tattoo of skeleton teeth over his knuckles.

Dolly felt like all her innermost desires and silly wants were visible in the redness on her cheeks. It made her feel small and exposed. She narrowed her eyes. 'No,' she said with a withering glare. 'I'm certainly not waiting for you.'

The guy laughed. Looked round at his mates. 'Feisty.'

Dolly rolled her eyes. 'Get on your bike and go.'

'But I've got my burger to eat and you to look at, sweetheart,' the guy said, and his mates laughed in unison like sniggering hyenas. 'Stunner like you. Bet you give it some.' He winked. His hair was too short and his skin held a trace of acne scars but his eyes were pale like wolves' and cut right to her core.

Under normal circumstances, this would be water off a duck's back. But Dolly felt ashamed of her pathetic fantasies, angry that she had dropped her guard in such a public place. Her lip curled. 'Before you go any further, I should warn you, I'm an officer of the law and I could arrest you for harassment.'

'Ooooooh!' The guy made a show of acting scared. His mates grinned. Then he leaned in real close and said, 'I like a woman in uniform.'

Dolly snarled.

The guy smirked. 'We could teach you a thing or two.' His mates grinned. He took the last bite of his Whopper and chucked the wrapper on the floor. He licked his lips. 'Girl like you. All nice on the outside. Bet you like it a bit rough, don't you? Bit nasty.'

Before he could say anything more, Dolly had swept his legs out from underneath him and had him pinned to the floor, her knee jabbed into his spine and his arm pulled round his back with her one good hand. The movement had been murder on her dislocated shoulder. His face was pressed into the gravel. His mates were frozen for a second in shock but then before they could react, Dolly muttered through gritted teeth, 'Any of you come any closer and I'll break his arm and arrest the lot of you. Got it?'

They watched, uncertain how to react. The guy's face was contorted in agony on the tarmac. 'Get off my arm, you bitch!' People were slowing to watch, panicked and intrigued by the drama.

Then she heard Fox's voice. 'What's going on?' His shadow loomed over them. 'Dolly?'

'Nothing,' she said, getting her breathing back under control. The guy's mates seemed less inclined to react now Fox was there, intimidated by the hulking great size of him. Dolly leaned forward so her mouth was close to the guy on the floor's ear,

'Watch your mouth in future.' Then she loosened her grip on his arm and stood up, walking away back to the bike like nothing had happened. Fox watched, confused. 'What's going on?'

The guy stood up, brushing gravel off his jacket. 'Your girlfriend's an effing psycho, that's what's going on!'

'Calm down, sir.' Fox held up a hand to pacify then looked between the pair of them. 'Do we need to talk about this?'

'Yeah,' the guy spat. 'I want her charged with police brutality.'

Dolly scoffed. 'Shut up.'

'OK, let's all take a moment—'

The guy did an imitation of Fox and made his mates laugh again. Then he said, 'Piss off, you twat.' And to his mates, 'Let's go. Good luck with the bitch,' he added, a sly smirk on his lips as they sauntered over to where their own bikes were parked.

'Dolly, you're suspended from duty. You can't have people on the floor. What did he do?'

'He was a prat. I was just teaching him a lesson,' she said, adrenaline subsiding, annoyed with herself for losing her cool over something so petty. The lecherous taunts merging insidiously with her childish fantasies. Riling her, making her forget all her training, making her embarrassed at her own weaknesses. What had she been doing pinning him to the floor?

'Great way of going about it,' Fox replied, shaking his head.

'Don't shake your head at me. You weren't there!'

Fox raised a brow. 'You're telling me whatever happened just then, it really needed to end with him flat on the floor?'

Dolly stared at him. 'Yes,' she said. 'Yes, it did.'

Fox blew out a breath. 'You need to learn to fight with your mouth not your hands.'

'Is that another Buddhist quote?' she asked snarkily.

Fox didn't deign a reply, just got on the bike and pulled on his helmet. Dolly got on behind and annoyingly had to wait for him to turn and help her on with her helmet.

They had to drive past the gang of guys to exit. Dolly heard them shouting and she gave them the finger.

'Dolly!' Fox reprimanded.

She felt like a child.

They pulled out onto the motorway. Clouds were blocking the glare from the sun. The traffic was mainly lorries.

Neither her nor Fox said anything. She could feel herself sulking. She felt the weight of irritation with her own behaviour. Replayed it a couple of times, thinking how she could have done it differently. She hated herself for her pathetic fantasy about Ruben.

Staring out at the countryside, Dolly saw an old billboard for Wookey Hole Caves, which she'd been desperate to visit as a kid. Then she saw her favourite Little Chef was now a Starbucks. She bit her lip, remembering stops on the way to London to visit Aunt Marge. Sharing toasted teacakes with Olive and blowing bubbles through their straws as their dad complained about the Little Chef coffee and went off on captivating tangents about espresso he'd drunk made out of civet poo. Their mum serenely sipping her tea, tucked snugly under his arm, so blissfully happy when the family was together as one.

It drove home the feeling of loss, of change. It reminded Dolly why the hell she hadn't wanted to come in the first place.

The rain had started to fall, fat and heavy, almost sizzling when it hit the tarmac.

She remembered the day they had left Willoughby Park. Their stuff rammed into overnight cases. Plastic bags of whatever extra bits they could fit in Aunt Marge's car. She remembered asking what would happen to the rest of it and no one answering. Like her voice had disappeared along with everything else. Driving away in Aunt Marge's ridiculously impractical white Mazda, straight past the Little Chef and Wookey Hole because Marge didn't stop, Dolly had still thought there was a chance they would return. What else would happen to their stuff otherwise? It was too terrifying to think that normality was no longer a possibility.

Suddenly she wanted to be off this long, monotonous road, away from its familiarity. She wanted to turn around but she wouldn't be able to explain why to Fox. She wanted a diversion. Anything.

Except the next minute, she got her wish and wished she hadn't. The loudest roar came up behind them. Dolly glanced round to see the gang of riders from the service station bearing down on them. The bikes had no silencers, the noise was ear-splitting. The leader, with his skull tattoo drove really close, his tyre almost scraping Fox's, goading.

'What are they doing!' Dolly couldn't believe anyone would be so stupid. She beckoned for them to shoo with her hand.

'Being dicks,' said Fox, tightly controlled tension in his voice, the muscles in his back taut.

'Go away!' Dolly shouted.

One was making funny faces at Dolly, inane, wide grinning eyes. She looked away. She wished she was in her police car with her nice siren and the actual legal ability to make an arrest. But her and Fox were ordinary citizens today.

'Just ignore them. They'll get bored.'

But they didn't get bored. They skidded through the rain, cajoling Fox to go faster, swerving really close.

The rain puddled on the hot, impenetrable ground, making the road like a skid pan and the bikes slide across the surface. Dolly could feel her adrenaline rise. She knew if she was in the driver's seat she'd be tempted to floor it, to weave through the traffic. Ego demanded it of her.

But Fox just ticked over calmly. Purred along at a steady speed, refusing to rise to the challenge. Recognising, overcoming and transcending, thought Dolly, who wanted to stick her leg out and kick the skull tattoo guy next to her off his bike. But then suddenly he was reaching across to grab her. Eyes laughing. She could feel him pulling her dislocated shoulder, the pain so sharp she could barely hold on with her one good hand. 'He's pulling me off, Fox!'

Fox glanced round. Taking one hand off the handlebars, he did a swift karate chop on the guy's outstretched hand to disentangle them. But as he did, a lorry up ahead pulled out from the slow lane, water spraying like a fountain off his tyres. Two of the bikers ahead shot dangerously through the narrow gap. But the one next to them was going too fast to do anything but swerve at right angles straight in front of Fox. Fox braked hard but it wasn't enough. Dolly could see the panic in the other biker's eyes. Rain streamed down.

Fox shouted, 'Hold on!'

Dolly gripped the wet leather of his jacket as hard as she could as he swerved sharp left, cutting between two giant juggernauts, missing the front grille of one by a hair's breadth.

Horns resounded. Their bike flew off the road through the bramble spikes of the grassy verge and then bounced down onto the furrowed earth of a cornfield, flattening six-foot-high corn as they powered forward in the driving rain.

Dolly gripped tight as she was thrown up and down in her seat. Her hands and neck were bleeding from the brambles. The corn was whipping past them. Fox wiped the rain off his visor, slowing as they went further into the field, looking around for where best to go but there were only fat green stalks like a jungle, then the bike suddenly hit a lump of earth and pitched them both forward, Dolly landing half beside, half on top of Fox, both under the full weight of the enormous bike.

'Shit,' Fox shouted. It was the first time Dolly had heard him lose his temper. He yanked off his helmet, wincing in pain as he tried with all his strength to lift the bike off their legs. 'Can you get free? Are you hurt?' He checked her first and foremost as his arms braced against the weight.

'I think I'm OK,' Dolly said, mentally scanning herself. Her dislocated arm surprisingly fine. Fox was taking most of the weight of the bike which meant she could wriggle herself free. 'Are you OK?' she asked, lifting her visor, unable to get the helmet off on her own one-handed.

Fox was trying to get out from under the dead weight of the bike. Dolly crouched down and using her good hand did her best to haul it upwards, creating enough of a gap that he could roll himself out, shuffling backwards till he was clear and she could let go, dropping the big lump of metal with a thud.

Fox lay back on the flattened corn. His eyes shut. The rain drenching them. Dolly sat down opposite. The pair of them hidden amongst the giant corn.

'Are you hurt?' she asked.

He exhaled once, then pushed himself up on his elbows and

said, 'No.' He looked like he was trying really hard to keep his composure.

The rain was trickling down Dolly's back. She looked down at her feet, away from his glare. She could tell he was steaming, trying his best to control the rage coiled tight inside. He stood up and tested his weight on his ankle, uncertain. With a vague limp that he clearly wasn't going to admit to, he walked silently over to the bike, inspecting it. Rain was dripping off his nose. With both hands on the handlebars, he heaved it up off the ground with all his effort. The other side had fared worse. The body was dented, the paintwork ravaged. Fox flicked out the stand and went round to have a look. 'Shit!' he said when he saw it, hands pressed in anger to the back of his head.

Dolly bit her lip. She stood up too.

He scrutinised the damage like he was inspecting a child, fingers soft on the scratches. He shook his head. She knew he blamed her without him having to say anything. She blamed herself. Her overreaction had been basic training stuff: had she kept a psychological advantage? No. Had she eliminated the need for excessive force? No. Had she let her pathetic childhood vulnerabilities cloud her judgement? Yes, yes, yes.

Lightning forked down the horizon and thunder rumbled overhead. Fox kicked one of the giant stalks of corn in frustration. 'Why couldn't you have just …' he stopped himself.

Hands on her hips, Dolly replied, 'Why couldn't I have what? Go on, say it,' her voice muffled by the helmet.

Fox turned to look at her, standing in the middle of the decimated corn. His expression changed from thunderous to confused, then softened into a satisfied smile. 'You can't get that helmet off on your own, can you?'

Dolly looked away in frustration. It was still raining. They were both soaked.

Fox sauntered over to where she was standing and stood in front of her, arms crossed over his massive chest. 'It would serve you right for me to leave you in it,' he said, and Dolly felt a sickening sense of claustrophobia at the idea of her head being stuck inside the helmet for the foreseeable future.

She looked up at him. He looked down at her, still mad.

She swallowed. 'Can you take it off, please?'

He paused, nostrils flaring with annoyance as he considered her request. 'You're an idiot, Dolly King,' he said, his eyes boring into hers. 'A child who needs to grow up. A hot-headed, temper-driven baby who has absolutely no understanding or grasp of her own emotions. Did you know that?'

Dolly didn't reply.

Fox reached over and yanked her helmet off with none of the care and attention he had before.

CHAPTER EIGHT

Down at the crumbling cottage, the sea lapping gently on the sand, Olive couldn't bring herself to follow Ruben inside. She was frozen in limbo on the well-worn doorstep. Zadie was already trotting through the dusty entrance hall nudging beer cans with her Converse-clad foot and trying to decipher graffiti. Olive feigned an untied shoelace, stalling for time.

She wondered what her dad would think of her, unable to set foot inside the house. He'd tell her about the night he broke into the catacombs of Paris. 'If you're not afraid of ghosts, then what's the problem? It's just dead people. And they can't harm you.'

But what if you are afraid of ghosts? Olive thought, the cool smell of the stone cottage invading her senses. She thought of Mark all cosy in his new home with mousy Barbara. What would her dad think of that? The fact she had grown up to live, however unknowingly, comfortably loveless. He would say something symbolically practical like, you move forward by putting one foot in front of the other, Olive. Yet going into the cottage felt more like an unwilling step backwards. Like a purge. Or that blood-draining that Victorians did. Or …

'I think it says, "Suck my—"'

'OK, that's enough.' Olive strode into the dusty darkness, dragging Zadie away from the lurid graffiti. Ruben was nowhere to be seen.

Olive was immediately assaulted by the views from every angle. The big French windows that framed the back garden. The hallway, once covered floor to ceiling with her mum's collection of oil paintings and sculptures. Zadie clamped to her side, Olive walked further down the corridor. She wasn't sure if she was breathing, so made herself take a breath. The kitchen was ransacked. The oven on its side. Zadie picked up a saucepan that had been burnt right through. The only thing unchanged was the view. The sea so bright it was almost white in the darkness.

Ruben appeared, spiderwebs in his hair. 'What a state!'

Olive nodded.

'I'm really sorry,' he said. He ran his hand through his hair and found the webs, swiping them away with a frown.

Olive shook her head. 'It's not your fault,' she said, and walked on so she didn't have to look at him. She poked her head into the living room, remembering the chair where her dad had had his daily nap when he was home. Piling logs into the wood burner in winter and rescuing little sparrows that had fallen down the chimney in summer. The shaggy lurcher, Everest, at his feet.

She paused in the doorway. Her brain was expecting rugs and lumpy soft furnishings, tasselled lamps and Persian rugs, sun-sparkling dusty air and a mantelpiece overflowing with jugs and ornaments. Instead, she saw a couple of disposable barbecues, crunched cans of Special Brew and an old Tesco bag. There was a distinct smell of mouldy wood and urine that made her want to cry.

Olive had no memory of it being cleared of their stuff. Who had packed away their belongings? It couldn't have been her mother. Maybe Aunt Marge.

As she stood staring, Ruben and Zadie came up next to her. 'This was the living room,' he said to Zadie, her nose wrinkled at the smell. 'It didn't look anything like this. It was all papered dark blue, even the ceiling.'

'Red,' said Olive, absently, half listening. 'It was dark red.'

Ruben frowned, 'Really? Sorry, red. And there were big pictures and all these colourful lights and cushions.'

Zadie looked around as if trying to envisage it.

'I am yet to see the point of a cushion,' Ruben continued, 'but I do remember a truckload of cushions in this room.' He glanced at Olive and she smiled half out of politeness and half because his presence, his jokes, did actually make it seem less bleak. 'And they used to throw the best parties,' he shook his head in awe at the memory. 'My God, they were fun. Think I threw up on gin for the first time at one of them.'

'Vodka,' Olive corrected.

'Was it vodka?' he looked unsure.

'It was definitely vodka. We never had gin in the house.' It was impossible not to remember what her mum was like after a gin fizz. It was Olive who had banned it from the house.

Ruben said, 'Well these parties, Zadie, you wouldn't believe it. The music, the dancing, the booze. The people. The whole bloody village was here.'

Zadie grinned. 'Really?'

'Oh yeah. And Olive's dad would put on an old tux, do you remember that?' he asked Olive, and she nodded, unable not to smile fondly at the thought of her dad donning his bow tie

99

and slicking back his hair. 'And her mum would have some big flouncy dress on and there was a band. Your dad was in the band, wasn't he?'

Again Olive nodded. She could feel an actual ache in her heart.

'See, Zaid, I'm getting it right,' Ruben joked.

Zadie couldn't help herself from smiling shyly at the use of a nickname.

In the room, everything was coming to life with his words and his memories. Different from Olive's own. As if slipping out from under a blanket of darkness. Her dad doing a jig in his moth-eaten tux, fiddle under his chin. Dolly with her rusty trumpet. Her mum clapping along, golden hair piled on top of her head, her dress cascading layers of home-stitched satin ruffles. Tables bowing under the weight of wine and glasses as the neighbours poured through the door.

Because, of course, that was what her family did when they got a bit of money. Her dad was always off somewhere hunting down the next big thing, the hidden cache that would make them rich – opal mining in Australia, a Spanish galleon sunk off the coast of Cartagena packed with King Philip V's gems, billions hidden in the jungle by an executed drug baron – all rumour and hearsay that had him packing his trusty camouflage bag. And on occasion he'd return with a big roll of folded notes in his pocket. But it never occurred to her parents to put it in the bank or pay the electricity bill. Oh no. Instead, they all got dressed up and went to Angelica's Trattoria and ate fresh spaghetti with giant prawns and endless scoops of multicoloured ice cream. And her mum and dad would get up and dance. Her mum all ruffles and flowers, her hair like copper in the cheap disco lights, her teeth gleaming as she laughed. And Dolly would grin at Olive, and Olive would smile back, but always with a knot of apprehension in the pit of her stomach.

Olive's mum had worked managing the small team that organised the public tours of Willoughby Park, her salary was minimal because it was pro-rata against a reduced rent cottage on the grounds. Her Christmas bonus went on booze and laughter for the village. Ironic, thought Olive, how determined she herself had been to never again live in fear of the electricity people knocking on the door and the hidden piles of red bills. Look where that had got her – abandoned by her supposed life partner, working in a job where new management hires she didn't respect very much took her idea and tweaked it to save costs, altered the fabric choices and chose less reputable factories in order to profit the shareholders. All for the sake of the safe option. What would have happened had she just relaxed and enjoyed the party?

Ruben nudged her on the shoulder and said, 'God, they were fun those parties, weren't they?'

Were they fun? She had a flash memory of Ruben dancing with her mother. And her dad dragging her to the Persian carpet for a turn. Dolly in a tutu. Sitting under a table, legs of guests all around them, Ruben swigging port from the bottle, passing it to Olive. Outside, strolling down the icy beach so they could look back on the cosy glow of the house. His hand wrapped firm and warm round hers. Olive looked across at him and something to do with the setting, with the memories at the forefront of her mind, for the first time since being back it was like looking across at Ruben de Lacy, the boy from the Big House. Same eyes, same crooked smile. She remembered his hand on her cheek as they kissed for the first time, hidden in the shadows, the clouds of their frozen breath mingling with the sea spray. A moment when it felt like the whole world paused just for her and she could shut her eyes and live pressed against his dark woollen coat forever.

But then Olive saw herself reflected in the cracked glass of a mirror on the wall behind him. The sight of her own sad eyes bringing with it other flashes of memory. The times she hauled her mother to bed and sat guard to check she was breathing or stroking her hair as she sobbed. The echoes of the silent weeping all around her. The soft hand that clutched hers so tight she thought her bones might crush. Constantly having to calm down Dolly and her million and one desperate questions. The lurcher pissing on the floor because no one had taken it out. She thought of the times she'd searched the house for money, gone through pockets of coats to scrabble together loose change. Unscrewed caps of Ribena from the larder only to smell the sweet acrid stench of wine. She remembered sitting on the swing, Ruben on the grass in front of her, swigging from a bottle of whisky stolen from his dad that he'd got a whipping for later, staring out at the sea saying, 'We've got to get out of here, Ruben, before it's too late.'

In the darkness of the ransacked house she heard Ruben ask, 'You OK?'

Olive had an overwhelming urge to be sick. 'I think I have to go outside.'

Ruben nodded, his brow drawn with confused worry. 'You don't want to go down in the cellar?'

Olive shook her head, fighting against the urine-scented air and the collapsing catastrophe of her childhood home. 'No, you go. It's fine. Look in the corner. That's where the coal was.' She was striding out of the cottage before he replied. Walking so fast she almost tripped, her shoulder bashing against the corridor wall, out the door, through the too-narrow gap in the metal hoarding so her T-shirt tore, and down onto the beach. Stopping only when her toes were nearly at the water's edge and she could breathe in lungfuls of sharp salty sea air.

It didn't take long for Ruben to stride out of the front door. Zadie skipping along by his side.

Olive was hovering on the path, half wondering if she should go back in. She hated being pathetic and defeated. 'Sorry about that,' she said as soon as she saw them.

'That's OK,' Ruben replied, 'you were right to get out, it was bloody terrifying down there.' His clothes were sheened with white dust.

'We saw a rat!' added Zadie.

'I wouldn't have liked to see a rat,' Olive shuddered, to Zadie's look of disgust.

'And you used to be so brave!' Ruben teased, swiping the dust off his shoulders.

Olive hated how hard the joke hit. Where had her courage gone? They were standing opposite each other on the sand. Ruben turned to Zadie and said, 'Do you know it was Olive who made us all camp out in the woods one Halloween?'

Olive frowned, she couldn't remember it at all. 'Did I?'

'Oh yeah.' Ruben seemed surprised she couldn't picture it. 'Your dad had that tent and you made us all drag out duvets and pillows. You must remember? The mad dog was there. And we told ghost stories that scared the crap out of Dolly.'

Olive put her hand to her mouth. 'We did, didn't we? Oh God, and that deer came over and we told Dolly it was a were-wolf or something.' She bit her lip guiltily. 'Poor Dolly.'

'Yeah, she never camped again.' Ruben did a deep belly laugh.

Olive tried to stop from smiling. 'We were really mean.'

Ruben shrugged. 'I remember being pretty spooked myself. I think you were the only one who made it till morning. Out of sheer stubborn determination!'

Olive remembered then, waking up alone in the tent, the sound of the birds outside as the sun rose and filled the warm canvas with a calm orange glow. A moment of paradise, before heading back into the chaos of the house.

It was strange seeing herself as he saw her. His memories cutting through her own. Would she have so willingly fled the cottage had they had this conversation first? She pushed her shoulders back, made herself stand taller. She was suddenly quite pleased that her hair was messy from sea spray and her uncreasable white T-shirt was torn and streaked with dirt.

Zadie said, 'So shall we read the next clue?' She turned to Ruben as she said it and picked a couple of old spiderweb strands from his shirt.

Olive had forgotten all about the clues.

Ruben seemed distracted from being preened by his daughter – torn between whether to shrug her off or let her continue to sort out his filthy shirt. In the end he stepped away slightly so he could continue the dusting off himself, which meant he handed the clue to Olive.

Olive was once again walloped in the chest by the sight of her dad's scrawling handwriting but this time rather than distance herself from it she allowed herself to fall into it. To see his tanned calloused hand as it held the pen, the speed with which he wrote, like everything was holding him back from life's adventures.

'There you are in the treetops. There you are in the sky. There you are in the water. Always nearby ...'

Ruben looked up blankly. 'Well, that's just gobbledegook.'

Olive wasn't really concentrating on the words because her mind was being flooded with images of her and her dad. Things she had just accepted as part of her childhood suddenly seemed exotic and crazy and completely unforgettable. The times he took her bouldering round the headland with the waves lapping beneath them, canyoning the hidden gorges and plunge pools. Just her and her dad – Dolly always left behind for being too young or for having whined one too many times that it was raining or too cold. But Olive had camped in mid-winter with little more than a bivouac of sticks and a blanket, fuelled by her dad's obsession to both overcome and become one with nature. They poached, they skinned, they cooked in ovens dug out of the mud. They rafted down vertical rapids on homemade rafts thrashed together with string. Whether she had done it to impress him or because she wanted to was never in question, she just went along because when he was home he invited her and it made her feel special.

Thinking about it now, it wasn't that she had forgotten those times, it was that she had taken them as normal, absorbed them as generic childhood events. Like the camping at Halloween. Yet now, looking back, the precious uniqueness of the trips left her with such a mix of sorrow and joy, it made her breath catch.

'What do you think, Olive?'

'What do I think about what? Oh sorry, yeah, erm ...' Olive stared at the clue, trying to get her brain to focus on the riddle. Then she laughed, more genuinely relaxed than she had been since she arrived. 'I have absolutely no idea.'

Ruben raised his hands in the air. 'Well, we're nailing this, aren't we?'

CHAPTER NINE

Dolly was sweating. Her leather jacket was draped over the bike seat along with Fox's, their helmets strapped onto the back with their bags. The rain had cleared. Disappeared like it had never happened. The sun burnt through the clouds like fire. The bike had refused to start when Fox had tried it. Dolly's phone had no signal and Fox's screen had cracked in the crash and was now half black and unresponsive.

All around them was corn. Stretching high up into the sky. Corn leaves, corn stalks, corn cobs trying to break free of their leafy green casings.

'I'm going to lift you up and you need to look around and see what you can see,' Fox said, wiping sweat off his forehead with the back of his hand.

Dolly didn't love the idea of him lifting her up. She was still smarting from Fox's little tell-off before he removed her helmet. Dolly wasn't used to being told off. Or rather, wasn't used to being told off and it resonating. Boring down into her body like a worm. When she was told off at work she just shrugged it off because she was usually right anyway. And she had never been told off as a kid. Her mum didn't believe in it. '*Raised voices crush the spirit,*' she would say, admonishing Olive for yelling at Dolly for something she'd done: going into her room without knocking or scratching a CD. Olive would stomp off in irritation while Dolly would shuffle closer to her mum and let her hair be plaited or lie on the carpet with her nose pressed up to their knackered old dog, Everest, while her mum dreamily sketched the pair of them.

'OK,' Dolly replied to Fox's suggestion because there wasn't really another option.

He came up behind her and put his big hands on her waist, lifting her up like an ice skater in a show. One minute she was on the ground, the next she was in the air. It was the strangest sensation; Dolly was strong and agile and independent, she wasn't used to being at another's mercy, but there was certainly a novelty to being hoisted effortlessly off the floor by big manly arms. The thought of it made her want to laugh.

'What can you see?'

Suddenly Dolly had the giggles. 'Nothing,' she said, trying to stop herself laughing.

'Dolly, stop pissing about, we're stuck in a bloody cornfield.'

'I know, sorry.' She put her hand over her mouth to try and contain the urge to snigger. 'Erm, what can I see?'

'Hurry up,' Fox urged. 'You're not light, you know.'

That made it less funny. She'd been imagining herself like a feather. 'All right!' She gave the horizon a once-over. 'It's just fields,' she said. Fox's arms were starting to waver.

'Can you see the road?'

'No.' She squinted towards a copse of trees in the distance. 'I think I can see a roof by some trees over there.' She pointed ahead of them.

'You think or you can?' he asked, voice tinged with irritation.

'I *think* I *can*,' she snapped.

Fox dropped her to the ground with an exhale of effort.

'All right, I'm not that heavy!' Dolly smarted.

Fox had his arms crossed over his chest, clearly wanting to keep to the point.

Dolly straightened her blue T-shirt, which was streaked with dirt and sweat. 'I think there was a roof. It was over there.' She pointed to where she'd been looking.

'So about thirty degrees due east?' said Fox.

'If you say so,' Dolly replied, one brow arched.

Fox shook his head, sighing with exasperation; he'd clearly had enough of her. She didn't want to think too much about the fact she'd managed to really piss off the most Zen unpiss-off-able police officer on the force. But at least he'd stopped quoting Buddhist monks at her.

The corn stalks were sticky and the leaves whipped annoyingly against their faces as they started to trudge thirty degrees due east in the heat. Fox was clearly having trouble with his ankle but wasn't going to admit it. Dolly's shoulder had started to throb. Sweat poured down her back and across her forehead. Fox's T-shirt was damp. The motorbike looked heavy to push. Dolly's trainers were rubbing her heels. She was thirsty.

Suddenly Fox stopped and held up his hand for Dolly to do the same.

'What?' she grumbled.

'Sssh!' he whispered, then pointing at the ground ahead of them said, 'Look!'

'What?' she whispered, concerned, looking to where he was pointing for imminent danger, only to see a tiny mouse nibbling on a fallen cob of corn, a kernel in its little paws.

Dolly frowned. 'The mouse?' she asked quietly.

'Yes, the mouse,' he replied, crouching as low as he could while still holding the bike so he could get a better look.

Dolly couldn't quite believe he'd stopped them to look at a mouse. There was a snarky remark poised on the tip of her tongue but something made her hold it back.

She glanced from the mouse to Fox, who was transfixed by the furry little creature. Dolly wondered if he would have stopped had he been with Mungo and Rogers. Probably. But they wouldn't have hesitated to quip something cutting in return, to stamp their feet so it ran away or joke about mouse kebab for dinner. They were who Dolly had made herself comfortable with on the force. They armed her with a sardonic shield of one-upmanship.

But Fox wasn't interested in any witty quip she might reply. He was too busy studying the fluffy little rodent. He didn't care about Dolly. He wasn't in it for the laugh. She was free, she realised, to crouch down next to him and look at the mouse too, but somehow, it took more effort than it would to clap her hands and guffaw, Mungo and Rogers style; to pause, silent and not care. It was something she did only in her own flat when she gave all her plants a bath, wiping their dusty leaves one by one, or bought nuts that she would never eat herself so she could feed them to the sparrows. It was the side of her that had scratched her legs creeping through bracken at Willoughby Park to catch a glimpse of the baby fawn. That cycled off before breakfast with a jam jar for tadpoles or made her own fishing rod to catch tiddlers in the stream.

How funny that a mouse could mean so much. Its little mouth and black beady eyes. She glanced again at Fox, who was still transfixed, and realised that it wasn't the mouse, it was the freedom to unselfconsciously enjoy a simple moment if she was brave enough to take it. No bravado, no jokey defence mechanism. She lowered herself down, shoulder to shoulder with Fox, and tried her best to watch in peaceful silence.

The moment, however, only emphasised the fact she wasn't at peace. She couldn't calmly watch because, she realised, her moral compass was askew. She owed Fox an apology and would be restlessly on the back foot until she gave it to him.

Sensing he was being looked at, Fox turned his head. The mouse caught the movement and froze. A second later it had disappeared into the corn.

'It's gone,' Dolly said.

Fox nodded. 'Let's carry on,' he said, hands on the handlebars, using the bike to flatten the corn ahead of them.

Dolly watched his back as he pushed forward in the heat. She looked at the dents in the side of the motorbike. She put her hands in her pockets. She breathed in through her nose, psyching herself up, 'Fox ...'

He paused and turned, 'Yeah?'

No, she couldn't do it. 'Nothing.' When she mulled the words over in her brain, it went against her every instinct. Admission of guilt felt like it would give him the upper hand.

Fox trudged on. The corn stalks fell. Dolly glanced behind to see how far they'd come. An arcing line like a crop circle behind them.

She saw how the rainwater collected where the corn leaves joined the stalk in tiny glistening puddles possibly for use by the plant later on. She wondered whether to point it out to Fox but realised she couldn't. It made her too vulnerable to ridicule.

She ran her fingers along the leaves as they walked. The sun beat heavy on her hair, burning her scalp.

How did he manage to have such an effect on her sense of right and wrong? He was so annoying.

Just apologise, Dolly, and be done with it! She looked up at the trickle of sweat between the muscles in his neck. 'Fox,' she said.

'Yeah,' he replied, pushing on with the bike, leaning forward now with effort.

Dolly took a breath, stealing herself. 'I'm sorry, you know, about what happened with the bikers, but I didn't know they'd follow us.'

She didn't know what she was expecting but Fox didn't even pause. Didn't even turn or say, 'That's OK.'

Unsure what else to say, she added, 'And, well, I'm sorry you're annoyed about the damage to your bike.'

He paused. 'You're sorry I'm annoyed or you're sorry for the damage?'

'Well technically I didn't do the damage—'

Fox held up a hand for her to stop and kept walking. Dolly had no choice but to follow. Her sense of wrongdoing no better than it was before. Worse possibly.

CHAPTER TEN

Ruben, Olive and Zadie took the shaded path through the woodlands back to the Big House, a little more bonded by the camaraderie brought out by the clues.

'I'm hungry,' said Zadie.

'So am I,' agreed Ruben, which clearly wasn't the answer Zadie was used to by the jut of her bottom lip. He imagined her mother kept a stash of suitable snacks in her bag for such occasions.

'We could get a rabbit,' he said, purely to wind her up.

Zadie's face fell in horror. 'What do you mean, get a rabbit?'

Ruben shrugged. 'Trap it. Skin it. Cook it on a fire. More likely a stoat around these parts, though.'

This was more than Zadie could endure. 'He's not going to do that, is he?' she asked Olive quietly, who shook her head, gesturing back towards Ruben, who was trying not to grin as he said, 'Maybe a fat pigeon if we're lucky.'

'Please make him stop,' urged Zadie, throwing Ruben a glare, at which he laughed and said, 'Just kidding, I wouldn't have the faintest idea how to kill a rabbit or a stoat.'

They walked on some more. Zadie peppering her pouts with the occasional desperate moan of 'I'm starving.'

Olive came to the rescue, pausing in the woodland to tear some berries off a bush. 'You can eat these,' she said, handing them to Zadie.

'What if they kill me?' Zadie looked very dubiously down at the fruit. 'I don't want to die before finding the treasure.'

Olive laughed. 'They're bilberries, they won't kill you.'

Zadie tentatively put one in her mouth. Ruben ripped a handful off the bush and scoffed the lot.

'They're quite tasty,' Zadie admitted, nibbling on another.

Olive bent down and picked a yellow chanterelle mushroom. 'You can eat these too, but it's better to cook them.'

'Wow, how do you know this stuff?' Zadie was impressed.

Olive said, 'My dad taught me.'

Zadie glanced across at Ruben as if expecting similar dad-like tutelage from him but he held his hands up and said, 'Don't look at me, kid, I'm as clueless as you. The only place I forage is Waitrose.'

Zadie picked some more bilberries. 'That's OK,' she said, mouth full. 'I learn loads already off my stepdad, Barry. He knows everything. And I really like acting and reading and he's in an amateur dramatics group.'

Ruben snorted a laugh at the idea.

Zadie frowned at him, her forehead furrowed in question.

Chastened, Ruben said, 'Sorry, I don't know why I laughed.'

They walked on through the dappled woods, light dancing on the leaves.

'So you like acting; do you want to be an actress when you're older?' Olive asked.

'Oh yeah, definitely,' Zadie replied without hesitation.

Ruben had to stifle a sigh.

'I love acting,' Zadie went on. 'Shakespeare especially. I think actually at the moment, I'd prefer to be a playwright. Or a poet. But preferably a playwright …' And she was off. Ruben wondered if it was a skill not to have to pause for breath. Maybe he could tout her out to *Britain's Got Talent*?

But Olive was listening, nodding, smiling. Was she humouring her or actually listening?

They crunched on through the dry forest. The smell of pine and sun-warmed bark all around them.

'I did want to be an actress but I get really bad stage fright, like totally frozen.' Zadie made a face as if she were mid-strangulation. 'It's because of all the overthinking. My brain just kind of short-circuits under pressure. But like, if there was no audience, you know, then I think I'd be a really good actress.' She nodded, as if enthusiasm could encourage Olive into agreement. 'My mum always says so.'

Ruben thought how mums were by far the biggest liars in the world. Not his mum. She was always straight to the point, no sugar-coating for the de Lacy boy. But other mums, normal mums, they were big fat liars. Half the world's problems could probably be traced back to the maternal softening of the blow.

Next to him, Olive was saying, 'I'm sure you'll be an excellent actress.'

'Not if she's got stage fright.' Ruben popped another bilberry into his mouth. The last thing he wanted to encourage was a fruitless and no doubt very expensive pipe dream.

Olive gave him a nudge as if he was being too discouraging, but Zadie was nodding. 'Yes. That's exactly right. Sometimes I go down to the beach – you know, on the pier – and just stand there and recite a monologue or a poem. I make myself do it.

It's really hard but sometimes people stop and listen. Once though, a group of boys from school stood in a line next to me pretending to be me, you know, mimicking me. I made myself carry on but …'

How could this girl be his daughter? No de Lacy in their right mind would do something like that. 'Why would you do that to yourself?' Ruben imagined himself as one of those schoolboys, thinking he was hilarious doing a mock Shakespearian bow next to the weird poetry geek.

'You can never give in to the bullies,' said Zadie.

Ruben was incredulous. 'But you can also not give them the ammunition.'

Zadie shook her head. 'That's victim-blaming,' she admonished.

Ruben rolled his eyes. 'No, it's common sense.'

The forest was getting denser. Brambles scratched their legs and arms. Well-trodden fox paths pressed the long grass flat.

'So what are you saying, Ruben?' Olive tipped her head, clearly intrigued. 'That Zadie shouldn't do something because a group of boys in her class can't handle it?'

'No,' he sighed, pushing a branch out of the way. 'I'm saying there are certain conventions of "normal" behaviour in life and if you're going to step out of them, you have to be prepared for the consequences.'

Zadie shrugged, completely unaffected. 'But I don't want to be normal. I want to be me.'

The statement seemed to stall Olive completely as she tried to detangle her jeans from a bramble.

Ruben held his hands wide as if defenceless. 'I'm just making the point that standing on the pier at twelve years old reciting Shakespearean monologues is never going to end happily.'

'It didn't end too badly,' Zadie said, pausing as she did battle with the leaves of an enormous fern. 'I made fifty-seven pounds in tips.'

'Really?' Ruben was impressed. Zadie grinned proudly as he helped her with the bracken. Maybe she was a de Lacy after all.

They popped out of the forest darkness into the bright manicured perfection of the south lawn. A poplar-lined avenue that led up to a lake with a fountain in one direction and the old orangery in the other.

'What's that building?' Zadie asked, pointing at the intricate fretwork of a dilapidated greenhouse.

Ruben looked where she was looking, then immediately turned to Olive to see her reaction. Olive had paused.

'That's, erm …' He'd lost his train of thought having seen Olive's expression. He'd avoided the orangery since he'd been back. 'It's where they used to hothouse fruit, like pineapples, in Victorian times,' he said, distracted. Beside him, Olive was silent. All Ruben could envisage were tangled, sweaty limbs. Steamed up windows, frantic hands and desperate kisses. It made him have to swallow before he could refocus.

'Wow, can we go and have a look?'

'No,' they both said in unison.

Zadie frowned.

Thinking on his feet, Ruben said, 'The structure's too dangerous.'

Zadie seemed placated by the answer and, turning towards the lake, jabbered on about how she much preferred pineapple to passion fruit but her favourite by far was mango. Olive walked silently beside him. Ruben wanted to ask her if she was OK but when they got to the lake, Zadie started jumping up and down, grinning gleefully in front of a statue of a woman bent forward standing atop big black and gold arches, a dog at her feet.

'Look, look it's Diana, I think,' Zadie squealed, swiping her hair out of her eyes. Then proved herself right when she got to the plaque and read it. 'Yes, look, Diana of the Treetops.' She pointed to the engraved words and then repeated the clue. '"*There you are in the treetops.*" And the sky part must refer to Diana as goddess of the moon.'

Ruben was very confused. 'How do you know all this stuff?'

'Because you can't study to be a playwright without knowing about Greek mythology.'

'You're twelve!'

'My mum thinks I'm very advanced for my age,' she said, leaning proudly against the side of the fountain but sticking her hand in a great blob of goose poo at the same time.

'Urgh, gross!'

'Advanced but completely clueless,' Ruben scoffed as Zadie wiped away the green poo on the grass. 'Enough of Barry and his amateur dramatics and Penny thinking you're a child prodigy, you need me, Zadie, to educate you in the ways of the world.'

It was Olive's turn to scoff with surprise, snapped from her silent reverie. 'Are you serious? What are you going to teach her about the ways of the world, Ruben?'

'I have lots to teach her. About how to act with people. How to chat. How to … dress …' He was running out of things to say that weren't just 'how to be cool', but he couldn't say that without sounding like a complete prat.

But Olive had perked up and wouldn't let the subject lie.

Instead, she was trying not to laugh. 'They sound like great life lessons. Stormzy would be proud.' She glanced at Zadie, who giggled.

'Yes, haha, let's all laugh at Ruben. Hilarious.' Ruben raised his brows heavenward. It had been a while since he'd laughed at himself. His tactic was usually to make the women he met laugh with him not at him, but, as he looked at Olive and Zadie both amused, both openly mocking him, perhaps that said more about the women he met. He didn't want to analyse too deeply the fact he was actually quite enjoying himself, so instead he squinted up at the lake statue and said, 'I always thought she was a mermaid.'

Zadie despaired. 'Why would a mermaid have a dog?'

Ruben shrugged. 'I don't know! I was a teenage boy. Why would I think about things like that? The only thing I remember is being able to see one of her boobs.'

Olive rolled her eyes.

Zadie blushed.

Ruben walked round the other side of the lake. 'See, boobs,' he grinned, pointing to one of Diana's exposed breasts.

Zadie shook her head at him. 'I don't think it's right to get all pervy about a statue.'

'It's not pervy,' Ruben protested. 'It's admiring.'

Zadie put her hands on her hips, calling across the lake. 'No. That's what all those groping old men say who don't like #MeToo.'

'Please don't lump me in with the groping old men.' Ruben was aghast. 'I'm very pro all that. I like strong women. I can just appreciate a well-sculpted statue, that's all.'

Olive seemed to have despaired of him.

Zadie narrowed her eyes. 'I've got some poetry I think you should read. To better yourself.'

Ruben opened his mouth to protest but seeing Olive watching him, recognising that look as one he had spent aeons trying to impress, that had always pushed him – as his daughter now seemed to be doing – to do better, to be better, to listen and question more. *'Ruben, what do you think about this in the news? What do you mean you don't have an opinion? Everyone has an opinion. OK, well think about it now, what's your instinct? Don't joke. I'm not going to kiss you until you give me a valid opinion. Yes, it is blackmail ...'* Realising suddenly that that look aligned with a time in his life when he was infinitely happier than he'd ever been before or since, he found himself holding his hands up and saying, 'Fine. Fine! Give me your books and your poems. I'd love to read them. Bring it on.'

Zadie responded with a smile of sweet satisfaction. 'Great. I've got some in my bag, we can look at them together later.'

Ruben came back round to their side of the lake, his shoulders stooped in acquiescence. 'Can't think of anything better.'

Zadie was delighted. 'And Shakespeare?'

'And Shakespeare,' he agreed through slightly gritted teeth.

'Hey look, there's a fish!' Zadie skipped off in the direction of the fish. Ruben blew out an exasperated breath.

Olive said, 'That was good. What you did just then.'

'Yeah?' Ruben felt his despondent body puffing up with pride.

'Yeah,' she said with the spine-tingling, well-done smile that Ruben had only ever thought he'd see again in his memories.

Olive turned towards the Diana statue in the centre of the lake. 'So this clue ...'

Ruben looked where she was looking, still basking in the glow of her congratulations, shielding his eyes from the glare of the sun, and he said, 'Someone's going to have to swim across.'

They stood side by side looking at Diana.

'I'll do it!' Zadie bounded back.

Ruben was about to agree when Olive shook her head. 'We can't send Zadie across.'

'We can't?' It seemed like an excellent idea to him because otherwise he knew which muggins would be swimming across in his Calvin Kleins.

Olive said, 'She's a child.'

'Oh right.' Ruben paused, then said for a laugh, 'Well that leaves you, Olive.' Knowing in a couple of minutes it would be him in the freezing lake because this new camel-jumper wearing Olive was not the type to breaststroke through grubby pond water.

But next to him, Olive was starting to nod.

Ruben made a face. 'Are you actually going to do it? Because I don't mind if you want me to …'

Olive chewed on her lip. 'I don't want to do it at all. But I think I *should* do it. You know, because I chickened out of getting the other one.'

'I wouldn't call it chickening out,' Ruben demurred, realising that he was actually quite keen to step in and prove his machismo by wading waist-deep into the lake. It might earn him some more brownie points, or at the very least would show off the abs he'd been working on with Peloton's 'Crush Your Core' session. What was the point otherwise?

But Olive had started to unbutton her jeans. 'I would.'

Ruben swallowed, completely distracted from any counter-argument by the fact she was about to strip off. He couldn't drag his eyes away. She untucked her T-shirt and pulled it over her head. Her skin was so pale it was almost white. He remembered the mole on her right shoulder blade.

Zadie shot him a look. 'You're perving.'

Ruben snapped to it. 'I was, I'm sorry. I hold my hands up.' He made a show of being ashamed of himself and Zadie shook her head with disappointment, swiping her overlong fringe out of her eyes.

Olive stood by the edge of the lake in her lemon-yellow bra and jeans. She glanced at Ruben and said, 'Turn around.'

'What?' Ruben was aghast.

'Turn around!' Zadie picked up the order like Olive's bodyguard as she started to slip out of her jeans.

Much to his disgruntlement, Ruben had to turn around. He was holding the T-shirt Olive had given him. Soft white cotton. 'Is this one of your T-shirts that doesn't crease?'

Olive sounded surprised, 'How do you know about my T-shirts that don't crease?'

'Google,' Ruben said as if it were nothing.

Olive said, 'You've googled me?'

'Yeah, so what? I've googled you,' he said, defensive. 'I bet you've googled me.'

Olive thought for a second, then said, 'No.'

Zadie laughed.

'Oh haha,' Ruben sighed. Was this to be his role between them? 'I'm glad *you* find it funny,' he said to Zadie.

Zadie's cheeks pinked as she carried on giggling. Then she said, more serious, 'You can turn around now.'

To Ruben's disappointment, Olive was already waist-deep in the lake.

'Oh my God, it's freezing!' she shouted. Then as it got deeper and she had to breaststroke towards the fountain, she said, 'There are reeds all round my ankle. Yuck! Oh, what was that?' she flipped over and pushed something away. 'Oh God, it's a giant bloody fish.'

'Be careful,' Ruben shouted back, 'it might be a pike.'

'What?' Olive swam quicker.

Zadie said, 'Do you really think they're pike?'

'No, but we don't have to tell Olive that.'

Zadie looked torn between her new-found hero Olive and being in cahoots with her dad. Ruben grinned at her, drawing her into a cosy pact of conspiracy, which made Zadie smile under her breath, satisfactorily silenced from telling Olive the truth. He tried not to think about whether this was father-daughter bonding or blatant manipulation as he cupped his hands together and shouted, 'Fast as you can, Olive!' spurring her into motoring in front crawl to the statue.

Olive got to Diana and hauled herself up onto the ledge. Ruben finally got to see her black lace pants but the notion of being an old perv had lodged into his brain and it wasn't as much fun as he'd hoped.

Olive squeezed water out of her hair. 'God, I hate fish.'

Ruben barked a laugh. Zadie turned away so she wouldn't be caught laughing too.

'Can you see the clue?' he shouted.

Olive had a cursory glance around the statue. 'No,' she said, clearly annoyed and embarrassed at her near-nakedness. She shuffled round the plinth to look on the other side. 'Nothing. I'm going to stand up. Don't watch me, Ruben,' she shouted.

'Olive, I've seen you in your pants before, you know.'

She frowned from the statue. 'A long time ago!'

Zadie cut in, gleefully, 'You two did used to go out!'

Ruben threw her a verifying wink that made her hop with excitement. Then he folded his arms and watched with growing amusement as Olive started climbing the statue of Diana, as best she could. She was all legs and arms trying to cling onto bits of bronze. Her hair was falling all wet down her angry face. It was like the clock had turned and there was fierce, teenage Olive doing what had to be done. He remembered the icy swims they'd do together in the winter. Goading each other through those first few punishing minutes that were always worth it for the glorious high of cutting through the glassy sea, just the two of them with nothing but miles of blue out ahead. Treading water and looking back at the snow-covered beach, picture-perfect when out of reach.

'Go Olive!' Zadie cheerleaded.

'There's nothing here!' Olive shouted. Then pushing her hair off her face, she looked back at Ruben and Zadie. 'Who are we kidding? Do we really think a clue my dad planted twenty years ago would still be here? And how the hell would he have got to the middle of the bloody lake anyway? What am I doing?'

They both looked at her in the middle of the lake, clutched onto the Diana statue in her underwear. It did suddenly seem very unlikely.

Ruben was about to shout as such when suddenly Olive went, 'Oh, hang on a minute,' distracted by something by Diana's foot. 'I think I have something. It's stuck ...' She dislodged a small black plastic box from between Diana's feet, like the tiny Russian doll version of the blue one Ruben had found the first clue in, and waved it at them. 'This is it! It's the clue!'

'Good girl!' Ruben clapped.

Zadie said, 'You shouldn't call her a girl, she's a woman.'

'I don't need any more of that from you, thanks,' he remarked, but not meanly, instead he found his tone more gently mocking, like this was their repartee. And he watched the unexpected pleasure on Zadie's face as she turned to cheer Olive.

Olive was now getting gingerly back into the soupy lake water. 'Urgh, the fish,' she cringed as she sploshed in. 'Oh, and it's even colder.' She half waded, half swam across to where they were waiting. And as she rose out of the water, for a moment, Ruben found himself completely entranced. Hair slicked back, determined in her bra and pants, expression like she dared him to comment, all he could see was teenage Olive. And he suddenly couldn't think of anything he had done with his life between those days and now. He liked his life, or he'd thought he'd liked his life but it seemed to disappear in a puff of smoke when he remembered his Willoughby Park days. The adventures, the company, the dares. The pressure to expand his mind, to be better, to try harder. Not because of school or his father. But because of her. Because of Olive and her opinion of him.

He found himself a little flustered by her semi-naked presence, whereas in contrast she seemed to have grown in stature and confidence. 'Do you want me to er ... Do you want to use my shirt as a towel?' he offered.

Olive gave him a look like he was mad. 'No, Ruben. I'll be fine.' She reached over to take her T-shirt from his hand – which he'd completely forgotten he was holding – and slipped it on over her damp skin. She had trouble with her jeans, her legs soaking, and winced as she tried to prise them up her thighs.

Zadie was watching Ruben watching Olive with much animation. Ruben shook himself, needing to nip those feelings in the bud, pronto. Olive was nothing like the women he dated nowadays, she was too terrifying. He'd never be able to relax for a second.

She said, 'I can't believe there are pike in a tourist lake,' tying her wet hair back off her face, her make-up all gone, still shivering.

Zadie said, 'They aren't pike. Ruben was lying!'

Olive opened her mouth wide, then thwacked him on the shoulder in admonishment, and Ruben said, 'You're meant to be on my side!' to Zadie, who giggled. He once again took note of the warmth inside him. Then he reminded himself that this set-up was transitory. He had been on enough holidays on yachts and secluded villas with friends to know that anything felt special in the bubble of amused camaraderie. It was in the real world where it fell apart.

CHAPTER ELEVEN

The roof of the house in the cornfield that Dolly and Fox were heading towards, thirty degrees due east of where they had crashed, turned out not to be the roof of a house.

'It's a barn,' said Dolly, shielding her eyes from the sun with her hand as she caught her breath. She was hot and dirty and gasping for a drink.

'It's not even a barn,' Fox said, parking the bike then standing to stare at the dilapidated building. 'I don't think it's been a barn for twenty years.'

Dolly walked forward into the shade of the collapsed galvanised roof, rusted holes casting beams of light onto old hay bales. A pigeon fluttered out when it heard her. A nest of straw on one of the big beams. In one corner was an old tractor, overtaken with ivy and a mesh of discarded rusty metal. There was a chair with a ripped plastic seat on the floor and a set of upturned metal shelves. Behind the barn was a small forest of pine trees and bare needle-strewn earth. Ivy grew up the side of the iron barn and threaded in tendrils along the path.

Dolly climbed up on one of the hay bales to get a better look out across the network of fields. A patchwork of green and yellow for miles around. The odd smattering of sheep. She saw a grey stone house in the distance, down the hill and back up the other side. 'The farm's over there,' she pointed straight ahead.

Fox didn't bother with any compass directions this time, he just nodded, 'Now she tells me,' and walked over to pick up the chair, his limp more pronounced now they'd stopped, and set himself down with a wince. The rickety chair legs wobbled and looked like they might give way.

'How's your ankle?' Dolly asked.

'Fine,' he said, untying his boot and pulling it off, teeth gritted against the pain.

'Looks fine,' said Dolly drily.

Fox didn't reply, just pulled off his sock and lifted his jeans leg up to reveal an ankle swollen up like a tomato.

'Shit!' Dolly said, looking at it in awe. 'You walked here on that?'

Fox shrugged. 'I've done worse.'

Dolly remembered the Swiss Army knife toe-cutting-off story.

'How's your shoulder?' he asked.

It hurt like hell. 'Fine,' she replied.

Fox nodded. He just sat there. Catching his breath. Then he shut his eyes.

Dolly sat on the edge of the hay. She checked her phone, still no signal.

'What now?' she asked.

He shrugged. Opened one eye. 'We roll back time to yesterday afternoon when I offered to give you a lift?'

Dolly bit the inside of her cheek. 'I've said I'm sorry.'

'I know you have,' he replied.

'Well, stop looking at me like that. What more can I do apart from apologise?'

Fox huffed, his expression incredulous as he got up and started to walk gingerly to the bike.

'What?' Dolly called after him.

He grabbed his bag. 'Nothing,' he said, limping to his seat.

Dolly could feel herself getting riled. 'What? Tell me! Come on—' She stood up.

'Sit down,' he ordered, annoyed at her temper. Then he sat himself, his big body lowered as gently as he could onto the feeble chair, and said with controlled anger, 'You didn't apologise for me, Dolly, you apologised for you. It was an insult.'

Dolly paused, caught off-guard by the truth. 'Well, I'm sorry, you're so bloody perfect.'

Fox undid his bag and got out a bottle of water. He chucked it to her.

'I don't want it,' she said.

'Don't be a baby,' he replied, sitting down and inspecting his swollen ankle.

Dolly begrudgingly unscrewed the water canister and took a long gulp. It was like heaven. Cool down her throat that was parched with heat and corn dust and midges. She stood up and placed it down next to Fox's chair. 'Thanks,' she mumbled.

Fox took a gulp of water himself, calmly screwing the cap on. 'I'm not perfect, Dolly.'

'I'm not perfect …' she mimicked with spiteful irritation, hands on her hips, looking up at an old pigeon's nest, the twigs meshed with bits of wire and tin foil.

Fox shook his head like she was a child.

'Don't patronise me,' Dolly sighed.

He raised a brow, taking another gulp of water, wiping his mouth with the back of his hand. 'Why not, when you deserve it?'

His every move annoyed her. His sanctimonious one-upmanship. Irritation bubbled inside her. She came and stood really close and said, 'What do you want to do? Do you want to hit me?'

Fox almost choked on his water. 'No, I do not want to hit you.'

'Go on,' she goaded. 'It'd make us both feel better. Come on, I'm as good as any of those guys in the ring,' she braced herself, good hand on her hip. 'Hit me.'

'Dolly, I am not going to hit a one-armed woman.'

'Yes, you are. Come on, stand up. You can be one-armed, too,' she snapped, trying to haul him up off the chair. 'Just hold one behind your back.'

Fox stayed where he was, refusing to budge, Dolly yanking at his arm. Then he started laughing. 'Dolly, I'm never going to hit you.'

'I want you to hit me,' she said, her anger morphing as she heaved him by the arm into almost crying laughter. 'Please!'

'No,' he shook his head, still smiling. 'No. I don't need to hit you. Nor do I want to hit you. I just want you to admit some weakness every now and then. Realise that not everything is a battle to fight.' He looked down at her arm still hooked on his. 'This being a case in point.'

Dolly sighed, her shoulders sagged. She drew her hand away and sloped away to sit on the edge of the hay. She took a deep breath, nodding. 'Yeah, I know.' Head hung, she glanced over at him. 'I know. I'm sorry.'

His face softened, almost in pity. 'That's OK.'

She bit her lip, glancing over at the trashed Kawasaki. 'I *am* sorry about your bike.'

'So you should be, that's travelled the bloody Himalayas with me and it never got scratched up this badly.'

Dolly looked at him with a questioning expression. 'You were really in the Himalayas with the monks?' In jeans and an old faded army T-shirt, big biceps and sweat-stained face, he didn't look like he'd fit in with the Buddhist monks.

'Uh-huh.' He nodded, reaching into his bag for a first-aid kit that of course he carried with him everywhere and unzipping it. 'And by the way,' he said, starting to bandage up his ankle, 'I really am definitely not perfect.'

Dolly frowned. 'I think that's a double negative.'

Fox shook his head. 'It wasn't. It wasn't good English but it wasn't a double negative.'

Dolly tipped her head. 'No, I really think it was.'

'Dolly …' Fox held up a hand. 'Let it go.'

Dolly took a breath to say more but stopped herself. Then in the pause she ran Fox's sentence over in her head and realised it was just bad English. She cringed at herself, then looked across at Fox to apologise again but he was just watching, smiling, knowing. Somehow though, this time it wasn't quite so annoying.

Dolly shook her head, embarrassed. 'I know I need to think more before I act.'

'It would help,' Fox replied.

Dolly found herself smiling. She leant against the big bale behind her, retying her hair so it was away from her neck in a knot on top of her head. She could see nothing but blue sky and the corn out ahead. The hay itched her back. She looked at Fox, retying the bandage on his ankle because it wasn't quite perfect, then pinning the cloth in place and putting the first-aid kit away in its proper place.

If she let it, there was something quite relaxing about being in his presence. Not just the whole military thing that let you know he was prepared for any eventuality, but a calm strength that didn't encroach. That just let her be. She never got that with men, usually. She never lolled about with messy hair and an admission of being wrong. She was always ready and fighting. In training she had her hair slicked and gripped to within an inch of its life. Even in bed she was up before them, barely having slept, never able to fully relax with someone else there with her.

'What are you thinking about?' Fox asked, and she realised she'd zoned out, silent.

'Nothing,' she said, sitting up straight, redoing her hair. Fox didn't push for anything more. 'How's your ankle?' Dolly asked, standing up, straightening her T-shirt, having another drink. 'Can you walk to the farm?'

Fox had pulled his boot on and stood up to give it a test. 'Yeah. I think it'll be OK. I'm going to have to leave the bike here, though.'

Together, they pushed it to the rear of the barn and camouflaged it as best they could under a mouse-chewed tarpaulin. Then they set off into the sun, their bags on their backs. This time though the walk was across lush grass for sheep grazing, tufts of wool caught on the wire fence, clover and buttercups springing up along the edges. The sheep eyed them with disinterest as they trekked slowly down the hill, the incline harder on Fox's ankle until Dolly found him a massive stick to use as support.

'Thank you very much,' he said, clearly surprised at the gesture.

But Dolly brushed away the moment with a 'Come on, Grandpa!' as he started to walk gingerly with the stick.

They trudged on into caramel wheat flecked with red poppies and darting butterflies.

Fox had to pause by a fallen tree. 'I just need a second.'

'That's all right.' Dolly sat down beside him. Not close, a person's width between them. They sat in silence. A beetle crossed the dry earth with painful slowness. Fox got the water out of his bag, had a gulp then handed it to her.

'Why did you join the police, Dolly?' he asked as she handed it back, the cool water still in her mouth.

She swallowed. 'To save the world,' she said facetiously.

He raised a brow.

She knew exactly why she'd joined the force, just never talked about it with anyone.

'Your record said you'd been arrested. Then you were given the option to go into training.'

She sat up straighter. 'You read my record?'

'I read the record of everyone I work with.'

'I haven't read your record.'

'That's not my problem.'

Dolly scowled.

'Come on,' he said, standing up and dragging a big stone over that he could rest his ankle on as he sat, 'Tell me, what happened? I'm genuinely interested. I have been dying to know since I read it.'

She looked across at Fox, still unsure how she felt about him reading up on her, but she was knocked off balance instead by the genuine interest on his face. The sitting and waiting for her to tell him. Not cutting in with his own story or half distracted by something on his phone. He was actually interested in her. She thought suddenly of the guys who wanted her to handcuff them in bed. The others who wanted the gruesome investigation stories but liked her in heels and a skirt when they went for dinner. She thought of all the faces she'd put on, the people she'd been to please. The questions she'd asked in order to deflect the very few, when she thought about it, that she had been asked in return.

But now, sitting on the fallen tree, the air still and silent, her skin warm, not a person but her and Fox for at least a mile, there was someone waiting to listen to what she had to say. Whose genuine expression of interest left her disinclined to lie – questioning, even, why she would even consider it.

'I joined because …' she paused, it was such unfamiliar territory, she had no well-rehearsed story ready to roll out. 'Because I didn't want to be living the life I was living any more.'

'What life were you living?'

'A lonely one,' she said with a half-smile. He nodded like he didn't actually need any further explanation; it was totally up to her if she wanted to continue. That was the thing about him, his presence was completely unthreatening, like he drew the judgement out of the air. She drank some water. 'I moved to London when I was about fourteen to live with my Aunt Marge – the one you met – and she wasn't necessarily the best with children. You could say I was quite lost as a teenager. I got in with the wrong crowd, you know, the cliché.'

Fox said, 'The wrong crowd? Is this the guy who put you off motorbikes?'

'One and the same.' Dolly nodded, not quite able to smile. She thought of who she was then. Too thin. Didn't wash her hair. Red-eyed from tears. 'There are certain people who can sense weakness,' she said.

'I couldn't agree more,' replied Fox.

Dolly thought of Great Destroyer Jake with his long hair and pseudo-Marxist politics. The sharp, angular beauty of his face. The dirty flat owned by his mum that he'd steadily trashed as a gesture of lazy anarchy. The feel of his hands on her face when her phone rang and he silenced it and slipped it into his pocket, saying, '*You don't need anyone else, babe. You've got me.*' Beautiful, awful Jake. A great destroyer.

'Well, me and the wrong crowd, we got into trouble. Stupid stuff …' She picked up a twig from the ground and started to strip it of its bark with her fingers.

Fox grinned at the idea of it. Dolly rolled her eyes. 'We protested everything. There was no agenda. Just destruction.'

'Sounds like a successful strategy.'

'Well, you know, when you're young …'

'I know exactly, Dolly.' He smiled, again totally without judgement. And Dolly found herself looking back on her younger self with a little more sympathy than she ever had. She said, 'They had found the address of some big corporate investor that they planned to, you know, go and smash a few windows and stuff. God, it's embarrassing recounting it.'

Fox nodded for her to continue.

'They swore that there was no one home and they were all there with bricks and started smashing the place up. But it turned out the wife was home with her little kid. It was awful. She called the police. The kid was screaming. I remember being like, this isn't right. But none of them seemed to care, they kept going till the police arrived. And when they did, the guy I was with, Jake – that was his name – and his mates all just legged it. We jumped on the bikes but he took off so fast and I hadn't got my grip properly.' She looked across shamefaced. 'I fell off. I shouted but no one turned back.'

'You were surprised he left you?' Fox asked.

'Yeah. No.' Dolly snapped the twig she was holding. 'I suppose if I really think about it, no.'

That was the problem with not talking about yourself, you could be taken aback by your own memories. 'Shall we walk?' Dolly asked, getting ready to stand up, thinking that was probably enough about her past.

'Not yet,' said Fox. 'So, you were arrested?'

'Yeah, and charged. They locked me up for the night. What I didn't know at the time was that Aunt Marge had very good friends on the force.' Dolly smiled wryly. 'She knows everyone. How she tells it now is that I needed to learn a lesson. I'd, er … pushed her to the limit, I think.'

'What lesson did you need to learn?' Fox asked.

'The pure terror of being arrested,' Dolly laughed. 'I think she just wanted me to stop wasting my life and had run out of ideas. This was the perfect storm. DC Molly Reynolds came to talk to me, who was actually – unbeknownst to me – one of Aunt Marge's closest friends. I remember looking up at her face in the interview room and she looked so cool and so together. She had these straight across eyebrows and this really sharp suit. And I remember the look on her face when she looked at me, it was *so* condescending. The pity.' Dolly sat up, chucked the bits of twig, and tried to tighten her ponytail one-handed.

'She impressed you?'

'She was amazing. Really strong, really confident. She showed me who I could be.' Dolly's eyes creased at the memory. The smell of the police station, the cheap coffee, Molly towering over her saying, *'No more excuses, Dolly. You answer to yourself and you alone. Yes!'*

Fox was watching her, mouth turned down, interested. 'Lucky escape.'

'Yeah,' Dolly felt the spark fade slightly as she thought about that time, considered how close she had come to disappearing into Jake and his friends. So desperate had her need been to feel something, anything akin to love.

Fox stayed quiet. The silence hung in the thick warm air.

In her head, Dolly suddenly replayed her fantasy of seeing Ruben de Lacy again. How she'd imagined the low whistle between his teeth. Practised her own pithy yet flirtatious comeback. Hoped he'd be wowed by her glossy hair and sculpted muscles. She'd never once considered a conversation they might have.

'Right,' said Fox, 'I think I'm OK to walk now.'

'Yeah?' Dolly stood up and brushed tree bark off her jeans.

Fox nodded and heaved himself up. Instinctively, Dolly gave him her arm to lean on. He took it to get his balance and she was suddenly really aware of his hand on her skin. She turned her head and their faces were almost touching. Dolly found herself noticing how dark his eyes were. Then Fox moved away and Dolly worried suddenly that she'd been staring.

'Shall we walk?' he said.

'Yeah,' she said, all casual nonchalance. Embarrassed that she had noticed anything about him. He might be willing to listen but he was still bloody annoying Fox Mason.

He looked at her, amused, like he could tell exactly what she was thinking. Nose in the air, she chucked her bag over her shoulder and walked off ahead.

CHAPTER TWELVE

Olive, Ruben and Zadie ate at Angelica's Trattoria in the village, which was still going after all these years. A dark nook with the same candles in Chianti bottles and pictures of old Italy on the walls that had been there when they were kids. The eponymous Angelica stalked menacingly out from behind the counter but softened the instant she saw Ruben and Olive. 'Just the same, the two of you! Oh, how lovely. I have missed you. And this is your beautiful daughter?'

Olive had to awkwardly explain that that wasn't the case, but then her phone rang and Angelica moved on, slinging her conker-tanned arm around Ruben and pronouncing him as handsome as Gregory Peck before ushering them to the best table in the house.

'Olive? Marge here,' her aunt's voice boomed out of the phone.

Olive followed Ruben and Zadie to the table, weaving her way through the restaurant diners. 'Hi Marg—'

'I can't get through to Dolly,' Marge bulldozed through Olive's greeting. 'I went to see her, told her to go on this hunt but then nothing and now her phone is going straight to answerphone again. I called her work and they said she's been suspended. Did you know that?'

Olive's back seemed to go into spasm whenever she heard from Aunt Marge. Like a Pavlovian stress reaction. Her late teenage years were basically spent teaching Marge how to be a parent while working furiously to get into art college and worrying about Dolly, who'd crashed off the rails spectacularly. Whenever Marge rang Olive it was always for her to sort something to do with Dolly that would leave Olive a tight ball of stress. In the whole time she'd known her, she'd never once rung Olive to ask her anything about herself.

'What's she been suspended for?' Olive frowned, then immediately smiled her thanks as Angelica drew out a chair for her and handed her a menu.

'Oh, I don't know, they don't tell you these things over the phone. What shall we do?'

Olive closed her eyes. It was all too similar to the times as a teenager – when both sisters were out of their depth in their new London life, struggling to make any sense of what had happened to them – that she'd sat up pleading with Dolly to go to school, to stop bunking off with the crowd of useless idiots she now idolised, panicking about the booze and pills, not with her mother this time but with her younger sister, holding her hair as she vomited in the loo, and Aunt Marge hovered in the background completely clueless. Being back at Angelica's Trattoria was almost laughably symbolic. 'Look, I can't really talk right now, let me think about it,' Olive smiled up at Ruben, who was watching with interest while Zadie was saying, 'They've got dough balls! Oh, and profiteroles!'

Olive turned away, 'She's probably just annoyed that she's been suspended and gone to the gym or something. You know Dolly, she never answers her phone …' Olive didn't want to get sucked into this, it made her heart beat too fast with familiar concern. The police had been Dolly's saving grace, Olive didn't want to consider what she'd be like without it.

Marge said, 'Possibly,' unconvinced.

In a momentary lapse of frustration, Olive sighed, 'Why does she always have to do this? Why does it always have to be a drama?'

Marge, who couldn't bear any sign of conflict, immediately cut in with a placating, 'Oh, I'm sure you're right. Perfectly decent explanation. I've got a supper tonight but I'll pop round her flat again in the morning, just to check. There's every chance she's on her way to you. She did say she might.'

Olive shook her head. 'I really doubt it, Marge. Dolly never does what you expect.' Then she hung up, taking a quick moment as she briskly opened the menu to get her breathing back under control and her stress levels down. She thought of all the times she'd walked the streets searching for Dolly, the hovels she'd elbowed her way through, the long-haired, greasy know-alls she'd done battle with just to talk to her sister. Surely Olive had done her time. Could she plead past kindness to offset future responsibility?

Zadie snapped her menu shut with a 'I'm having dough balls, a margherita pizza, a Coke and profiteroles for pudding.' Then sitting back in her chair, said, 'OK, we can read the clue now.'

Zadie had wanted to prolong the excitement by saving reading the clue till dinnertime.

'Are you sure?' Ruben quipped.

Zadie nodded. A young waiter came over to take their order while Olive dug in her handbag for the little black box, prised it open and pulled out the clue, which had been sealed in small a ziplock bag.

'*You know the maiden rocks that guard the southern bay. But did you know their heart of stone they one day threw away?*'

Next to Ruben, Zadie was practically bouncing out of her seat. 'I know where the maidens are. I read about them when I looked the area up. Three rocks in a perfect straight line – there used to be four but one eroded – they were thought to be the daughters of drowned fishermen sent to guard against the shallow rocks!'

'Yes, well done, they're round the headland on the tip of Trevellyn Bay,' said Ruben, impressed. 'Maybe you are a genius.' Then with a cheeky grin, he added, 'You take after your father,' throwing out the remark as casually as he sipped the glass of red wine set down by the waiter.

But Olive watched Zadie absorb Ruben's words like a keepsake, ready for her diary later that night. 'Dear Diary, everything is going exactly as I'd hoped. Daddy is so handsome and funny and thinks we're so alike …' She could see her desperation in those huge blue eyes. The fairy-tale reunion. The beaming smiles and the twirling hugs. The galloping unicorns and the twinkling of stardust.

Ruben however had already moved on to the next subject. 'What was that earlier on the phone. What's happened to Dolly?'

'Oh, nothing,' she said.

'Come on!' he laughed. 'Clearly something's going on.'

Olive found herself not wanting to mention Dolly's suspension and Aunt Marge's concern as to her whereabouts. It felt too much like the past. As if their family were still as haphazard and chaotic as they always were. 'Honestly, it's nothing,' she said, sitting up straight, taking a sip of her wine, remembering for some reason the look of disdain in Ruben's father's eyes when he looked at her, the riff-raff on the estate.

Ruben smiled like he could see straight through her. 'You've become very prim, Olive.'

Olive felt her cheeks flush again. Hating the fact she was coming across as uptight. She thought of Mark; he would be perfectly happy to let the matter lie. For a moment, she wished Mark was here, to hell with what he'd done. Just for the simple comfort of familiarity in moments of weakness. He'd have deliberately changed tack when he saw her get flustered, possibly put his hand on her leg under the table and given it a squeeze. She missed the intimacy of their silent understandings. 'Could we talk about something else?'

'If you want,' said Ruben. 'Zadie, name your number one holiday?'

Zadie took the bait without question. Chuntering on about the many endangered corals of the Great Barrier Reef while also desperate for a trip to the Christmas markets in Bruges. Ruben caught Olive's eye and offered a nod of apology. She shook her head like it didn't matter but she could feel he still had one eye on her while Zadie pontificated.

Then the food appeared, giving Olive a much-needed reprieve. As she ate, she could still smell the lake water on her skin, even though she'd showered. It occurred to her that if she'd been with Mark, he'd have been cringing as soon as she'd jumped in the lake. Embarrassed. Worried what people would think and mortified himself by the draw of attention. In fact, were she still with him, she too would have been embarrassed. Together they lived by life's rules. Quietly. A little sardonically. Never drawing attention to themselves or away from the status quo.

Yet climbing on that statue, searching for the clue, she had felt the most herself she had in years.

It made her wonder if perhaps they had lived together in such perceived normality so they never had to examine anything even remotely below the surface. Instead, they ticked the boxes of a relationship. They read the same newspaper, discussed the same politics, laughed at and derided the same TV programmes. Both escaping the lives they'd had – don't get her started on Mark's bizarre family history – and as recompense let this neutral, vanilla way of living lead the way.

In Angelica's Trattoria, Olive, Ruben and Zadie gorged on garlic bread and margherita pizza, red wine and Coca-Cola, tiramisu and profiteroles. Lashings of everything while Italian opera bellowed in the background and Angelica popped over for the occasional chat, brandy in hand, squished up cosily next to Ruben, demanding their life stories but interrupting with her own.

And as they talked and laughed, firmly in the moment, Angelica delightfully loud and brash, Zadie wide-eyed with delight, Ruben indisputably charming, Olive thought occasionally of the algae-covered, bone-chilling lake water. The giant fish circling her legs. The cool ripple over her skin as she kicked hard underwater, feeling less like the luxury fabrics executive and more like the girl who cut her hair in the bathroom with the kitchen scissors.

It made her think of Mark sitting at his computer, his heart lighting up when he got a message from mousy Barbara, and for the first time, instead of incredulous disbelief and self-pitying anger, she saw a manifestation of his own unhappiness. An escape from the humdrum of reality. Both of them – Mark and Olive – together but apart, their real selves squashed to the corners of their existence in order to live prosaically as one.

Back at the Big House it felt strangely like they were a family. The evening having smoothed their edges. A sense of easy familiarity between them. Zadie was exhausted. After calling her mum she changed into her pyjamas and trotted off to bed. Zadie slept with Harry Potter on her headphones – 'I know it's too young for me but I love it.' To which Ruben replied with some confusion, 'Too young? They're the only books I've ever read, and I only finished the last one last year.'

Zadie seemed the most pleased with this answer than any other he'd given and went off smiling.

'Do you fancy another drink?' Ruben asked Olive.

From his tone, he clearly expected her to say no, and she would have normally but instead Olive said, 'Yeah OK,' reeling slightly from the liberation of self-honesty coupled with an underlying concern about Dolly. She wasn't ready to go to sleep yet.

Ruben said, 'The best wine's in the cellar. Want to come down?'

Olive followed him through the impressive, ornate corridors of the Big House. Past rooms she'd never been in, only imagined. The wine cellar was down a spiral staircase of beautifully restored stone walls and into an arched room with racks and racks of wine. Olive looked around. 'You can't tell me you're not affected by being back here.'

'Oh, I'm affected,' Ruben said, running his finger along the various wines until he came across one he approved of and selected a dusty bottle. 'A great vintage of my father's,' he said, wiping the label clean with his hand. 'He would turn in his grave if he knew we were drinking it like plonk.' Tucking it under his arm, he started up the stairs, saying over his shoulder, 'I'll admit, I was affected in the forest. It was sad being back there. And I was affected in the cottage, but I'm just not affected here,' he clarified, gesturing towards the austere corridor ahead of them. 'I don't massively like it. It means nothing to me.'

Olive closed the door to the cellar stairs behind her and followed Ruben across the Persian carpets and past museum-esque antiquities, considering all the unhappiness he had experienced within these beautiful walls. 'I'm not sure I believe you,' she said, thinking how she hadn't even been able to go down into the cellar at the cottage.

Ruben laughed, ushering Olive into the sitting room and, grabbing two glasses and a corkscrew from a lacquered drinks cabinet, they went outside through the French windows to sit at the patio table. In contrast to the stuffy stately-home smell of the house, the night air smelt of honeysuckle and fresh mowed grass. The view was out over the lake. The statue of Diana with her bow poised and glinting in the moonlight. 'You're the one who said you were completely fine being here,' he said, opening the wine with a pop.

Olive looked out over the gardens. Ruben placed a glass down in front of her. A fox padded through the beam of the outdoor light. In the distance she saw the roof of the dilapidated orangery. 'I was lying.'

Ruben snorted into his wine.

Olive found herself smiling. She felt light from a desire for honesty. 'Everywhere I look I see things I don't want to see.'

There was a pause. Ruben took a sip of wine and said, 'Christ that's good.' Then to Olive asked, 'Like what?'

Olive gave him a look. 'You know exactly what. Everything. The mess at the cottage. The bench you slept on. And I saw you, you didn't want to go to the orangery either.'

The orangery. The site of so much happiness and yet absolutely hideous at the same time. When he met her eye she could see that he could see it all too. All the moments they spent together hidden by the vines and the palm trees so tall they'd broken through the already shattered glass. The building, decrepit and forgotten even then, had become a haven for their forbidden relationship. Where they sat with their fingers entwined and listed the countries in the order they would visit them when they escaped this place, where they snuggled under blankets and she buried her head against his smooth skin, where he kissed her hair and said, *Without you, I don't think I would be me.*

Ruben looked away back out at the night-lit garden; he opened his mouth to say something but changed his mind, lowering his head a touch. Olive wanted to say that he didn't have to say anything, that she was thinking what he was thinking, but she didn't feel she knew him well enough any more to risk such assumptions.

Ruben turned his head to look at her, his mouth tipped in a sad smile. 'All went a bit wrong, didn't it?'

Olive nodded.

It was at the orangery – their special place – that they learnt it was another couple's special place, too. That someone else had taken advantage of the tangle of vines and the giant overgrown leaves. It was there that Olive and Ruben had discovered his father and her mother having an affair, approximately two minutes before her father discovered it and another thirty seconds before her little sister discovered it. The revelation was a flash of time that lived in Olive's brain, drawn to the foreground as little as possible. 'I'm not sure I can even go over there,' Olive said, pointing to the greenhouse roof. 'Just looking at it, all I see is my mother lying on the floor grasping at his ankle. I mean ...' She rubbed her forehead with her hand. 'What was she doing? How could she have got so low?'

'I don't know.' Ruben shook his head, sitting back in his chair. 'You wouldn't catch me grovelling at that bastard's feet.'

Olive looked at him; his jaw tight, blue eyes brimming with displeasure. She wondered if he never thought about it either, closed himself off to emotions as well. What safe status quo had he lived by – that of the carefree Lothario from the looks of his Instagram.

Olive would never forget the sight of her mother, cast off by Lord de Lacy as soon as their clandestine affair was no longer clandestine. Limp and broken. Sobbing, inconsolable. Olive had stared frozen, unable to comprehend what she was seeing, so many questions in her head. Why would you do this when you are so loved? Why ruin everything? She remembered feeling a guilty mix of pity and disgust. But then it had all been overshadowed by the ensuing angry confrontation between her lovely dad – just back from his best adventure yet – and Ruben's. And then as he had stormed away, a new focus. That of Lord de Lacy's eyes on the tightly clutched hands of Olive and Ruben. The dawning realisation that while he'd been shagging the riff-raff, so had his son. *'Over my dead body will you throw your life away on her!'* All to a backing track of her mother's delirium at being cast aside. Detested by Lord de Lacy for the weakness she represented in him.

It made Olive's stomach tighten to think of it. The haughty disgust of his words aimed at her family. At her. It brought into stark relief the chasm between them. The Lord and his servants. He'd spat. Lord de Lacy had actually spat in distaste near where her mother was lying. '*For Christ's sake, get up, woman.*' Olive had let go of Ruben's hand to haul her mother up. To her it marked the moment when everything ended.

The treasure hunt Olive's dad had laid, hopping with excitement that he'd struck it rich, was forgotten. His camouflage rucksack that had been dumped in the hall, '*I'm back, girls, back for good this time!*' gone when they returned to the cottage. Olive half stumbling under the weight of her uselessly sobbing mother. Her dad was gone and they never saw him again. He died three weeks later. Aunt Marge had come to stay with them, Olive's mother too wrecked to be of any use. Olive had been the one to cover Dolly's ears as Marge sipped Martinis and said things like, '*He knew he wasn't coming back from that trip. You don't kayak the roughest river in the world and imagine you're coming home to tell the tale.*'

Sitting at the patio table, Ruben gulped down the last of his wine. 'If only they could have kept their hands off each other.'

'I know!' Olive inhaled, surprised by the feelings conjured up by the chat. 'What was she doing with him? It still makes me really angry. More angry than I thought it would, actually. I've just never been able to understand what she was doing. She ruined it all, and for what? He didn't love her. My dad, he loved her!' She finished her wine, a little embarrassed at her rant. Ruben topped both their glasses up. She thought of the chaos that had ensued. Her mother's catatonic breakdown. Aunt Marge's haphazard attempt to reassemble the lives of two teenage girls. The de Lacys packed up and gone. An eviction notice placed on the cottage. All of it a mess of grief and anger and resentment.

'If only I had known what was going on with them – with my mum and your dad. Done more to stop it. I feel like if I'd just seen the signs—'

Ruben scoffed. 'Oh, come on, you can't honestly be blaming yourself? There were no signs. Your mum was like the perfect mum. No one would have known.'

'I should have known,' Olive said, tipping her head back to the starry sky. 'I knew what she was like.'

Josephine King was the kind of mother who threw tea parties for the teddies with homemade lemonade and hot cross buns. Who spread patchwork eiderdowns on the ground and gathered her girls close for fantastical fairy tales. To anyone looking on it was an idyllic childhood. To Olive though, it felt like her mother was so good with children because really she was always just a child herself. She would stubbornly refuse the burden of reality, referring to herself as the dreamer and Olive as the sensible, practical one. But it was tiring being responsible for someone else's whimsy.

'Then there's my dad, he was locking me in the park, for God's sake! They were all nuts.' Ruben shook his head, draining the last of his wine with a sardonic grin.

Neither of them spoke.

The fox trotted back across the grass. Olive watched it pause to stare at them, then disappear into the trees.

Ruben turned to look at her, elbows on his knees. 'What do

you think would have happened if we'd gone? You know, like we talked about, running away together, leaving this all behind.'

'Your dad would have found you and dragged you with him to where it was he went.'

'New Jersey.'

'New Jersey,' Olive remembered. 'As far away as he could possibly get from any of us.'

Ruben waved a hand like that didn't count for now. 'Just suppose he didn't.'

'But he would have done. You would never have been able to get away. And I think you would have regretted it if you had.'

'I would not.' Ruben was aghast.

But Olive was too old to believe in fairy-tale fantasies. 'You would. You would have lost all your opportunities. You would have lived thinking what if. I mean, think about it, you know your dad was an asshole, but I bet you still think if you hadn't messed up your exams he wouldn't have kicked you out of the house that first time, don't you? You don't think he'd have found something else to complain about? That he was just a bully. He would never have let you be happy with me. And you wouldn't have been able to be happy because you'd have wanted to prove something to him.'

Ruben narrowed his eyes as he thought. 'No,' he said with a shake of his head. 'You're right about him being a bully, I've never thought that. But you're wrong that I wouldn't have been happy. I wasn't happy in America, so …'

Olive raised a brow. 'I think you had a pretty OK time in America.'

She watched his lips twitch as he recollected his time at the New Jersey boarding school. 'It was OK.'

Olive sat back, that admission enough to satisfy her that no mistakes were made. 'And whatever happened, I had Dolly to look after. And my mum. And … I don't know, I felt like I'd taken my eye off them for one minute and it all collapsed. And it wasn't your responsibility. It was my family.'

'I would have made them my responsibility.'

Olive shook her head. 'Come on, we were sixteen. And we were too different.'

'We weren't different.' Ruben made a face. Olive wondered if he believed what he was saying or just arguing to win. 'We agreed on everything.'

'Your dad thought we were different.'

Ruben looked down at his glass. 'Yeah,' he said, 'but there was nothing I could do about that except apologise.'

Olive looked away, she remembered Ruben standing on the cottage steps. She remembered the feeling of being seen as nothing, as scum. Of saying to Ruben, 'I don't think I can get over the way he looks at me. You can walk away from this but I can't.' And Ruben saying, 'That's unfair.' And Olive nodding. 'Yes, I know it's unfair. But what is it your dad says? "Fairness is a childish concept."'

At the patio table, after a moment's pause, Ruben seemed to pull himself back to his adult self and said, jokily, 'So you don't think we could have been blissfully happy?'

Olive laughed. 'No. We were so young. We wouldn't have been able to stay together through all that. I was really hurt by everything your dad said. Now I'd probably be able to get over it. Not probably, definitely. But I was only sixteen and it felt real. What I said earlier about thinking about the what-ifs, even if you hadn't, I would have done. I would have thought how I was holding you back. And it was pretty bad at Aunt Marge's. Pretty bad with Dolly. It's inevitable we would have drifted apart. That's the reality, isn't it?'

'Ever the pragmatist, Olive.'

Olive felt herself bristle. She was too used to being seen as the cool, rational one. 'No, I just think it's too easy to imagine the alternative as perfect. We didn't know who we were outside of this place.'

Ruben held his hands up in defence. 'Don't worry, you've persuaded me! I agree. We were sixteen. Babies. Idiots.' He laughed.

The moment had changed. The gap between their old and new selves had widened again. They both had their new personas back in place. She said, 'So what have you been doing with your life?'

Ruben topped up their wine glasses. 'This and that,' he said casually.

'You can do better than that,' said Olive, looking out at the garden. 'Have you been married?'

'I've not yet had the pleasure.'

'What work are you doing?'

'This and that,' he said, a little cocky and laissez-faire. 'I made quite a bit when I sold my company a little while ago so …'

Olive internally rolled her eyes. 'What did the company do?'

'Just data analysis.'

'Just data analysis?' Olive mocked. 'It was obviously more than that to make you "quite a bit".'

Ruben shrugged, acting coy at the attention. 'It was a programme we built that was geared to Formula One racing but essentially you could use it in anything. Sport, the military, online shopping. Whatever you want. It was very targeted but could be adapted across a variety of sectors, that gave it its value.'

'So a little more than just "this and that",' Olive said with a shake of her head, like she'd caught him out in his humble bragging.

Ruben laughed, more bashful, 'Yeah, I suppose so. And to prove your earlier point, when I rang my dad to tell him about the deal, he said, "Sounds like a fluke, Ruben."'

Olive winced.

Ruben shrugged like it was nothing. 'He didn't believe anything had any value if it wasn't in law or banking.'

'So is the whole rich playboy thing you living up to his disapproval?' Olive's lips twitched with a smile.

'How dare you!' Ruben barked a laugh. 'Why do you think I'm a playboy?'

'You have Stormzy tickets, Ruben. You wear the sunglasses eighteen-year-olds wear. You drive a fast car and you live in some swanky penthouse.' Olive felt herself falling into their old familiarity, their easy banter. She remembered suddenly moments lying on her back looking up through the dazzling lemon yellow of the leaves in sunlight, laughing till her stomach ached and she could barely breathe, Ruben cracking up beside her.

'I like Stormzy,' he said, then he stopped, thought for a second and added, 'How do you know where I live?'

Olive swallowed. 'I don't,' she said. 'It was just a guess.'

'No, it wasn't.' He grinned. 'You've looked me up. You've been on my Instagram.'

'I have not,' she lied, feeling her cheeks go red.

Ruben's mouth stretched even wider into a very satisfied smile. 'I think you're lying, Olive King.'

Olive huffed. Not liking the feeling of having been caught out, the smugness of his expression making her feel like one of the adoring women she knew he had queuing up. She didn't like the loss of control. It derailed her. The vulnerability of it made her uncomfortable. Perhaps she wasn't actually ready for real honesty.

In an act of self-preservation, she altered the course of the subject by saying, 'You are going to take Zadie to that Stormzy concert, aren't you?'

Ruben smirked, his confidence now sky-high, 'I think it's called a gig.'

'Whatever. Are you going to take her?'

He shrugged. 'Maybe.'

'Is that your answer for everything?' Olive felt more comfortable with her disapproval. 'You know she thinks you're a hero, don't you?'

Ruben shook his head. 'I'm not a hero.'

'*I* know that,' Olive quipped.

Ruben raised a brow like he could see straight through her. Then he said, 'I don't want to be a hero. The kid knows not to expect too much.'

Olive blew out an incredulous breath. 'You really think so? She's spent twelve years building you up to some godlike status.'

Ruben ran his hand through his hair, ruffling it out of place. His eyes drooped. 'My life's not really set up to have a daughter.'

Olive sighed. 'This is a chance, Ruben. They don't come round very often. Don't mess it up with her,' she urged, feeling justified now in her desire to sabotage the earlier moment.

Too quickly, Ruben said, 'Yeah, of course.' Then he got up, rolling his shoulders as if reacquainting himself with his true self.

The moment for honesty between them was over.

Ruben stretched his arms above his head and yawned. 'Time for bed, I think.'

CHAPTER THIRTEEN

Dolly and Fox received an exceedingly warm welcome at the farm at the bottom of the valley. It was owned by Matilda and Duncan. She was West Country born and bred. He was an Aussie who'd come over to pick fruit one summer and never left. 'You can borrow the van, mate,' said Duncan when Fox explained the situation over a cold beer in the garden. Matilda had strapped an ice pack round his ankle with a tea towel. 'Sleep in the back, that's what we do. The only problem is there's a bloody great crack across the window where this idiot' – Duncan pointed to his son, Brad, a tall, sweet-looking blond kid standing by the back door – 'hit a bloody buzzard, but you'll be right.'

'Are you sure?' asked Dolly, naturally suspicious of anyone and anything, especially favours. She was sitting across from Duncan, her own beer dripping condensation on the wooden outdoor table.

'Yeah! Definitely, no doubt about it,' Duncan waved a work-gnarled hand. 'Take it, pay it forward and all that. We'll go and get your bike now. Leave it here with us. Brad here's done a bit of mechanics, he'll have a tinker with it.'

Brad nodded from where he stood in the shade by the door.

'Well, I mean, that sounds perfect,' Fox said with a swig of his beer, clearly much more inclined than Dolly to take people as he found them. 'Thank you.'

Duncan tipped his head in acceptance and then clinked his beer with Fox's. 'Happy to help.'

Matilda came out with a plate of freshly baked scones and jam. 'You can't drive on that ankle,' she said, nodding towards Fox's tea-towel-bound foot.

Fox made a face. 'No, probably shouldn't.'

'Definitely shouldn't,' Matilda scolded. 'Stay here tonight, we've got some B&B rooms set up. Leave in the morning.'

This was way out of Dolly's comfort zone. All this kindness of strangers. She even gave her shoulder a test to see if she could get behind the wheel but it still sent shooting pains through her when she lifted it above forty degrees.

She could feel Fox watching her. His expression like he could tell how uncomfortable all this made her. This having to rely on others, to accept help. 'This is all very kind of you,' he said.

Dolly shifted in her seat.

Next to her, Matilda shook her head, mouthful of scone. 'It's nothing. And there's a giant leg of lamb that's been in the barbecue oven for the last six hours that needs eating. You'll be helping us out.'

Fox sat back with a grin in Dolly's direction. 'It gets better and better!'

After their drinks, Matilda showed them to one of the B&B rooms. All beautifully decked out in country cottage chic. As she made to leave, Dolly said, 'Oh no, sorry we need two rooms.'

Matilda looked surprised and said, 'I thought—' at the same time as Dolly said, 'We're not together!'

'Sorry, love. Just figured with a chap like that …' then winked at Fox, who lapped it up with a grin.

Then feigning sad, puppy-dog eyes, Fox added, 'She'd never have me.'

Matilda made a face at Dolly. 'You're mad.'

Dolly tried her best to laugh along with them. Then Matilda went off to get the key for the other room and Dolly glared at Fox.

'What?' he said, all innocent.

'Don't,' she warned.

He grinned. 'Chill out, Dolly. You've got to learn to relax. Laugh. Have some fun.' He leant forward and whispered, 'It's not a crime to enjoy yourself.' Then he walked away into his room, kicking the door shut behind him and she heard a sigh of pleasure and the sound of him flopping down on the huge squishy bed.

Once she'd been let into her own room, Dolly had a shower, washed her hair with the little bottles of lily of the valley shampoo and conditioner and changed into soft blue joggers and a raspberry-pink T-shirt. All the while she was overly conscious of the fact Fox could hear her through the wall, because she could hear him. She didn't want to be aware of him. She wanted to go back to hating him but something about him asking her a simple question about herself – not to mention him handing her the water before he'd taken a sip – had thrown a trip switch inside her that set her off kilter. He had got her talking about herself without even really trying. That never happened. It was only then she remembered that was Fox's skill. He'd been a hostage negotiator. This was what he was trained for. Listening effectively was part of his job. What was it they called it? Dynamic silence. She tried to think what he'd done. He'd labelled her emotions, definitely, oldest trick in the book – *You sound surprised, Dolly*. Oh God! She'd totally fallen for it. He found people's weaknesses, their interests, their emotions and used them to burrow under their skin.

She had a flash forward to Brogden patting Fox on the back saying, '*I don't know how you did it, but you've cracked her. And she was a particularly tough nut. Fox Mason, you've more than earned your bonus.*'

Dolly made a face at the wall when she heard him creaking about next door. She felt as foolish as she did unwittingly relieved to have spoken about things she never mentioned. It all seemed immediately less negative now she had said it. But still she felt tricked, and when he opened his door and knocked softly on hers she pretended not to hear. It was petty, she knew, but she needed to regain her autonomy.

Dolly waited five minutes then followed him downstairs and out into the garden. The light had started to fade. The table was piled high with food and drinks and in the centre, a big vase of sweet-smelling jasmine and ivy tumbled down onto the tablecloth. Over by the barbecue Duncan was making a show of basting the lamb shank. Fox was discussing motorbikes with Brad but when he saw Dolly he gave her a nod. She purposely didn't join them, instead she went to where Matilda was mixing drinks. 'Prosecco with homemade elderflower cordial,' Matilda said, handing Dolly a champagne flute with a few tiny white elderflowers sprinkled on the surface.

Dolly took the drink and found herself a seat that didn't have a dog or cat or chicken sitting on it. On the step by the

French windows, one of the many children was playing the violin, the others fought over a Nintendo Switch. The view was all patchwork fields and pale dusky sky. Just one sip of the elderflower cordial and Dolly was back home. Back running behind Olive. Back standing on her tiptoes trying to reach the biggest of the million white flower heads for her mum to dip them in batter and sizzle into elderflower fritters that they'd eat piping hot and burn their mouths. Back to Ruben lifting her up so she could pluck the flowers from the very top. Back to sitting on his shoulders while he said funny things to impress Olive. Back to lying in the grass watching him, watching how close his fingertips were to Olive's. Back to barbecues on the beach, fairy lights and homemade bunting strung between two surfboards, the music, the dancing, the dog chasing rabbits and the dark black evening sky. They were days bathed in sunlight. Memories shrouded with fine gold thread. All of them together. The smiles. The laughter. Her mum's blonde, blonde hair, the curls heavy like silk. The tilt of her head as she danced with their dad. His infatuated eyes entranced. The waft of her perfume. Next to them, she saw Ruben bowing to ask Olive to dance, all over the top like a costume drama on a Sunday afternoon. Olive shaking her head in refusal, above the jest of it all. Faux broken-hearted, he would move on to Dolly, who jumped up quicker than a kangaroo. She would press her head to his shirt and inhale. She would tip her head, hoping her frizzy curls might somehow cascade down her back, and see Ruben's eyes locked not on her like her dad's were with her mum, but on Olive, who sat watching with mild amusement and her customary watchful concern. Olive was the one who stopped the fallen candle setting fire to the table, who made sure the barbecue wasn't burnt, who checked the dog was fed. Who took their mum away when she suddenly stopped laughing.

Sitting on her kitchen chair at the farm, Dolly sipped the Prosecco. The little girl's violin was stuck on the same chord. Over and over, she played, making the same mistake each time. Stamping her foot. Clenching her teeth in frustration. Duncan abandoned the roast lamb to go over and encourage her to change tune. But she burst into howling tears instead and Matilda hurried over to usher her inside to bed.

Dolly watched the histrionics. Seeing the girl's little face screw up all red, she could taste the flavour of gasping, frustrated tears. Dolly could sense Fox watching her out of the corner of his eye. She looked away, reaching down instead to give a wiry Jack Russell by her feet a stroke.

She wanted to stop the reminiscing in its tracks. To turn her brain off and go over and join the ensuing chat about tired pre-teens and whether the Kawasaki would beat Brad's souped-up dirt bike. But she couldn't switch it off that easily. Even as the Jack Russell woke up and started weaving between her legs in excitement, she remembered the day she saw Ruben and Olive sneaking away, his hand pressed firm on the small of her back. She knew in that moment that they were more than just friends. She remembered the all-encompassing fear that she had lost them to each other; her idolised big sister and the boy she loved so much it made her heart ache. Dolly, the little fool on the outside who didn't know. She remembered following them through the woods, watching from behind a big fir tree as they took their own secret path down into the tangled, derelict mess of the orangery. Her own face crumpling as she watched

Ruben cup Olive's cheek, sickened with jealousy at the utter adoration.

The Jack Russell came back with the stick between its teeth but refused to give it up when Dolly bent to take it. As she wrestled it from him, she was struck by the memory of running so fast she tripped on snaking brambles that lacerated her legs. Found by her father freshly back from 'the best adventure of them all', out rallying the troops because he'd laid the treasure hunt to end all treasure hunts. She found it hard to remember his face. She knew he was grinning. High on life. He'd changed into normal clothes but he still had the sunburn of an explorer. If she had one wish it would have been to look at him properly in that moment of his radiant happiness. To have stood up and grinned back, rather than sobbed inconsolably into his open arms about love and deceit and her evil sister at the orangery. Her pride was hurt along with her heart and she wanted justice and attention, dialling it up a notch to get Daddy onside. If only she had brushed down the bramble cuts, wiped her face and smiled. He wouldn't have gone marching to the orangery to see what Olive had done to upset her sister. Nor would he have seen as Olive and Ruben discovered his wife, Josephine King, in the arms of Lord de Lacy. He wouldn't have witnessed, broken-hearted, the shameful, vitriolic showdown, nor come to blows with Lord de Lacy. He wouldn't have picked up his still-packed rucksack and never returned. Had she just smiled, the worst thing to happen in Dolly's life would have been simply an unrequited crush on her sister's secret boyfriend.

At the barbecue, Dolly felt suddenly dizzy. The memories colliding like snooker balls. The ground like a listing ship. She focused all her attention on the yappy little dog.

'Dinner's ready!' Duncan shouted, declaring the lamb finally perfect. Everyone came to take their places at the table. Matilda got the sharp knife from the kitchen. 'Won't need that,' Duncan said, carrying the steaming tray of barbecued lamb in front of him, 'this is so tender, meat'll fall straight from the bone.'

Dolly stood up, steadying herself with the back of a rickety chair. Fox came to stand beside her. 'Everything all right?'

'Yeah,' she said, blinking hard to get herself firmly back in the present, 'never better.' Then to the rest of the table, with her best smile in place, said, 'This looks delicious, I can't wait.'

CHAPTER FOURTEEN

Ruben de Lacy found it nigh on impossible to sleep after his drink with Olive on the Big House veranda. He lay in bed, tossing and turning, listening to the howl of the fox and the hoot of the damn owl, missing his London apartment noises. He wanted helicopters and fire engines, drunken revellers and idling Ubers.

He kept replaying the conversation over and over in his head. Before she had shot him down with the belief that they wouldn't have stayed together, he had actually been building up to saying that he had missed having her in his life. He put the pillow over his face. Thank God he hadn't!

When she had said that he'd have lived his life thinking *what if*, Ruben had wanted to grab her by the arms and say, *What do you think I did?*

He could vividly remember the days of lying on soft grass looking up at blue sky, talking about anything that came into their heads. How Olive was going to be a millionaire. How he hated the word 'pamphlet'. How Olive thought that the moon was on the back of the sun till she was at least eleven. How Ruben liked raspberries but thought strawberries overrated. He thought of the shared cigarettes in the rain. The malt whisky he stole from his dad and got flogged with his belt when it was found missing, but every whip was worth it for the dusky evening spent drinking it with Olive, the fit of giggles that made his stomach muscles hurt, the stupid dancing, the rambling stories and that moment when his mouth first touched hers. A kiss that still ranked in his top ten. OK, top five. He stared up at the crack in the ceiling. Top three. Who was he kidding? Top one. The best kiss of his life.

But sitting next to Olive on the patio, he had felt strangely hollow. He thought of the times he had sat on his bed at school in the early morning, her phone number dialled but never made the call. The evening after the affair had been discovered, Ruben had snuck out to see her at the cottage. She had stood on the doorstep and said, 'Our lives are too different, Ruben.' He had begged her not to end it but she'd been unwavering. He hadn't fully understood why until she'd spelt it out just then on the patio. Not just her hurt at his father's words but for him, so she didn't hold him back.

Ruben ran his hand through his hair. Christ, how frustrating a rationale! Why didn't she let him decide?

But then he remembered the email he'd sent from his American boarding school where his accent, clean-cut good looks and self-destructive disregard for authority catapulted him immediately to the top of the tree. Motivated to hurt perhaps, or to get her jealous, he'd recounted all his wild and crazy escapades. She had replied with a stark précis of her current life. He thought of his paragraph on getting suspended for doing mushrooms at homeroom. Hers that she had had to sit up all night with Dolly who, since the death of their father and breakdown of their mother, had stopped being able to sleep.

Ruben sat up contemplating the past. Why had he never read between the lines and considered other options for her rejection? Because, he realised, he *had* been too young. Olive was right – as always.

When the sun rose, Ruben got out of bed and made himself a coffee. He sat on the back step of the kitchen, the buddleia still held the scars of his fall from the roof, ahead of him the sun streaming onto the lush grass where the black cat was curled in a knot of legs and paws, completely oblivious to the rabbits lolloping on the lawn. Ruben looked out towards the sea. He thought of the Olive who had turned up the other day, all polished and pressed. He thought of who she must have been, her good job and her neat little flat. She drove a Volvo, for Christ's sake. The Olive he had known would never have driven a Volvo.

She was definitely right, he realised. They couldn't have stayed friends. They *were* too young. They didn't know who they were. Life would have got in the way. Because look at who they had become.

Yet he had loved her. More than he'd loved anyone. There was a lump in his throat as he thought of it. Ruben was most unused to this sense of emotion. This sentimentality. Maybe he was getting old. Maybe it was just that Olive's family had felt like the only proper family he'd ever had. It occurred to him that he'd spent the last twenty years essentially alone. Tied to nothing and no one. And while he enjoyed himself very much, life was definitely lacking that sense of guarantee. The idea that there was always somewhere else to go where you would be welcomed into the warm, fed and watered and entertained. And loved.

But no, she was right, it would have been a disaster. Just the chaos and tragedy that had gone on here was enough to prove it so. From his experience, relationships always ended in disaster.

Suddenly there was a presence beside him. Zadie squashed herself into the small space left on the back step, a bowl of cereal in her hand, dressed in another of her bizarre ensembles. 'Morning!' she chirruped. 'Oh, you can see the sea from here! I just love the sea. I swim in the sea every day at home. There's literally nowhere I like better than the sea.'

Ruben was on the cusp of limiting her to three sentences a day. He suddenly understood stressed mums everywhere as she interrupted his precious me-time. 'Yes,' he sighed, 'you can see the sea.'

Next thing, Olive arrived and the morning started. She busied herself getting coffee, burning toast and trying to decipher the clue, while Ruben hovered awkwardly, unable to relax around her after his night of soul-searching. His movements felt rehearsed and wooden. When she asked him to pass the Marmite, he slammed it down on the table too hard for no reason other than he'd forgotten how to use his hands. He was completely distracted by things he wanted to say to her, questions and clarifications about the past. She asked if he wanted coffee, he couldn't look at her. Who knew if he wanted coffee? Not him, that was for sure.

Olive was frowning at him, clearly about to ask why he was being so weird, when the doorbell rang. A giant gold bell that tolled when someone pulled the metal handle outside.

'Who's that?' squeaked Zadie, jumping up to go and look.

Ruben followed, opening the huge door as Zadie peered through one of the side windows saying, 'It's a really pretty blonde woman.'

When he opened the door he heard a voice say, 'Well, Ruben de Lacy, look at you.'

And standing on the step was quite possibly one of the most beautiful women he'd seen in years. Blue eyes, rosebud lips, hair like a cornfield on a summer's day. A sight for sore eyes, to say the least. Had they dated once? If not, he'd damn well find out why not. He looked her up and down – denim shorts revealed long tanned legs, simple yellow vest, hair could perhaps do with a brush but on the whole the perfect specimen. This was more like it. This was more Ruben's type of woman, enough of Olive's prim, righteous condescension. He was all about fun, not self-flagellation. 'Hi there,' he drawled to the hot blonde, a self-assured smile on his lips.

The woman paused. Her eyes narrowed. 'You have no idea who I am, do you?'

Ruben shrugged it off. 'Give me a second and it'll come to me.' His smile grew wider. All thoughts of Olive and her unreachable expectations, Zadie and his failure at fatherhood, flooding away as he stepped firmly into familiar territory.

The woman watched, hand on her hip, waiting, smile widening (perfect teeth).

Ruben's grin grew as he played for time, trying to place her. He was sure they'd dated. She brushed a stray lock of hair from her cheek. She liked him, that was for sure. Praise the Lord.

Then suddenly Olive appeared behind him. Damn. All he'd needed was five minutes more. He didn't need Olive's judgement towards his desire for some much needed harmless flirtation. But then Olive stepped past him and said, 'Oh my God, Dolly, why didn't you tell anyone you were coming?'

All the humour drained from Ruben's face. 'Dolly?' This was not the staunch policewoman he was expecting.

'Hi Ruben,' the woman in front of him grinned, stood there in the golden sunlight seemingly lapping up his surprise before glancing briefly, dismissively, at Olive and saying shortly, 'Aunt Marge made me.'

Ruben was 100 per cent speechless. What a transformation! If Olive hadn't confirmed it there was no way he would have believed this stunner was Dolly King.

Next minute, from a beaten-up van in the driveway, a great hulk of a man appeared, saying with a scolding voice, 'Dolly, what are you doing? Why aren't you wearing your sling? You're going to do permanent damage to your arm!'

Ruben watched Dolly's cheeks pink as the guy handed her a tatty old sling and then helped truss her up with it. 'What were you thinking?' he was saying.

Dolly mumbled something sulkily incoherent, and suddenly Ruben could see little Dolly again. Beside him, Olive quipped, 'Looks like she's already taken, Ruben.' A little dig at his obvious approval of adult Dolly.

'No need to be jealous, Olive,' he drawled quietly. 'Just appreciating a fine thing.'

Olive scoffed at the mention of jealousy and it gave Ruben a little buzz.

Ruben had always had a soft spot for Dolly. He'd always enjoyed her tagging along. She was easy to wind up but also laughed at his jokes. She'd been funny and sweet and adoring. He never forgot the time he'd found her on her own, trying to rescue some baby robins that had fallen out of a nest. She had them all scooped up in her hands but couldn't reach high enough to put them back. He'd only come out for a fag but ended up embroiled in the rescue, popping each one back as the mother robin went nuts in the background.

When all the fluffy little baby birds were safe in the nest, he'd turned to Dolly for a friendly high five, only to find her on tiptoes, clasping his face in her sweaty palms and kissing him hard on the lips with fervent desperation. Feeling a little like a cat held too tight by a small child, Ruben had struggled to extricate himself and catch his breath. At the moment when he should have let Dolly down gently, he was so gasping for air that he had laughed instead. Oh, he could still see it now, the painful humiliation in those big wide eyes. Poor little Dolly. When Olive had come out looking for him, he'd had to explain what happened, worried about Dolly on her own in the woods. Olive had winced. 'She can't just go around kissing people. God, she's as nuts as Mum.' Ruben had sprung to her defence, 'No, it was sweet. Don't have a go at her!' Olive had started walking into the woods already. 'I'm not going have a go at her, I'm just going to teach her a bit about what to do with boys.' Ruben had thought it would be best for Dolly's self-esteem were he not to tag along for that chat. When he'd walked home he'd seen her curled up at the base of one of the giant oaks, sobbing into Olive's sleeve. Olive had winked at him as he'd tiptoed past and he knew he'd see her later at the orangery. That was all the two of them had cared about at that time, those snatched meetings. Maybe it *had* made them blind to everything else.

Now, on the doorstep, the big hulk of a man thrust out his arm, shaking Ruben's then Olive's hand. 'Fox Mason,' he said. 'Colleague of Dolly's.'

'What, are you here to arrest somebody?' Ruben quipped

and instantly regretted it when no one laughed. It felt like a real dad joke when he noticed Zadie wince. Clearing his throat, he said more seriously, 'Ruben de Lacy.'

A very unsubtle look passed between Fox and Dolly. Ruben wondered if it was something to do with his dad joke.

Zadie squeezed herself to the front and said, 'I'm Zadie, Ruben's daughter.'

'You have a daughter?' Dolly said with surprise.

Ruben said, 'It's a long story.'

Olive made a confused face. 'It's not that long.'

'Anyway, come in,' Ruben ushered them inside, ignoring Olive, feeling like she was being deliberately obtuse, niggled, he decided, from coming across as jealous earlier. That was the benefit of knowing exactly how another's brain worked.

'Have you spoken to Marge? Told her you're here? She rang me, she's worried about you,' Olive was asking.

'She's fine,' said Dolly, waving away the concern. 'She knows I'm here.'

'She doesn't.'

Dolly turned. 'Olive, she does.'

Olive looked away with a shake of her head.

Zadie was running about like a hyperactive puppy. 'We answered the first two clues. We've got the third, but we don't know what it means.'

Dolly said, 'You've done the first two clues?' Surprise in her voice, almost hurt.

Olive said, 'Well you couldn't expect us to wait when we didn't even know if you were coming!'

Dolly visibly bristled. 'I didn't say I wanted you to wait.'

Olive raised a brow.

Ruben said, 'Can I get you a coffee? Toast?'

'We've had breakfast,' said Fox, all deep and authoritative, making Ruben feel like a weedy schoolboy.

Dolly said, 'I'll have toast and coffee.' Her tone pedantic, like she was deliberately going against Fox for having spoken for both of them.

Ruben clocked the interaction with interest. As did Olive. Fox just seemed unfazed.

When Ruben came back with the coffee and toast, they were all sitting at the long kitchen table. Olive was saying, 'So you've been suspended from work, dislocated your arm, you've written-off a police car and, Fox, your bike is in a barn somewhere?'

Fox chuckled. 'I know, can you believe it? I've been to war-zones less stressful than working with Dolly.'

Dolly sat back a little sulkily with her good arm crossed over the bad.

Olive blew out a breath. 'Blimey, Dolly, what are you doing?'

Fox said, 'Has she always been like this?'

'Yes,' said Olive, eyes wide for emphasis.

'I have not!' Dolly defended herself.

Ruben put the coffee and toast down in front of her. 'I don't think she was always like that,' he said in Dolly's defence. Half because it was true and half because it seemed like Olive was being a bit mean. She'd always looked after Dolly in the past. Now she seemed overly stressed, riled by her sister's presence.

'Oh please!' Olive scoffed.

Fox said, 'She's jinxed,' but his addition was good-natured, whereas it was clear to anyone who really knew them, there were undercurrents between Olive and Dolly.

Dolly stood up, the coffee spilled. 'I am not bloody jinxed.'

'Dolly, calm down,' said Olive.

'*Dolly, calm down*,' Dolly repeated patronisingly, faux-soothing.

Fox looked surprised by the interaction. 'Dolly, why are you getting so annoyed? It's just messing.'

'It's not just messing. It's always like this. No wonder I didn't want to come. Five minutes we've been here and you can't help yourself. Always telling me what to do, like you're my mum.' She waved a hand in Olive's direction.

Zadie's head was flicking from side to side, like she was watching a tennis match.

'I can't help myself?' Olive pointed to herself. 'Are you kidding me? I had Aunt Marge on the phone last night panicking that you weren't answering your phone and you'd lost your job, ready to go round and check your flat. Do you realise that all around you, you have people constantly pent up with worry?'

'And do you realise that you pick at me for any justifiable reason you can get?' Dolly huffed. 'And I haven't lost my job, by the way, I've been suspended. Completely different things.'

Olive rolled her eyes. 'Can you hear yourself?'

Dolly narrowed her eyes. 'Very clearly.'

After a pause, like two wild cats facing off, Olive said, her voice neutral, 'Nice to see you've grown up, Dolly.'

Everyone round the table looked embarrassed.

Dolly ran her tongue along her top lip. Then she turned to Zadie, who was watching the whole thing entranced, and said, 'What's the clue?'

'*You know the maiden rocks that guard the southern bay. But did you know their heart of stone they one day threw away?'* Zadie recited it by heart, her voice small in the room. 'We know the maidens but not the heart of stone.'

'OK fine,' Dolly snapped. 'Leave this one to me and Fox. We'll find it.'

Olive sat back in her chair, hands spread wide. 'Fine. You do that.'

'Fine,' said Dolly. 'We will.'

And the next thing Ruben knew, Dolly had grabbed Fox by the arm and was storming out of the house. Olive watching with a tight-lipped shake of her head. The coffee sloshed all over the table. The toast untouched.

Olive got up to get a cloth and clear up the spill.

Zadie's phone rang. 'Oh, that's my mum!' And she disappeared outside where the black cat was still sunning himself.

Ruben said to Olive, 'What was all that about?' Surprised at what he'd witnessed between the two sisters. The immediate lack of humour over the current predicament.

Olive chucked the cloth in the sink and cleared the plates. 'What do you mean, what was all that about?'

Ruben leant against the sideboard. 'You sound like you're mad at her.'

Olive started to wash-up. 'I'm not mad at her. We don't speak enough for me to be mad at her.'

Ruben found himself incredulous at the very idea. 'Why don't you speak? You were so close.'

'Because she's like that,' Olive said, gesturing towards the door that Dolly had left through. 'She's never grown up.'

'She must have grown up. She's an officer of the law,' Ruben replied, as he took a plate from the sideboard and started to dry up. After a few minutes of silence he said, 'I really can't believe you don't get on. She was such a sweet kid.'

'Yeah well, things changed.' Olive paused washing-up. 'I just get a bit fed up of the Dolly show, you know. She never thinks about anyone else. All anyone's ever done since we left here is bail out Dolly. She's never had to take responsibility and she never will. She acts like a child, OK!'

Ruben tipped his head. 'It's not her fault everything went wrong.'

Olive rinsed the last plate of washing-up suds. 'I know it wasn't her fault but …' she paused. 'Sometimes it feels like it was. That she was so young and mollycoddled, that she went crying to my dad because she'd seen us together—'

'Hang on, that's very unfair. You said last night that it wasn't my fault about my dad and what a nasty piece of work he was. Well, then how can any of it be Dolly's fault? Your mum *chose* to have an affair.'

'It's not about the affair,' snapped Olive. 'It's the fact that all she ever thinks about is herself.'

There was a pause where Olive seemed to presume the conversation was over.

But Ruben didn't think it was done. She'd been on her high horse last night about his potential failings at fatherhood and he felt justifiably high-horsed now in return. She was being so petty. 'Don't you think, maybe …' he proffered, feeling his heart rate rise in what was possibly a fear of reprisal but he refused to kowtow, him and Olive had always told it to each other straight, 'it's you that's being a bit childish?'

Olive turned from the sink to glare at him.

Ruben stared back. Unwavering. He could tell from her

expression that it was a long time since she'd been challenged. He could see all the colours of her furious eyes. The flick of her lashes as she tried to harden her stare. Inside he wanted to smile – it was like one of their showdowns as kids. The adrenaline was addictive but he just kept on looking, calm and composed, holding her steady, watching every tiny flicker of her face. She looked really pretty when she was annoyed.

Then suddenly Zadie came skipping inside. 'That was my mum; she's having a great time on her honeymoon. They've swum with dolphins. Can you believe it? I swam with dolphins once but they were like really far away.'

Ruben kept one eye on Olive, watched as she wiped her hands angrily on a tea towel. He could feel his heart thumping.

Zadie was still talking as Olive swept past him, with clearly the best comeback she could rustle up in the time. 'Why don't you just focus on your daughter?'

'Will do, Olive. Will do.' Ruben grinned.

CHAPTER FIFTEEN

The morning sky was white like a fluffy roll of cotton wool. Seagulls snoozed on the ice-flat sea in the distance. The park was still. A kite hung limp in the branches of a horse chestnut.

'You seem tense, Dolly,' said Fox as he strode alongside her.

'She's so righteous!' Dolly stomped through the lush grass, past grazing deer and sprawling ferns. 'Always acting like some pseudo-parent, going on about how I've never grown up. I'm a grown-up, look at me, grown up!' Dolly turned to Fox outraged as she gestured to her adult self.

'Did you ever feel like a parent?' asked Fox, walking next to her, feet sinking into the thick grass, a trail of deep dewy footprints behind them.

'Don't start all that on me. It's not going to work. "Do you feel this, you seem that." I'm on to you, Mason. None of your hostage negotiator stuff on me, got it?'

Fox smiled under his breath. 'I don't know what you're talking about.'

'*I don't know what you're talking about,*' Dolly mimicked. 'Don't act the innocent with me.'

Fox didn't reply, just kept his annoying half-smile on his face. Dolly looked ahead at the landscape and tried not to think about anything to do with her mum and dad. Many years ago, she had perfected the ability to shut her thoughts down completely. Through a dogged determination to conquer meditation, she could now turn her mind into a simple canvas of blue. Nothing else but blue. Like the sea. But it wasn't working right now. 'And no,' she huffed, 'I never felt like a parent. *I* felt like a child.'

Fox didn't say anything.

Above them, the sun was working hard to peek through the shredded clouds.

'Olive had everything she wanted,' said Dolly, still on the warpath.

Tiny birds darted in and out of the bushes.

'Did she?' questioned Fox.

'Yeah.' Dolly tied her hair up with her good hand, twisting it angrily into some semblance of a ponytail. 'She had everything!'

They walked a little further. Hands behind his back, Fox mused, 'Do you think maybe she had everything *you* wanted?'

Dolly glared at him. 'What's that supposed to mean?'

Out on the horizon, fishing boats were coming in after a night at sea. The sunlight catching on the rigging and the tinfoil sea.

Fox turned away so his gaze was fixed on the boats. 'Well, she had the guy – Ruben. She had the upper hand in terms of your relationship purely from her age.' Fox shielded his eyes from the growing glare of the sun to get a better view of the fishermen. 'And I'm assuming – based on the school of thought that she was the parent figure – clearly everyone in the family listened to her. So she had authority, which is always enviable.'

Fox looked back in Dolly's direction.

It was her turn not to say anything. To consider instead what had been said.

Fox took a chance and said into the silence, 'You can be jealous of someone, Dolly, and still empathise with them.'

'Shut up, I'm not jealous!'

'Right you are,' said Fox.

Dolly could sense he was biding his time now. Storing away details.

What was so annoying was the initial meeting with Ruben de Lacy had left Dolly punching the air inside. She'd kept her face straight, she'd played it cool, she'd even managed a little aloof flirtation. The long-awaited face to face with Ruben had gone even better than her wildest fantasies. She had done it. She had wowed him. She had him eating from the palm of her hand. She'd felt high as a kite. Dear God, it had been a miracle. Then bloody Fox saunters up with her sling and Olive does what Olive does best, which was tell her off.

'So where are we going?' Fox asked.

'Trevellyn Bay,' said Dolly. 'It's round the headland. When the tide's out there's miles of rockpools. We used to go there as kids.'

'And you know the way?'

''Course I know the way!'

Fox got his smashed phone out of his pocket and tried to load Google Maps. 'No signal, damn it.'

'Honestly, I know the way,' Dolly laughed.

'Dolly, I don't want to be rude but your navigation skills so far haven't been much to write home about,' he replied without looking up.

'What?' She sucked in her cheeks. 'Well, I was going to let you try my phone but now I won't.'

He gave her a withering glance. 'You've just claimed that you're not a child.'

Dolly turned away, chastened.

It was hot. The sun was getting higher, brilliant ketchup rays cascading the horizon. Sweat was trickling down her back. They came to a fork in the path. One way led through the woods and the other snaked up towards heather-strewn rocks.

Dolly said, 'It's that way,' pointing at the rockier terrain.

'You're sure?' said Fox.

Dolly rolled her eyes. 'Of course.'

They hiked on. Higher and higher into the wild landscape. The rising limestone rocks. The pink heather. The patchwork grass. The yellow gorse. In the distance, the sea bashed roughly at the headland. Stretched dark and blue out to the horizon. 'Is this still Willoughby Park?' asked Fox.

'Oh yeah. It's Willoughby Park for miles.' There was moorland as far as the eye could see. Gorse bushes and intermittent stone tors. 'I'm thirsty,' said Dolly, pausing to get her bearings.

Fox wiped his brow. 'Me too.'

'Don't you have any water? I thought you were always prepared.'

'I am but you rushed me out of the house.'

They walked for another half an hour or so.

Dolly said, 'We need those sticks that tell us where water is.'

'Divining?' Fox asked.

'Yes!' she replied, sweat trickling down her temples. 'Exactly. Don't they teach you that in the Marines?'

Fox chuckled. 'Considering we were amphibious troops, there wasn't much call for it.'

Dolly yawned. She was thirsty and hot and still bristling from her run-in with Olive. There was no shade. And what had seemed like a short hop to the top of the hill was taking a deceptively long time. 'What do the monks do when they're really thirsty?'

'Well, I think in this situation they would advise positivity. Believe that you will find what you are looking for and you will,' Fox replied, his own T-shirt soaked with sweat that he'd wiped from his brow.

Dolly nodded. Then she said, 'I'm just collecting saliva in my mouth and drinking it.'

Fox laughed. 'Nice.'

Under different circumstances the view ahead of them would have been idyllic. Rocky outcrops up the tumbling hill. Grass as green as emeralds. Tufts of yellow gorse and a row of trees bent almost double against harsh winter winds. But to Dolly it was looking very unfamiliar. She paused, glanced around to get her bearings. She couldn't see the house any more. Nor could she see the sea.

Fox paused too. 'All right?' he asked.

Dolly winced. 'Yeah.'

Fox said, 'What?'

'I think I might be a bit lost.' The sun looked less beautiful, the landscape less picturesque. Now it looked hot and barren and exempt of shade.

'Oh, you're kidding?' Fox smacked his forehead. 'I knew not to trust your directions.'

Dolly was about to defend herself when Fox bent down to touch a pile of earth. 'Molehills,' he said.

'So?'

'Moles prefer ground that's damp. More malleable. Means there's water near here.'

'Are you making this up?' Dolly asked, eyes narrowed with disbelief.

Fox shook his head, deadly serious. 'No!'

Dolly wasn't sure whether to believe him. They trekked on. Fox taking the lead. The hillside terrain was harder than it looked. Uneven and dotted with old grass-covered molehills that jarred the ankle. Ahead of her, Fox looked like he was starting to limp slightly again.

The sun was merciless. It felt like a cricket bat thwacking her further towards the ground. Searing her skin while the grass itched her ankles.

'I can't believe this is happening to us, again,' Fox said. 'Everything I do with you goes wrong.'

Dolly raised a brow. 'Everything *I* do with *you* more like!'

'No,' he wasn't having any of it. 'I'm sensing you're definitely the weakest link here.'

Dolly shook her head, eyes reprimanding. 'I don't think your Buddhist monk would approve of that accusation.'

Fox ran his hand over his super short hair and sighed. 'No, you're right.' Then he bowed slightly and said, 'I'm sorry.'

Dolly laughed again. 'You don't have to bow to me.'

Then suddenly Fox stopped short, still half bent over. 'Oh Christ,' he muttered.

'What?' Dolly said.

There was clear panic in his voice as he hissed, 'Don't move. It's a snake.' He sounded almost like he might be hyperventilating.

Dolly said. 'Is it poisonous?'

'I've got no idea,' he snapped, really trying to calm his breath. 'It's a snake. That's enough, isn't it?' His neck had gone blotchy red.

Dolly frowned. He was getting awfully ruffled for someone usually so calm. She peered round him to look at the killer beast that had provoked such a reaction in the unflappable Fox Mason. Curled up, basking in the sun, completely uninterested in the pair of them, was a grass snake, the kind Dolly used to catch in a bucket and take home to study.

But, she assumed from Fox's general quivering demeanour, he didn't know that. Dolly grinned to herself. 'Oh God,' she said, voice low.

'What?' Fox turned his head, his pupils the size of pennies.

'Stop! Don't move,' Dolly ordered, feigning serious calm. Two could play at his all-knowing smugness.

'Is it poisonous?' he whispered, face pale.

'*Very*,' said Dolly, trying really hard to stay serious when he was frozen in terror next to her. 'You need to put your hands on your head and walk away very slowly.'

Fox started to lift his arms. Then he paused. 'Why do I need to put my hands on my head?'

Dolly felt her straight face give way. 'Just for my amusement,' she laughed, then bashed him on the shoulder and said, 'It's a bloody grass snake. Totally harmless, and it's fast asleep!'

Fox blew out a breath, his shoulders slumping. 'Dolly!'

She laughed again, steering him away in the opposite direction of the snoozing reptile. For the first time since she'd met him, Fox allowed himself to be led.

'Don't laugh,' he hissed. 'That wasn't funny.'

'I'm not laughing.' The laugh escaped through her nose. 'It *was* funny for me.'

Fox shook his head, face still drained of colour.

Dolly walked them back and then across and up in the direction of the rocky outcrops at the prow of the hill.

Once they were a good twenty metres away from the snake, Fox gave himself a shake and with his hands on his knees as he took calming breaths, said, 'The one thing I'm really scared of is snakes.'

Dolly tried to hold in her smile but couldn't. 'So I gathered.'

Fox clocked her expression. 'I'm glad my fear gives you such entertainment.'

'It really does,' she said, laughing freely now, stomping on through the thickening grasses, her feet getting stuck in boggy earth. 'Best thing to have happened all day.'

Fox huffed, unable to muster a comeback. Then he looked at Dolly, his face exhausted from the adrenaline come-down. 'That was more excitement than I can take.'

'You should lighten up,' said Dolly. 'Then these things won't have such an effect.'

The climb was arduous. Steep and slippery, rocks tumbling under their feet. At one point, Dolly lost her balance and slid a foot or so down, only to be caught by Fox, reaching to grab her good arm. 'Thanks,' she said.

'Don't mention it.' They carried on up. Fox looked back over his shoulder. 'Do you mind if I ask why you and your sister don't seem to get along?'

To her surprise, Dolly found she didn't mind. She was still tickled at having brought Fox down a peg or two with the snake, which in turn made confiding in him not such an abhorrent idea, as if through witnessing his vulnerability they felt more like equals.

'We weren't always like that,' she said.

'No?'

'No. She used to really take care of me. Would always be there. We bickered, you know, like sisters do and she was always ahead of me, but if things went wrong, I knew I could go to Olive.'

Fox didn't say anything.

Dolly said, 'You can say it, you know.'

'Say what?'

'Like a parent.'

'I wasn't going to say that, Dolly. I was going to say that it's sad that it's changed.'

'Yes.' Dolly paused, surprisingly wistful at the memory, almost choked. She put her hand on her chest. 'God, I'm thirsty.'

'Keep talking and you'll forget about it,' Fox said without looking back.

'Is that some hostage trick?' she asked.

'No, it's a desperately thirsty and quite interested trick,' he replied.

She thought they were nearing the top of the hill but it was like a mirage; it just got further away the more they walked.

'You said she took care of you. What were your parents doing?' Fox asked.

'My dad was away a lot. He was an explorer.'

'Wow.'

'Yeah.'

'Did he take you exploring?'

'He took Olive,' said Dolly. 'I was too young.' She could picture it, watching them setting off from her bedroom window. Jealous and frustrated. To make up for it, her mum had taken her off on little adventures. They'd play games in the woods, collect tadpoles, bake biscuits and eat them on colourful rugs in the caves on the beach. Just making sure this little person had the best time they could growing up. Trying to counter any unhappiness.

It wasn't lost on Dolly how much her mum would have loved this hunt for the clue. The freedom of the climb. The beauty of the sun in vermillion lines like a starburst. The fresh smell of ozone.

There was no person Dolly adored more than her mum. She sometimes went into the department stores just to smell the perfume she used to wear at the fragrance counter. Would stand eyes closed, inhaling, while the sales assistant asked her if she needed any help.

'And your mum?' asked Fox.

'My mum was …' Dolly didn't quite know how to describe her. In Dolly's head she was like an ethereal figure strolling through bracken, deer feeding from her outstretched hand.

Walking in silence, birds swooping in black murmurations, Dolly found herself remembering the moment when Ruben's dad and her dad were bellowing at each other like rutting stags. Her mother broken and discarded on the ground. Dolly remembered holding her tight under her arm and lifting her with Olive to guide her back through the woods to the house, gently. Silently.

She had wanted to remove her from the crude insults and the implications. She didn't want her sullied and degraded by Lord de Lacy. She didn't want her foolish and deceitful and at his mercy. They had settled her vacant-eyed mother on the chair in the sitting room and for a split-second what was real wasn't real. And who her mother was wasn't her mother. But then the moment had vanished when she had looked up and said with such soft sadness, '*What have I done?*' And Dolly had crouched down and rested her arm round her mum's shoulders and together they had sat for five minutes, maybe half an hour. Until the chaos blew in and their dad stormed out and Aunt Marge took them away.

The memory made Dolly have to shut her eyes for a second. To pull herself together.

'You all right?' Fox asked.

'Yeah fine,' Dolly said, eyes flying open, embarrassed that he'd caught her lost in a moment.

'I was just thinking that I hadn't felt thirsty since you started talking,' Fox said to Dolly's relief, choosing not to push it.

'Admit it,' she replied, 'it's my spit trick, isn't it?'

He laughed, deep and rumbling.

They walked some more. Almost reached in the crest of the hill.

'How old were you when you moved?'

'Fourteen,' said Dolly. 'I was very young though. Very naïve.' She laughed at the memory of herself.

They walked on. Fox checked his phone as they got higher but there was still no signal.

Dolly thought about those first few weeks in Aunt Marge's house. How much her mum hated it. How she'd walk around saying how dark it was. Flinging open curtains – 'There's never enough light,' she'd cry with despair. And then there was the call to say her dad had died. Swallowed up by the rapids. And her mum got even worse; schlepped around in a pair of purple leggings and a shapeless cream cardigan for an hour a day until she didn't get up at all.

Fox cut in on her thoughts. 'Are you sure you're OK?'

'Yeah, I'm fine,' Dolly said quickly. 'Absolutely fine.' The sun sizzled their skin. Burnt like they were on the barbecue. The yellow tufts of grass stretched on either side of them, dry and arid. She looked at Fox's broad back and his triathlon T-shirt. She couldn't believe that once again he'd got her thinking about things. She hadn't noticed a tactic. But he'd most likely used distraction. This time though, she found she wasn't quite so annoyed, more relieved in a way, that, while she hadn't said anything out loud, she could finally call to the fore some of the things she'd buried deep down in her head.

Fox glanced across. 'What?' he asked. 'Why are you looking at me?'

Dolly said, 'My mum wasn't really suited to real life. To any life away from here and my dad. She died soon after we left. I think of a broken heart. Olive would say she drank herself to death.' She rubbed her eyes. 'It was a really rubbish time.'

Fox nodded.

Dolly immediately wanted to take it back. She didn't want it to sully the memory of her mother. Not that Fox had any memory of her, but her own. Like, now it had been said, it was real. Even though it had been real all along.

'You're not going to tell anyone any of this, are you?'

'Tell them what?' he asked. 'You've hardly told me anything.'

'Just ...' Dolly felt like he knew everything in her head. 'Swear on Buddha you won't say anything.'

He snorted a laugh. 'I swear on Buddha himself.'

Dolly nodded.

Fox said, 'Do you hear that?'

'What?' Dolly paused to listen.

'That's a waterfall!' he said, face lighting up. 'See, Dolly. Think positive and thee shall find.'

'I wasn't thinking positive,' she said.

'I was.'

'Well, how do we know which one of us was right?'

'You can riddle that one out on your own,' Fox said, as they crested the hill and saw the glistening waterfall below them, a secret cove where the twinkling brook tumbled its way down black rocks and lime-green moss. 'I am going to have myself a cool drink of water.'

Fox and Dolly practically ran down the other side of the hill, skidding to the waterfall, whooping like giddy children.

'Race you!' Dolly shouted.

But Fox did one better. Without warning, he scooped her off her feet and ran with her to the cascading water.

'What are you doing? Put me down!' She whacked at his hands. 'Fox, you can't just pick me up! Put me down.' But he took no notice. Instead, when he got to the fastest point of the waterfall, he stuck both their heads underneath the running water.

'Put me down, you great oaf!' She smacked his chest with her good hand, coughing and spluttering with surprised laughter as he put her back on her feet. There was water up her nose. Her hair was soaked.

Fox was lapping water with a big grin on his face.

Dolly slicked her wet hair off her face. 'I can't believe you just did that.'

'Believe it, baby,' he replied, dark eyes twinkling.

Dolly had to look away. It suddenly felt too friendly, like she'd told him too much. She felt trapped, unused to someone having so much on her.

She cupped some of the running water and drank it in parched gulps.

It wasn't that she didn't have friends. It was that her friendships were all on her terms. She chose what they saw. How close they got. She glanced surreptitiously up at Fox, who had moved on to other things. Climbing the rocks to explore. He, however, seemed to magically coax out information and that unnerved her. He paid no attention to her glib retorts that usually worked to ward off anyone treading too close. He even laughed at her. It was uncomfortable new territory for Dolly and she couldn't say if she liked it or not.

CHAPTER SIXTEEN

On the pretence of a walk, Olive had stormed off on her own. It amazed her how well she knew the paths of Willoughby Park. Knew all the nooks and crannies, all the memories etched on her brain. She avoided the path to the woodland and the beach, and the other to the orangery and instead went in the direction of an area that was roped off. Personnel only. Piles of chopped logs and bonfire remains, a compost heap and a green four-wheel drive. She got closer. There was a polytunnel with raised beds on either side with exotic-looking plants. A couple of giant palms in pots ready to be heaved into the ground. This was where Terence, the old groundskeeper, worked his magic. And where her dad, when he was home, earned a bit of extra cash.

At the entrance to the polytunnel she paused, peeked her head in and took a sniff. Warm manure and the tang of summer. They were hothousing lemon trees, figs and clementines. She put her hand on the wood. She remembered her dad building the frame. Felt bittersweet pride at the fact it was still there. Her stomach tight with nostalgia. She walked on, the concrete floor was even more cracked with grass growing through the crevices. The damson tree still overhung the shed at the far end, sticky fruit staining the floor purple. She felt her steps get slower as she reached the door of the shed. The smooth plastic of the handle was as familiar as skin. The smell hit her like a wave. She stood on the threshold, savouring for a moment the scent of her youth – her happiness, time spent here with her dad eating sandwiches and drinking tea – before her nose became accustomed to the smell and it disappeared.

She felt like she was trespassing. The chairs and table and the shelves were the same. The little Calor gas stove was probably a replacement but still the same. Chipped mugs hung on nails alongside bits of twine and labels and dirty teaspoons.

Olive sat down in one of the chairs, positioned such that she could see out of the window over to the rolling hills, the deer camouflaged in the bracken, the oaks in the distance, the wide path that led round the trees to the fountain. She closed her eyes and thought of the times she'd walk down here carrying a basket of sandwiches for his lunch when her mum was working. Everest, his beloved lurcher, barking. His hands ingrained with dirt. Of the hair-raising tales he'd tell of his various scrapes and near-misses across the globe. Little treasured moments. The lukewarm tea and a KitKat. The pair of them blissfully alone, unreachable.

'Coo-ee.'

Olive opened one eye. Tottering in her direction in a gold bomber jacket, leather leggings and L'Oreal's best flame-red hair, was Aunt Marge.

Olive jumped up out of the chair. 'Marge, what are you doing here?'

'Hello, Olive darling, I went to the Big House and Ruben and that lovely little girl thought you might be down here.' Marge approached with her arms open for a hug, Olive felt herself step back, Marge then lost her nerve and reached to squeeze her shoulder instead. She smelt of talcum powder and hairspray. 'Dolly texted me last night to say she was on her way and I worried that I might have stirred up a bit of tension. I know what you two can be like and I thought, my girls, I'm not sure they're going to be able to do it on their own.'

Olive frowned. 'Why didn't you tell me that Dolly texted you?' Thinking of how she'd chastised her earlier for the worry she'd caused.

'I did.' Marge got her phone out to prove it. The message had indeed been sent but unread. 'How is one meant to do anything in a place with no mobile phone reception? I got sent the most hilarious meme on the way here. I'll forward it to you when I've got Wi-Fi.' Aunt Marge's memes always came three weeks after they'd had their heyday. She put her phone away with a 'Oh well, no harm done,' and then giving Olive a beady stare said, 'How is it? How's it going?'

'It's fine,' said Olive, always a little wary in the presence of Marge.

'You fibber!' Marge grinned good-naturedly. 'Now, let's get the kettle on, I'm gasping. Drove the whole bloody way at about nine hundred miles an hour and only got flashed once. Good eh?'

Olive made the tea on the Calor gas stove, completely bamboozled. She was all fingers and thumbs. Nervous for some reason. Marge was faffing about with her phone, holding it up outside the shed, trying desperately to get some signal, all the while Olive sensed she was sizing the situation up. At the very least it was suspicious that Olive was alone in the shed and Dolly was off over the other side of the headland.

When she was handed the cup, Marge wrapped her hands round the warmth and took a long, piping-hot sip. *'Teflon mouth, that's me,'* she used to say, as teenage Olive and Dolly quietly, miserably, cupped their mugs of out-of-date hot chocolate in Marge's haphazard flat.

'So,' Marge said, 'tell me everything. How's Ruben – aged well, hasn't he? Still very handsome. And, more importantly, how are you and Dolly getting on?'

Olive gave her a very précised rundown of events so far. As she rounded off with the arrival of Dolly and the argument, the great black cat sauntered into the shed and Marge gave it a sneer of disdain, 'Get out of here, shoo!' she snapped. The cat ignored her. 'I hate cats,' Marge grimaced, looking utterly disgusted as it leapt onto her lap. She sat with her arms crossed, glaring at it. Olive remembered Marge's little dog, Bernard, an insane and very unfriendly pug. The reason they couldn't take the lurcher with them when they left. One of many things Olive stacked up against living with Aunt Marge.

'So, not a roaring success so far,' Marge said as she tried to heave the cat off her lap, glancing up at Olive, lips pursed in wry amusement.

Olive shrugged. 'You could say that.'

Marge laughed. The lines on her face creased deep. Years of suntan and cigarettes carving their grooves in her skin. 'Poor Olive,' she said.

Olive felt foolish for coming across like she needed sympathy, especially from Marge, who had always relied on her to be the strong one. 'I'm fine, really.'

'Oh, I know you are, darling. You're always fine. Always were.' Marge smiled, eyes creased. 'Superwoman, Olive.' The cat nudged at Marge's hand for a stroke. 'I felt terribly sorry for you when you had to come and live with me – like a little tightly wound ball. Far too young to have all that responsibility and baggage, and then there was me, a terrible parent. It's shameful. None of us would have coped without you.' Marge was directing her conversation to the cat. Like she knew, instinctively, that Olive wasn't one to cope well with the direct weakness of empathy.

'You weren't terrible,' Olive replied quickly, while her brain whirred in the background wanting to say, 'Hang on, can we just pause. Can you just say all that again, please?' Because she couldn't really believe what she had heard. An actual acknowledgement of the way it had been.

'Oh, I was. I was.' Marge sighed, giving in to the giant cat with a reluctant pat. 'I know it. You don't have to be polite. I'd have been feeding you both champagne for breakfast if I hadn't had you there. It was a terrible time that I handled very badly.'

Olive's instinct was to jump in and defend her, but Marge held up a hand to preempt it. 'Don't deny it, Olive. I'd got a bit better by the time it was just me and Dolly, but not with you. I'm sorry.'

Olive shook her head like it was nothing but her heart was thumping. 'Please don't apologise. You took us in, Marge, you gave up your life for us.'

Marge was absently scratching the purring cat. 'Yes, but I did what any good person would do. You were both lovely. And it was all so tragic. My bloody brother and your mother needed a good kick up the behind, both of them.'

Olive turned away. 'Don't say that.'

Marge lifted the cat from her lap and got up to stand by

Olive. 'I'm sorry, I don't want to upset you. They were your parents and you loved them.'

Olive glanced across at her. 'But?'

Marge smiled, looked down at the steaming mug of tea. 'But they both certainly had their faults.'

Olive shook her head, she wasn't going to allow history to be rewritten. 'But it was my mum who had the affair.'

Marge paused mid-sip of her tea. 'Is that how you see it?'

'That's how it was,' Olive replied, feeling the hairs on the back of her neck stand up in defence of her family.

Marge nodded, taking another sip. She looked out the dirty window. 'Oh look, a deer.' They both watched, a stag had lifted its head from the wilderness, bracken draped over its antler. 'Do you remember the time your dad left you and Dolly in the wilderness to find your own way back?'

'And my mother totally overreacted!' Olive replied, knowing she was coming across as tart, but she couldn't help it. She didn't want the memory of her dad brought down in any way. 'It was fine. It was fun.'

Marge tipped her head, uncertain.

Olive huffed and looked away out of the window, trying to recall properly the event Marge was referring to. She remembered her new red shorts and the compass that her dad took great pains to teach her and Dolly how to use. She remembered him grinning and saying, 'Right. It's three o'clock now,' handing her his hand-drawn map, 'you aim to be home by teatime. Yeah?'

Olive had nodded, hopping with excitement. She could feel Dolly's hand clutched tight in hers. He'd ruffled their hair, said 'Good luck, my little adventurers!' and then he'd gone. And Olive had felt so proud that he'd trusted them alone. That he'd believed they could do it, aged ten and seven respectively. Both of them with their giant backpacks – pocketknife, waterproofs, sandwiches, banana, compass, foil blanket, torch. Prepared whatever the weather.

She'd been afraid, of course she had, there were sounds in the undergrowth, but that was half of what being an adventurer was all about. Ahead of them the sun danced on the sea and the gorse was bright yellow and the heather pink like witches' sweets.

Of course, Dolly had started to cry. But Dolly cried at everything. Olive remembered knowing that she couldn't let go of her hand. Dolly was holding so tight – her infamous imagination, that already had her left at home when their dad wanted to camp out at night or explore the cave on the beach, kicking in now with a vengeance. Olive smiled as she recalled trying to get her backpack off and the compass out, all one-handed, all contorted as Dolly clung on like a monkey.

In the shed, Marge started to flick through a crumpled magazine. 'Oh look, Monty Don. He's very practical.'

Olive didn't say anything. She barely saw Marge nowadays, outside of Christmas and birthdays, even then Marge always had trouble squeezing them into her social calendar so a quick drink in town or a hasty supper was the norm and Olive was fine with that. They didn't have a great deal in common and, more often than not, if Dolly was there, Olive felt like the third wheel.

Marge closed the magazine. 'You don't take my opinion very seriously, do you, Olive?'

'I've never said that.'

'You don't have to say it. I know. And I know it's well

deserved. I let you down. I allowed you to shoulder far too much. But I'll tell you one thing. I knew my brother. And I knew your mother. And I knew what was going on between them much better than a child would see.'

Olive felt her jaw tense.

'Your father was a good man, there is no denying it. But he was also a very selfish man, always had been. And he shouldn't have buggered off round the world at the drop of a hat, leaving your mum at home in the middle of nowhere with two kids.'

'Please, Marge, don't do this.' Olive wanted to put her hands over her ears. 'She had the affair.'

'Because she was lonely!' Marge insisted.

'My dad loved her.'

'Yes, and she loved him. That was the trouble. Your parents' weakness as a couple was her inability to cope without him and his inability to put anyone's needs before his own. They were both equally to blame.'

'No!'

'Yes!'

Silence.

Marge sighed, folded her arms across her chest, heavy gold bracelets rattling on her thin wrists. Olive didn't look at her. 'This isn't going quite the way I had planned,' Marge acknowledged. 'One of the things I've always wanted to say to you, Olive, is that their faults were their own responsibilities. Not yours.'

Olive closed her eyes.

Marge sat back down on her chair. 'They were never your responsibility, Olive.'

Olive stared down at her untouched cup of tea. Marge

reached forward and picked up the magazine again, started to leaf through the pages. Outside the stag stalked away.

Olive thought again about the adventure her dad had set her and Dolly on. She remembered flinching at every animal noise as they trudged to the higher ground. Every crack of branch. It was exciting. They were brave explorers. They ate their sandwiches and fed the crumbs to the blackbirds. She had a vague memory of popping out at the road and a car with two guys inside pulling over to ask if they needed a lift. They had backed away then, her and Dolly, knowing exactly how to disappear into the denser undergrowth to hide. A bit scary but a good learning experience.

You wouldn't get away with something like that now. The *Daily Mail* would have a field day, reporting on someone dropping their children deep in the woods and challenging them to get home in one piece. But it was exhilarating. Character-building.

She remembered the light failing. The cold creeping in. It was well past teatime. They'd eaten their bananas. They'd drunk their water. Dolly's fingertips were cold.

Olive remembered the massacre of the sheep's carcass in the torchlight. Left bloody and dismembered by whatever animal had ripped it apart. Olive had stupidly forgotten all her dad's wilderness training at that moment. She'd forgotten everything she'd learnt the entire ten years of her life. Ask her her name and she wouldn't have been able to answer. All she remembered was shouting, 'Run, Dolly! Run as fast as you can!' Then hurtling through bracken and bushes and brambles, faster and faster, her heart burning in her chest. Dragging Dolly behind her, the thumping sound of an animal chasing behind them. Sweating, bleeding, crying. And then suddenly, ahead of them in the trees was this shed and the polytunnels. And a door that Olive could slam shut behind them and drag an old table in front of and lean against with all her weight as she panted to get her breath back in the pitch darkness until finally she could tell herself there was no beast giving chase and it was stupid to be scared when they were simply here in the shed.

She could picture Dolly's broken little face though as she put the torch on her. Seeing that she'd wet her pants in fright. Knowing they had no other clothes. Unsure of the way back to the cottage from here in the darkness. Hearing the scuttle of mice or rats as they curled together wrapped like a burrito in their foil blanket. Waking with a spider crawling across her face. Silent in horror so as not to wake Dolly. Cold and damp from morning dew.

That was where the police found them. Huddled in the shed. Their mother sobbing with relief. Their father feigning remorse but chucking Olive a wink and a thumbs-up when no one was looking, proud that she'd managed to find a good place to bunk down.

She had always wondered if things would have been different if she'd got them home by teatime. Whether her dad would have been prouder. Whether he would have been proud enough to stay. Certainly there wouldn't have been the massive row between him and her mother that saw him overseas for six months. That was probably when her mother's affair started, for all Olive knew. If only she'd been able to get her and Dolly back by teatime.

With his knuckles rapped, their father never left them alone again, but his tasks and challenges persisted. There was always a frisson of danger that she learnt never to admit to their mother. Every adventure that bit crazier than the one before. It was sink or swim. No whining allowed. That was why Dolly always got left behind.

Thinking about it now, it was possibly a bit nuts to deposit your children alone in the woods. She'd be furious if Ruben left Zadie out there and she wasn't even her daughter. But it wasn't so simple. To Olive, while maybe it was madness, she couldn't escape the fact her father had made her who she was. Over time, what had once instilled terror became instead excitement. Fear became adrenaline. Life had been exciting. She was suddenly gripped by sadness so acute she struggled for breath. That had been her childhood. Her fearless father. Her – perhaps justifiably in retrospect – emotionally wrought mother. Her little sister. Her big eyes and plump hand. She remembered the smell of Dolly's hair as they were wound up in their burrito blanket in the shed. Like cherries, it smelt. Cherries and childhood.

Olive closed her eyes again. She could feel the hovering threat of tears. But she wouldn't cry here in front of Marge. The impact of loss however seemed to be catching up with her like a fast-forward button. Images fast and blurred.

She heard Marge's chair creak and felt her come and stand next to her. 'I didn't want to upset you, I'm sorry.'

'You didn't,' Olive replied.

Marge smiled.

Olive surreptitiously dabbed at the corners of her eyes with her finger. She remembered the day her dad came back for the last time. Gold supposedly weighing down his pockets. *'This is it, girls! I've hit the big time!'* he shouted, unable to contain his excitement, dashing off to lay the clues before he'd even unpacked. The treasure hunt was meant to mark the end. He was home to stay this time. They were going to be a family. It occurred to her now that all their lives they had fitted around him and his restlessness. Him being with them had felt so much like second best that she had done what she could to make it great. To make his time free from boredom. Is that what her mother had done, too? Was that why there were the parties? The beautiful frilly dresses and the long, long blonde hair. She thought how they had lived with nothing, waiting for him to return with riches. And he'd finally done it. He'd proved himself right. There *was* gold at the end of the rainbow.

But would he really have stayed? Or would he have always chased the next adventure? He used to cup her cheek and say, *'I'm doing it for you, kiddo. For you and your sister and your mum.'*

She wondered now if she might reply, *'No – you're my dad and I love you – but you're doing it for yourself.'*

The life of an explorer was, she realised, an addiction to the thrill of possibility and, however hard he tried, it always came before all of them.

'Neither of them were perfect, Olive, but that didn't make them bad people,' Marge said softly, her hand tentatively coming to rest on Olive's arm. 'They let you down, they built you up. But in the end, they were just human and you have to forgive them. We're all just human.'

CHAPTER SEVENTEEN

Dolly walked along the side of the rocky stream fed by their little waterfall. Ten or so metres further on the stream tumbled into a larger waterfall that plunged into a dark pool of jagged rocks and giant ferns.

Dolly sat with her legs dangling over the edge, feet hanging over nothingness. Leaves of the moss-covered oaks reflected back at her in the glassy black water below. Spray from the waterfall splashed her legs.

She felt Fox coming to sit beside her. 'Can I ask you another question?' he asked, leaning back on his hands, his arm muscles bulging, his fox tattoo grinning.

Dolly looked at him, on guard for subtle negotiator tactics. 'If you must.'

He chuckled. He sat up, rubbing the earth off his palms, resting his elbows over his knees and looking out over the waterfall. Dragonflies swooped in the air. One landed on a big gunnera leaf next to them, brilliant blue against frozen pea green. 'What the hell is going on with you and your sister and this Ruben guy?'

Dolly bristled. 'Nothing.'

Fox studied her. 'Your reaction tells me otherwise – pupils

dilated, cheeks reddening, sudden uncomfortable body move-ments. Do you know how you tell if someone's lying, Dolly?'

Dolly sighed. 'Look at their movements when they're telling the truth.' Basic training.

Fox tipped his head as if she'd nailed it.

Dolly ran her tongue over her top lip. 'I don't want to talk about it.'

'Can I guess?'

'No,' she said, shifting so she was facing away from him.

Fox rubbed his hands together with what looked like glee. 'OK. You didn't want to wear the sling when you saw him so I'm guessing that's because of vanity. Was there something there between you?' He bit his lip and thought, 'No. His reaction would have been different. You're the youngest, so ... I'm guessing it was a crush.'

Dolly huffed. 'Can you stop, please?'

'Yes!' He punched the air a tiny bit like he'd sailed through the first round. 'Now you said you were young and naïve for your age, so did something happen—'

'Stop!' said Dolly, holding up a hand, feeling her cheeks burn as her brain did a speedy run-through of her failed clinch with Ruben. Of watching him with doe-eyed adoration as he took all the little baby birds that had fallen out of the nest and talked to them jokingly as he gently put them in one by one, stroking their fluffy heads. He was such a hero. She'd thought her heart might burst out of her chest that very moment. He was her absolute perfect man and no part of her could conceive that with hidden feelings so intense they might not be reciprocated. God, in retrospect he'd just been bunging some birds back in a nest and there she'd been gearing up to pounce. She covered her face with her hand. 'I was fourteen, all right. I misread all the signs. He was in love with my sister. He was basically really nice to me because they were together – which I didn't realise. I attempted a very misjudged seduction. It was a humiliating moment in my past that I'd rather not talk about. All right?'

A grin spread across Fox's face. 'Oh, please do.'

'No!' Dolly felt like her whole body was on fire. Why did this guy have to be so good at his job? She could barely bring herself to replay the event in her head, let alone talk about it; occasionally snapshots of it popped into her mind at inopportune moments, winding her with momentary embarrassment.

'Are you thinking about it now?'

'Yes!' said Dolly, half laughing. 'Stop asking me about it!' It was like watching some excruciating moment on TV between half-closed fingers, while quietly dying inside. Her infatuated heart thrumming like the wings of the baby birds. The feel of his lips under hers. The touch of her palm to his cheeks. His mortifying laugh of shock. And then of course he told Olive, who gave her the most humiliating talk about relationships, made worse by the gentleness of her tone. All the while hiding the fact that Ruben would never love Dolly because he was in love with her, Olive. The shame when Dolly discovered that they were an item. But it wasn't a patch on the discovery of her mum and Lord de Lacy. Dolly had retched every time she shut her eyes and pictured her mother's affair. She hadn't slept for what felt like months afterwards. All these clandestine relationships merged into the dark, destructive secret of adulthood that Dolly and her childish romantic fantasies would always be on the outside of, would never fully understand.

'And now you want to show him you're all grown up and gorgeous?'

Dolly arched a brow. 'You think I'm gorgeous, do you?'

It was Fox's turn to blush. 'You're not ugly,' he conceded.

Dolly turned away, a smug little pout on her lips.

Fox stretched out in the sun. 'Do you know the definition of madness?'

Dolly said, 'No, but I'm guessing you're going to tell me.'

Fox spoke looking up to the sky, 'Doing the same thing over and over and expecting a different result.'

Dolly opened her mouth to reply but found she had no rebuttal, afraid what he was saying was too close to the truth. Instead, she said, 'You're so smug and annoying. Do you know that?'

'You have told me on a number of occasions,' he replied.

'Right, well now it's my turn,' she said, riled. 'Shall I try and guess what happened to you?'

'If you want,' he said, rolling so he was lying on his side, propping himself up on his elbow. 'This should be good.'

Dolly ran her tongue along her teeth as she thought. She took in his open, smiling face. His calm. 'Well, you said you left the Marines and went on your bike to the Himalayas to recuperate. So it can't have been something good.' She paused. 'I don't know if I should guess because it's going to be something bad.'

Fox shrugged, non-committal.

Dolly raised her eyes heavenward. 'You're so annoying.'

He chuckled.

'Well don't get upset if I say something insensitive, OK?'

'Dolly, you're always saying things that are insensitive.'

'Shut up!' She gave him a playful shove. He rolled onto his back then sat up. 'Come on, keep guessing.'

Dolly narrowed her eyes to scrutinise him, as if the answer were on his face. 'I don't think you were fired. The suspension from work was too much of a shock for you to have been through it before. I reckon you left voluntarily because of something that happened.'

Fox tipped his head, 'Correct.'

Dolly grinned smugly. 'I could be a negotiator.'

'I wouldn't go that far.'

Dolly paused, reassessing him to prove her prowess. 'You're quite brooding so I think whatever it was, it was something you felt responsible for,' she mused, searching for an example. 'You know, like in one of those films when someone blows up their best friend or something hideous like that, but not that obviously.'

Fox tilted his head. 'Why not that?'

'Oh my God.' She put her hand over her mouth. 'That's not what happened is it? I'm so sorry. I shouldn't have said anything.'

'Dolly, it's fine. It's dealt with. It's OK,' Fox replied.

'No but …' She felt awful. 'How can you have let me guess?' She bashed him on the arm.

Fox grinned. 'I shouldn't have done.'

'No,' she said, blowing out a breath before turning to look him in the eye. 'I'm really sorry.'

'Dolly, honestly, it's fine. It was a long time ago. A very good friend of mine had been taken and I was the one trying to get him out. I made a judgement that turned out to be wrong.'

She winced. 'Oh God.'

He shrugged. 'I've come to accept that whatever had happened, I don't think we would have got him out alive. I just … Well, I've learnt that you can drive yourself crazy with what-ifs.' He ran his hand through his hair, then let his arms flop over his knees.

'Wow,' said Dolly after a moment's silence. 'No wonder you're like how you are.'

Fox laughed. 'How am I?'

Dolly made a face, unsure how to put it into words. 'I don't know, like, closed. Unemotional.'

'And you're not closed?'

'Oh, I'm closed,' Dolly laughed. 'But I make that obvious. You hide it behind Buddhist quotes.'

Fox frowned.

Dolly laughed. 'It's not a bad thing. It's good. It's good to be calm. To not feel stuff. I wish I didn't feel anything.'

Fox said, 'You know there's a difference between not feeling things and having felt them and come out the other side? I'm not closed, Dolly, I'm just considered, careful.'

Neither of them spoke.

It seemed suddenly so silent, despite the rush of the waterfall. The earth warm under her hands. Her feet over the side weightless.

'You see feeling things as a problem?' Fox asked, moving forward so his legs were hanging over the side, too.

Dolly licked her dry lips. 'Maybe,' she admitted.

Fox glanced across at her. 'Do you know I went nuts for a bit? Like totally renegade. I'm lucky I wasn't court-martialled. There's no way of not feeling stuff, I can tell you that for nothing; I suppose I've just learnt how to channel it.' He kicked the rock under his heels. 'Because it comes out, you know, whatever?' He paused, smiled. 'Like pinning blokes to petrol station floors. Bitching at your sister and getting angry with your heroic new partner at work.'

Dolly rolled her eyes.

Fox laughed.

There was a pause. Then he said, 'Just don't ever think you can outrun something.'

'No,' said Dolly with blasé certainty.

But as they sat there, side by side in silence, the words did something to her body. She tried to shift position to make the feeling go away but she couldn't do anything too obvious. She was too aware of his all-seeing presence. But her mind was being flooded with images that she felt an overwhelming compunction to flee from. Dark beasts that had lain waiting, baying in the wings. The things she was constantly avoiding from the moment she woke up in the morning to the time she went to bed. If she woke up in the night, it was with a dread that the darkness might pin her down. Dolly was always moving forward. She outran. That was what she did. Her feet hadn't touched the floor in years.

Sitting on the edge of the waterfall, she had to put her hands up to her mouth. The sudden, unexpected emotion was like a torrent. She had absolutely no control over it. 'Oh, God!' she said with surprise.

'What?' Fox turned, concerned.

'Nothing, I just ... what you said, about outrunning things.' She moved her hands to her cheeks, warm and suddenly wet, wiping away tears that she couldn't dry fast enough.

'Dolly, why are you crying?' Fox's brow creased. 'What's going on?'

'I don't know,' she said, through hiccupping sobs. 'I don't know. God, what am I doing? I'm crying.' It was like her brain was collapsing. Like a stomach held in by a belt and trousers suddenly spilling forth. She saw the moment her dad had seen her mother and Lord de Lacy together, the sun blinding off the broken glass of the greenhouse. The tree stump she tripped over as she took a step back. The look of fury that Olive gave her that punched deep into her core and never left. Seeing her great heroic dad crumple into incoherence. Olive trying to reason with him. Olive phoning Aunt Marge. Olive putting their mother to bed. Dolly running round like the world was on fire, crying, clutching anyone she could find to ask what was going to happen. Then add straight-talking Aunt Marge into the fray – *'Always destined for this kind of mayhem.' 'No one kayaks those rapids without death in mind!' 'I warned him, you can't leave a person for months on end on their own; loneliness is akin to madness.'* She saw herself as a child running through burnished bracken behind Olive and Ruben, breathless to catch up. She thought of perching on her tiptoes in front of Ruben, the smell of cigarettes on his breath, in her head whispering, 'I love you,' before pressing her lips to his. She thought of her eager anticipation of her dad walking through the door, dirty and rugged and laden with silly souvenirs. She thought of watching him and Olive yomping off on their own, waiting one day to be invited, always second best. Willing herself not to be the weak one who was scared of the dark and the noises and the heights. She thought of the loneliness of living with Aunt Marge in a flat in the city. Wishing for the acres of green space and freedom of Willoughby Park. Wishing for her mum. The mum of her childhood who stroked her hair and hugged her tight. She thought of Jake – The Destructor – and his motorbike and the time he ripped the phone out of the wall when he caught her using it. Of the cigarette burns on her skin. Of the first time she arrested someone for domestic abuse and wanting to smash his face against the floor so he'd never be able to smirk the way he smirked at Dolly as she cuffed him. She saw her whole life from a cherished childhood innocence bursting with love to a gaping hole of nothing, filled only with hatred and anger and loss. A hole she'd never quite been able to climb out of.

She saw it all. Like a merry-go-round. Dolly frantically brushed at her cheeks to make the tears stop. 'I'm really sorry. I don't know what's wrong with me.'

'Stop press, Dolly King is crying.' Fox smiled. 'Dolly, no one cares.'

She sniffed. 'I care. Imagine Mungo seeing me now.'

'Screw Mungo.'

She laughed.

'You really care what Mungo thinks?' Fox was incredulous.

She shook her head. Then she nodded. 'I don't know.'

'Dolly, you'd be a better policewoman if you didn't care. Own it and you'll stop being afraid of it.'

She nodded again.

Fox looked at her closely. 'Don't let fear win.'

'No.' She wiped her eyes with her T-shirt. 'Is that another Buddhist mantra?' she quipped.

'No, it's a common-sense mantra,' said Fox. His black eyes smiled.

Dolly wanted to thank him but couldn't bring herself to say it. She also wanted to lie down and have someone drape a blanket over her. Instead, she peered down at the waterfall, at the swirling mass of frothy blue. Then she turned to look at Fox, who was settling back, resting his hands behind him onto something that didn't fit with the calm idyllic nature of the place, onto what Dolly suddenly realised was a bloody great adder. Ominous black zigzags along its back. 'Fox! No!' she shouted, just as his hands pressed onto the scaly flesh and the sudden movement made the adder dart forward but Dolly had already grabbed hold of his arm and with all her weight yanked him with her over the edge of the waterfall.

They plummeted fast down the cascading water, smashing through the black, bubbly surface feet first. Deep and icy cold. Dolly's shoulder jarred on impact, the pain ricocheting through her. She let go of Fox. She opened her mouth to scream and water rushed in. She was still sinking. Down, down. She couldn't find the surface in the darkness, all she could feel was the agony from her shoulder suffuse through her body. She couldn't see Fox. When she kicked, her foot thumped against jagged stone. Then her head smashed against a rock, scraping the skin raw on her temple. She wondered if she was going to die.

In the darkness, she saw herself as a little girl in her home-made dungarees and her thick wild hair. All that talking about the past. Dolly wondered what this kid would think of her now, of who she had become.

She struggled in the water. Too dark and disorientated to work out which way to swim. Too tired and breathless. Instead, all she saw were her memories swirling thick and bright in her mind. And for the first time, she found herself looking directly at the feelings – the shame, the guilt, the fury. She tried to do as Fox had said, to own it rather than be afraid of it. And she found that laid out before her, they all became valid emotions. She could pick them up, turn them over – like sizing them up in a shop. Yes, Dolly, it was OK to feel second best when your dad left you behind because you cried. Yes, of course it was shameful to try and kiss your sister's secret boyfriend, but you were young and blinded by infatuation.

It was a novelty to be able to pick these tangible feelings up, examine and explain them and simply put them down again rather than carry them furtively in the back of her mind, where they weighed down her every move. And soon she felt other things creep in. Sympathy. Sadness. Even gratitude. She found herself more and more distanced from that little girl in the homemade dungarees. She was able to look at her and smile sadly rather than banish her from her mind in horror.

Disorientated and slightly delirious in the murky water, Dolly found herself stretching out to trace the little girl's face. She was so innocent and trusting it made her heart hurt. *'If only you could see how lovely you are,'* Dolly whispered, voice choked as she saw all the feelings – the hopes and vulnerabilities, the sweet enthusiasms – so visible on her round young face. She reached to clutch the little girl's hand. *'Don't change,'* she urged, knowing it was fruitless but saying it all the same, *'Please don't change.'* The frizzy-haired reflection just grinned at her, confused about why she ever would. And Dolly found she wanted to burst into tears, but then the hand grabbed tighter to hers. Much tighter and with much more strength than Dolly would attribute to a little girl. Suddenly she was being hauled from the water. Rising fast through the bubbling waterfall and gasping for air when she reached the surface. And she found that it was Fox dragging her up from the dark depths. Bubbles of relief rose from her mouth as he hauled her up onto the bank and they both lay, panting, side by side like gasping fish on dry land.

'You couldn't make it up,' Fox said, when he'd caught his breath. 'Life with you.'

Dragonflies darted in the air around them. Birds dipped their heads and drank from the edges of the lake. A lizard stood motionless on a rock.

'Life with *you*,' Dolly replied, wincing as she tested the movement in her shoulder.

Fox laughed. Rolling his head so he was looking at her. 'Are you OK?'

Dolly nodded, sitting up and trying to retie the sling with her teeth. Fox took over. She was exhausted. Her shoulder throbbed. Her throat hurt. Her temple was bleeding. But as she let him help her to her feet she was overcome by a strange lightness inside herself. It came, she realised, from the belief that possibly she was OK.

She had a sudden desire to smile. A new kaleidoscopic appreciation of the nature around her. She held in the urge to point out the radiance of a butterfly. The bitonal colours of an uncurling fern. If she searched in her brain for something to panic about, nothing tangible appeared. She thought of the little girl – young Dolly – and she wanted to draw her into a hug. To sigh together and console each other. To kiss her on the top of the head and tell her that she was loved. That she, Dolly, loved her.

In the verdant undergrowth, next to the waterfall, Dolly stood taking a few calming breaths, swiping her hair from her eyes, feeling all the aches and pains on her body. Gazing at the dappled sunlight through the canopy of leaves, she suddenly saw exactly what she was meant to be looking for. 'That's it,' she said, pointing ahead at a giant monolith half hidden by moss and overgrown vines, carved into the shape of a near-perfect heart. 'That's the maiden's heart of stone!' *Think positive and thee shall find.* Maybe Buddha was right after all.

CHAPTER EIGHTEEN

Ruben de Lacy had had enough of the King family and their treasure hunt. He decided instead to prove to Olive that he was in fact a very admirable father and took Zadie to the beach.

The main beach was a short walk round the headland from the crumbling cottage. The sun beat down on their skin. It was quickly apparent that Ruben had not packed adequately for the trip when they arrived at the busy stretch of golden sand and Zadie said, 'Can I have the suntan lotion, please?' as if by magic he had thought to bring it.

Ruben said he didn't have any. Zadie frowned. In Ruben's bag was a paperback, a small hand towel to sit on and dry his feet should they get sandy and a bottle of water, for himself.

The noise of the waves thumped gently on the sand. Bodyboarders in the surf shrieked with laughter. A little kid was crying. Ruben glanced around, everywhere he looked were families with windbreaks, abundant towels, toys, cool boxes. Even fold-up chairs. Enough paraphernalia to sink a ship. The kind of beach-goers he used to mock.

He hadn't even put his swimmers on – Ruben was a tropical bather, he did not swim in the chilly English sea. Zadie on the other hand was stripping her T-shirt and shorts off, underneath which she had on a fluorescent green swimsuit covered in sequinned strawberries. He hovered next to her, not even that keen to take his trainers and socks off. 'Do you want an ice cream?' he asked for something to do.

'Yes please. Vanilla please,' said Zadie, plonking herself down directly on the beach, making Ruben wince at the very idea of being covered in all that sand.

'Vanilla? Really?' he asked. 'You don't want anything more exciting, like bubblegum or something?'

Zadie stared up from the sand. 'No way. Vanilla's the best flavour.'

'No,' he shook his head in objection. 'No one actually likes vanilla.'

'Everyone I know loves it,' she replied. 'Barry calls it the Coca-Cola of ice-cream flavours.'

Ruben shook his head. 'No, I'm sorry, I couldn't disagree more. The Coca-Cola of ice-cream flavours would be mint choc chip.'

Zadie laughed like the very idea was preposterous. 'No way! I don't know anyone who likes mint choc chip.'

'I like mint choc chip,' Ruben said, stubbornly defensive. Annoyed that Barry and his boring vanilla flavouring was what *his* daughter took to be the norm. 'I'll ask the ice-cream man.'

'OK,' said Zadie with grinning confidence.

Ruben came back ten minutes later with two ice creams, a bottle of Factor 50, two rattan beach mats to sit on and a towel with 'I heart Cornwall' written in bright yellow on blue.

Zadie looked up from her sand sculpture, blinking against the brightness of the sun.

Ruben handed her an already melting vanilla ice-cream cone.

She thanked him as he tried to lay the mats down and stop the ice cream from dripping. Once their little patch was all looking a lot more comfortable and Ruben was seated – away from direct contact with the sand – Zadie said, 'Well?'

'Well what?' he replied.

'What did the ice-cream person say?' she asked, on a lick of her ice cream. 'They said it was vanilla, didn't they?'

Ruben licked his mint choc chip. 'Might have done,' he grinned.

Zadie sniggered. Ruben smiled.

They ate their ice creams watching the boarders. Seagulls cawed as they circled over the surf. When she got to the waffle cone, Zadie said, 'I don't really like these cones. I like those other ones. You know, the ones that taste like cardboard.'

Ruben looked at her incredulous. 'I specifically bought you the better cone because the other one tastes of cardboard!'

'Oh,' Zadie smiled. 'That's nice. Thank you.'

'You don't have to thank me for something you didn't want.'

'I'm thanking you for thinking of me,' she said.

And Ruben wasn't quite sure what to do with that.

Zadie finished off her ice cream and said, 'I'm going to go for a swim. Wanna come?'

Ruben made a face. 'Absolutely not.'

'OK,' said Zadie, and she skipped off.

Ruben thought for a second then called her back. She stopped and turned. She stood a bit like a duck, tummy sticking out, feet apart, but didn't seem to care in the slightest. It actually made her quite endearing – her intrinsic confidence with who she was. 'You can swim, right? Your mum, she'd let you go in on your own?'

'Oh yeah,' Zadie nodded eagerly. 'I love swimming. My mum reckons I could swim before I could walk.'

'OK, great. Off you go.' Ruben waved her away then settled down with his paperback.

Every few minutes he glanced up to check she was still alive. At one point he couldn't see her and got a bit panicked, trying to work out how he'd explain it to her mother. He stood up, scanning the shoreline in front of him for someone who looked like Zadie. The only person who fit the description couldn't have been her because she was hanging out with a group of body-boarders and was about to have a go on one of their boards. But it had to be Zadie, no one else stood the way she did, nor did he imagine there were many fluorescent lime swimming costumes in production. Ruben watched her, wondering how she'd managed to befriend this cool-looking gang so quickly. He supposed she was quite endearing, sometimes. She said such ridiculous things that on occasion were funny. He saw a tall blond boy laugh at something she said after she pulled off a pretty impressive ride on his board. Much better than anything Ruben could manage. But then, he consoled himself, she lived by the sea and Ruben didn't. He shaded his eyes with his hand so he could see better, he wanted to make sure the loping youth kept his hands to himself. Having been one, Ruben knew exactly what teenage boys were like and he considered striding over just to let them know that he was on to them. But to her credit, Zadie didn't seem bothered at all, holding her own, even going back for another turn on the guy's board. Ruben raised a brow in respect as he watched her carefree prowess. Maybe she did have some de Lacy genes after all.

Keeping one watchful eye on his daughter's potential suitors made lying on the beach reading his book much less relaxing. Ruben's contentment was further shattered when a dripping shadow was cast over his sun-warmed body and Zadie's voice said, 'Do you want to come and have a go?' She was holding a black bodyboard with a skull and crossbones printed on the front under her arm. Apparently one of the dudes had a spare and she'd been deemed a worthy recipient.

'I'm OK, actually,' said Ruben, shielding his eyes from the sun, looking up at her grinning silhouette.

'Oh, go on!' Zadie pleaded. 'It'll be fun. I'll show you what to do.'

Ruben held his hands up. 'No!' He was emphatic. 'I don't have my trunks.' He stood up, uncomfortable with the dynamic of Zadie towering over him.

'You could go in your T-shirt and pants. That's what I do sometimes at home.'

Ruben was not going bodyboarding with a load of cocky teenagers in his pants. Nor for that matter did he think Zadie ever should – he'd have a word with her mother.

'Pleeeeeease?' begged Zadie.

'No,' he tried to laugh, hoping it would all go away. Just then one of the lanky youths whistled and shouted, 'Yo, Zadie!' beckoning her to rejoin them. Ruben narrowed his eyes. When he looked at the boy, all he could see was raging hormones and swaggering teenage lust. This, coupled with Zadie saying, 'You know, Barry always goes in with me. He's really good on a surf board,' made Ruben tip his head up to the sun and say, 'Fine. Fine. I'll come in.'

Zadie whooped.

'But I'm not doing it in my pants. I'll go and buy some shorts.'

Five minutes later he was back wearing a pair of turquoise

board shorts with giant pink hibiscus flowers all over them. 'Don't laugh,' he said, 'it's all they had.'

Zadie beamed with delight at the shorts. 'I think they're great.' Which was exactly what worried him. 'Right.' He braced himself for more humiliation, 'let's get this over with.'

'It'll be so much fun,' she replied, gleeful as they walked over the wet sand to the sea.

Ruben looked down at her grinning face. 'I can't believe you've managed to get me to do this,' he said with a shake of his head.

She looked up at him, all innocent big eyes. 'You'll love it.'

Ruben found himself snorting out a little laugh himself. 'I very much doubt it.'

The water was freezing. The surf like pellets of ice splashing against his very white calves. All the cool young kids were messing about on various contraptions. Some surfing, some paddleboarding, others on something you chucked on the shore and rode on. 'Want a go on that?' Zadie pointed to where a girl in a red swimsuit was careering through the shallows. All Ruben could think about were the potential chiropractor bills should he place one foot on it. 'No thanks,' he shook his head at the kid who held it up for them when she'd finished her ride.

Ruben had never felt so old. His luminous turquoise and pink flowery shorts didn't help. All the others were in bold block colours. And any hint of a pattern was a skull or marijuana leaf. No one was wearing hot-pink hibiscuses this season. Except the dad.

And his tan was so shameful. His white T-shirt marks and pale chest compared to those who'd spent the whole summer in the surf. Usually before a holiday, Ruben went to visit Tatiana on the King's Road for a quick all-over spray tan. Not that he'd ever admit it out loud. The salon was very discreet.

'OK?' Zadie was babbling on next to him with instructions.

Ruben hadn't been paying the blindest bit of notice. Too busy comparing himself with a load of teenage boys. Pitiful. 'Sorry, just run it past me again.'

Zadie sighed. 'Right …'

Off she went with more instructions. Ruben listened this time. She was very clear. Very patient. The water had warmed up now where it splashed round his thighs.

'There's a good set of waves coming in now. Want to try these?' Zadie asked.

Ruben shrugged. 'Why not.' And he waded out further, looking ahead of him at what seemed to be growing into fairly ginormous blue waves. 'Do you think these are maybe a bit big?' he called out to Zadie where she watched in the shallows.

'No! You'll be fine,' she replied. 'Just enjoy it.'

Ruben clutched his board too tight. His knuckles were white.

'Start paddling!' she yelled.

A couple of the dudes had paused to watch. He could sense their sniggers. He was distracted. His hair had flopped into his eyes. The wave was looming. He tried to paddle but the board popped out from underneath him. He spent so long trying to reposition himself, Zadie shouting, 'Paddle!' that by the time he started a kind of frantic attempt at swimming, the lumbering wave was teetering over his head ready to crash. Which it did. Hard. Walloping Ruben and the board under the surface, rolling him around as it tumbled to the shore. Sand filled his trunks. His arms scraped the shore. He eventually surfaced like a dying fish, coughing and gasping, hair everywhere, sand-burnt, tangled in the board rope.

Zadie had her hand over her mouth in giggling pity.

Ruben tried to gather himself together. Wiped the snot and spit off his face, relieved his shorts of the sand. He panted as he got his breath back. Checking around him to see who had seen his humiliating wipeout. It was only then that he realised no one was looking. The kids were all doing their own thing. The only one glancing in their direction was the boy who seemed to be trying to impress Zadie rather than paying a blind bit of notice of Ruben. To them he was invisible. He was the old dad. He was meant to make a fool of himself. He was on a whole different strata of life to them. He wasn't one of the cool kids.

Ruben swept his hair out of his eyes. The realisation, while depressing, was also quite liberating.

Zadie crouched next to him, concerned. 'Want to try again?' she checked, tentative.

Ruben looked out at the tumbling surf. 'Yes,' he said. He would conquer this beast. 'Yes I do.'

Zadie grinned.

Three more attempts. Three more catastrophic wipeouts. But on the fourth attempt, Ruben got it. He caught the wave just after it reached its crest and was carried with it like a gliding mermaid right up to the shallows. He felt euphoric. So much so that he jumped up with a genuine whoop! One of the dudes sniggered, but Ruben didn't care. He was a convert. He had potential to be a pro. He was thirsty for more.

'Fun?' asked Zadie.

'Brilliant,' he replied, unable to mask his delight with any form of subdued cool.

Zadie clapped. Then rushed off to where the gang of teenagers were lolling on old towels, listening to music, comparing notes on their phones and came running back with another board. 'We can do it together,' she beamed.

Ruben didn't care who he did it with, he just wanted to get back out there in the waves.

Together they raced, side by side, into the dark blue water. Ruben, eager for another ride, kept flinging himself on every wave that came his way, ignoring Zadie when she told him to wait. After one too many disappointing rides, desperate for his euphoric high, he finally conceded that she might know better and decided to listen.

'Leave this one,' she said.

'Really? But it looks great.'

She shook her head. 'No.'

Ruben had to force himself still. He watched it rise up and up to a beautiful crest. He was about to shout, 'See, it's a good one,' until it suddenly fizzled out into nothing and he was glad he kept his mouth shut.

Then suddenly Zadie was turning on her board, shouting, 'This one! This one! Dad, get ready!'

And Ruben did exactly what he was told, waiting, poised for more instruction.

'Hold on, hold on,' she called. Then, 'Go!'

And they both paddled like daemons. Side by side, powering forward as the wave rose and rose behind them, hung suspended in the air and then crashed into the perfect rolling galloping white horse propelling them faster and faster towards the shore. Ruben found himself whooping. Zadie was grinning. Spray splashed into their faces. He didn't care about his flowery shorts.

He didn't care about being watched. He cared about that exact moment. Just him, her and the elements, free of all pretence, united together in this wild ride. He hadn't even minded when she'd called him Dad. He looked over and saw her laughing. He was laughing too, both giddy with enjoyment. She caught his eye. Her round little face and equally round eyes, excitable, exhilarated. In that moment he caught a glimpse of himself in her. In the way her mouth quirked when she smiled.

And the recognition made his whole body go rigid. His chest tightened as if crushed. He couldn't get his breath. He wasn't looking where he was going and his board hit a rock in the shallows, jarring his head and neck with a crick, pushing him over into the water so his back scraped along the sand.

He tried to right himself but the shallow water made it clumsy and awkward. His foot got caught in the cord of his board. He stumbled getting up. Zadie was there next to him, her arm outstretched to help.

'Are you OK?' she asked, concerned as he coughed and spluttered.

He waved her hand away. 'Yes, yes, I'm fine. Fine.' He stood up, rolled his shoulders, trying to iron out the pain in his neck. 'Stupid rock,' he laughed, fake and forced. 'Well, I think that's it for me.' He unstrapped the Velcro cord from his ankle and handed Zadie the board. 'Great fun. Yes. Jolly good.' Ruben wondered why he suddenly felt like his father. All brittle and reserved. Zadie was watching, confused. 'OK then. You carry on. Take your time with your new friends. I'll see you up at the beach.' He was still doing it, talking in clipped monotone. 'Good,' he added for pointless good measure.

Zadie stared at him in puzzlement for a second then one

of the surfer kids – the one who'd been trying to impress her earlier – came over and asked her if she was going back in, gesturing for the spare board. Zadie seemed torn, on the cusp of trying to persuade Ruben not to call it quits yet but also flattered by the blond guy's attention.

'Great, yes,' Ruben said. 'You go. Have fun.' He thrust the board in the boy's direction and added with a slightly menacing whisper, 'No funny business, I'll be watching you!' to the lad, before walking backwards for a couple of steps up the beach then turning and increasing his pace to a jogging stroll.

His brain was in overdrive. One half urging him to run away as fast as he could, the other half desperate to turn around and watch his daughter carve up the waves.

He could almost see his lovely easy life being sucked away from him like the tide. What if something happened to her, if she got ill, would he suddenly have to sit by her bedside at the hospital, life grey with worry. What if she got pregnant? Did he have to go and hunt down the culprit? What if she wanted to live with him? It wasn't like some bad Tinder date that he could bat away with a casual, *Believe me, I'm really not worthy of you.* But maybe he didn't want to bat her away. Maybe he'd just had more fun than he'd had in as long as he could remember.

He felt his chest tighten again. Did Zadie know CPR?

Calm down, Ruben, it's fine, he told himself. He had the best of both worlds; it was just two weeks and then he deposited her in Hove or Brighton or wherever it was she lived before any of this started. It was all fine. So why did he feel like he had something caught round his neck, desperate yet strangely reluctant to shake it off?

CHAPTER NINETEEN

Dolly and Fox found the clue in a small red plastic box wedged into the nest of stones encircling the base of the huge heart-shaped stone. The box was cracked, water had leaked in over time and half the writing was obscured. Dolly had spent a moment or two staring at the remaining handwriting before she was able to speak over the lump in her throat. Seeing the words was like momentarily having the person back. It made her remember the letters he'd sent that her and Olive would argue over. Dolly had snuck one into her room and slept with it under her pillow until Olive found it and took it away.

'So what does it say?' Fox asked, his clothes still damp from their foray into the waterfall.

Dolly read out what was legible of the clue: *I am the only thing stronger than fear. I am treasure worth more than gold.* She had no idea what that meant. She looked up at Fox. 'Sounds like your kind of thing – are those Buddha's words?'

Fox huffed a gentle, tired laugh. 'No. Not that I know of.'

Dolly frowned. She had really wanted to nail this one. 'OK, well let's head up to the house, see if they know.'

But by the time they navigated their way through the tropical valley, through the gorse bushes and back to the Big House there was no one there. It took another ten minutes circling the house trying to find a spot with at least two bars of signal. Olive's phone went straight to answerphone, so Dolly called Ruben, who had a vague grainy connection where he was down at the beach.

Ruben repeated the clue to make sure he'd heard it correctly, then huffed and said, 'Sounds like a bloody Hallmark card. I don't remember the clues being this difficult in the past.'

The unconscious ease with which she'd called Ruben wasn't lost on Dolly. Just twenty-four hours ago, her palms would have been sweating at the very idea of dialling his number. Before she could think much about it, in the background she heard his daughter's voice squeaking with excitement. 'I know what it is!' she shouted, 'I know! I had a pencil case with it written on. It's hope. Hope is the only thing stronger than fear!'

'Blimey, well done!' said Ruben with obvious astonishment. Then he thought for a minute and said, 'Could it be the Hope and Anchor?'

'Oh yeah, possibly,' Dolly replied, still marvelling at the fact she was chatting so casually with Ruben. 'Is it still here?' The Hope and Anchor had been the only pub in the village.

'Let's hope so!' said Ruben. 'We'll meet you there.'

Dolly tried Olive again, then sent her a text updating her on their whereabouts. Part of her was quite relieved she hadn't been able to get through.

They got to the village to discover that the Hope and Anchor was still in existence. Not only that, the whole place had been given a facelift. Still charmingly old-fashioned, but it no longer smelt nostalgically of stale beer and salt and vinegar crisps. Dolly remembered sitting curled in the window seat with a colouring book and her Barbies, while her parents chatted to everyone they knew. It was all raucous and animated and people would always slip her and Olive a pound each for the fruit machines. Now the tables were polished rather than sticky, and the floor was gleaming wood rather than swirling cigarette-burnt carpets.

Fox went to the bar to get the first round. Dolly, Ruben and Zadie found a table in the corner by the mottled window. Where there had once been fraying fake carnations in white vases on the tables, there were now fresh-cut posies of wild flowers. But the newly painted dark red walls still had the black-and-white pictures of shipwrecks and comfortingly there was still scampi in a basket on the menu. An old toothless sea dog in dirty blue overalls, a relic of the past, snoozed into his pint at the bar and a middle-aged couple in the corner sipped quietly on gin and tonics.

'Not quite like it used to be,' said Ruben, glancing around at the polished wood and artful displays of classic hardbacks and coils of fishing rope.

Dolly shook her head. She tried to conjure up old images of him as they spoke. Him leaning dark and louche against the oak trees in the rain, tendrils of cigarette smoke in the air as he bitched about his father. Olive straddling a tree branch, stretching forward to pluck the fag from his fingers. Dolly perched on a crumbling picnic table in awe.

She tried to overlay the image with the one sitting next to her now, trying to sort Zadie out with the Wi-Fi code so she could play a game on his phone, while at the same time trying to make polite chat with Dolly. He looked remarkably dad-like.

He'd filled out, no longer the sinewy skinny rake, still no muscle tone. His clothes were quite showy. All labels that Dolly had never heard of. His phone was top of the range. His watch looked like it weighed a tonne. His car keys had an Aston Martin fob. As much as Dolly wanted it to, none of it chimed with the way she lived her life. The hours she spent in the gym. The hours she spent working. To her, his car was just a police report waiting to happen.

'And so how have you been, Dolly? I hear you're in the police. It must really suit you, you look great,' he was saying, half distracted by Zadie, who couldn't get what she wanted to download.

This was exactly what she'd dreamed of, Dolly thought, the admiration, the clear appreciation. But in reality, the feeling inside was like the deflation after unwrapping all the Christmas presents; however good the gifts inside, nothing could ever live up to the anticipation.

Zadie suddenly put the phone down and said, 'I have to go to the loo, I'm bursting!' Ruben helped her clamber out of the window seat. Dolly found herself struck by a realisation that was far stronger than the feeling of deflation. It was relief. The heart-tightening humiliation and adoration was gone. She was free from the grip of the crush. It made her want to laugh. It did in fact make her giggle.

'Are you all right?' Ruben asked, sitting back down with a bemused frown, uncertain of the joke.

'Fine,' said Dolly, trying to wipe the smile off her face.

'What's so funny?' Ruben asked, self-consciously checking his shirt and hair. 'Is it something to do with me? Do I have something on my face?'

'No.' Dolly held up a hand to stop his paranoia. 'No, sorry, it's nothing.'

'No, go on, say what it is,' he urged.

Dolly had got her giggles under control. She shifted in her seat and said, 'It's nothing, seriously, it's just, all these years you've been there in my head as like the perfect guy. And now I'm here with you, I don't fancy you *at all*!'

She watched Ruben's face fall.

'Right,' he said, 'good to know.' Then sitting back, he added, 'Christ, I didn't realise I'd aged that badly.'

Dolly cringed. 'No! I didn't mean it like in a bad way. You're very good-looking and stuff.' She felt her face get hot as she floundered. 'It's not an insult. Just, you know, for me it's a good thing that there's nothing there, no attraction …' She could feel herself digging further and further into a hole as he looked more and more hurt and offended. 'Oh God, sorry Ruben, I didn't mean …' Dolly scrabbled for words, her cheeks crimson.

Ruben held up a hand. 'It's not a problem, Dolly. Think no more about it,' he said, seeming to visibly lift himself up and force his jovial charm back in place. 'I am delighted to be of service.'

Fox came over with the drinks, putting them down on the table. Aware he'd missed something by the awkward silence in the air, he looked from Dolly to Ruben. 'All good?' he asked.

'Tickety-boo,' said Ruben, reaching for his pint and taking an extraordinarily long sip.

Dolly nodded, now suppressing awkward, nervous giggles.

Fox sat down, clearly deciding to rise above it all and lifting his glass said, 'Well, cheers, here's to the next clue and finding a needle in a haystack!' just as the door flew open and in bustled flame-haired, gold-lamé-clad Aunt Marge.

'Hello, darlings, darlings. We're here, we made it. Darned phone signal.'

Dolly jumped up, frowning. 'Marge, what are you doing here?'

'Oh, I came to keep an eye on my girls.' Then she turned around like she'd lost something. 'Where's Olive gone?'

'I'm here,' said a tired and slightly exasperated voice from behind her as Olive entered the pub.

Dolly looked away.

Olive looked at everyone but Dolly. 'Anyone need a drink?'

'I could murder a port and lemon, darling,' said Marge, then spotting Fox at the table she gave a little whoop of glee and snuggled down next to him in the booth. 'Oh, I'm glad you're here!' She gave his arm a squeeze. 'I do like a man with muscles,' she winked, which in turn, across the table, seemed to make Ruben look even more dejected.

Oblivious to any tensions, Marge settled herself down, leather leggings crossed, hot-pink talons thrumming the table. 'So the clue is somewhere in this pub, is it?' she asked, looking round pleasantly surprised at the updated interior. 'May as well give up now,' she chortled.

Zadie trotted back from the toilet and took her seat again next to Ruben.

'And here's the pretty young thing!' said Marge. 'Look at those fabulous shorts!'

Zadie beamed, dipping into an almost curtsy to show off her blue striped shorts printed with giant roses. 'We've just been in the BEST waves. They were like higher than us! Da— I mean Ruben did a massive wipeout, it was so funny!'

Marge said, 'That sounds tremendous. I still can't believe

you have a daughter, Ruben.' Then to Zadie she added, 'Do you know I took on Dolly and Olive when they were not much older than you? How my life changed. It was quite eye-opening, I can tell you. All those hormones. Phew.'

Olive came over with drinks for her and Marge and took a seat on a spare stool.

Marge took a gulp of her port and lemon. 'Just what the doctor ordered.'

Dolly said, 'We weren't that bad, Marge.'

Marge reached over and squeezed Dolly's hand. 'No darling, you weren't bad at all, it was me. I was used to living the single life. Girl about town. Man in every port, you know, nudge nudge, wink wink,' she elbowed Fox, who couldn't help but good-naturedly grin. Marge put her glass down. 'It was a baptism by fire to suddenly have two teenagers in the flat. Squabbling away. I'd never had to get up so early. I remember I'd haul myself awake and there was Olive making breakfast and getting school uniforms ready.'

Next to her, Olive was picking at a beer mat and she glanced up briefly. Dolly wasn't certain if they made eye contact or not.

Marge carried on. 'I was dreadful,' she said over the table to Zadie, 'didn't know whether I was coming or going. But I got there in the end. I worked out what I was doing, didn't I, Dol?'

Dolly nodded, more to make Marge feel good rather than it being true. Remembering Marge in her satin dressing gown, packet of Benson and Hedges and a black coffee, head in hands over how early it was, while Dolly scraped mould off the strawberry jam.

'We had fun, didn't we?' said Marge.

Dolly said, 'Yeah, we had fun.' Because sometimes it had

233

been fun. Like living with a socialite. All sequins and feathers and pink gin. Just a little bit less cosy than home had been, and a little bit more lonely.

'Kids,' Marge added, scrunching up her nose and patting Olive on the leg, 'they turn your life upside down but always in a good way.'

Across the table, Ruben had paled. 'Actually, Zadie's just staying with me for the fortnight. While her mother is—'

But Marge cut him off. 'Oh no, it's never just a fortnight, Ruben. You might think it is, but oh no. It's for life. Like puppies,' she added. 'Not just for Christmas and all that.'

Ruben was looking significantly less jovial than he had been earlier that day when Dolly and Fox arrived. He patted his trouser pockets, clearly looking for his phone, a safety-blanket to dive into, then realised Zadie had it. He excused himself to go to the bathroom.

Just as Ruben was going, Fox stood up and said, 'I'll get another round. What d'you want, mate?'

'A gun to the head,' Ruben replied morosely.

Fox gave him a sympathetic pat on the arm. 'I'll get you another pint.'

Ruben nodded and sloped off to the loo.

Dolly watched him go. She felt like she was having an out-of-body experience. Being in a pub with Ruben de Lacy, unconsciously having dealt him a blow similar to the one she'd experienced years earlier. Validating Marge's attempts at parenthood. No interruptions, bizarrely, or contradictions from Olive. Dolly felt weirdly powerful. 'So where do we think the clue's going to be, then?'

Zadie put Ruben's phone down and said, 'It could be any-where.'

Olive said, 'And there's nothing more in the clue?'

Dolly handed it to her. 'You can read it yourself. The rest is all blurred.'

Olive took it without saying anything. Kept her eyes on the water-damaged text.

Marge peered over her shoulder. 'Oh, I see what you mean. What the devil does it say?' She plucked the paper from Olive's fingertips and, putting her reading glasses on, peered right up close, trying to decipher the writing. 'If we can't work it out then the whole treasure hunt is over, isn't it? And you've come so far!'

Suddenly the old sea dog snoozing at the bar perked up and said, 'Treasure hunt?'

Dolly swung round to look as he staggered to a stand, criss-crossed his way to their table, wispy grey hair sticking out at all angles, pint sploshing as he walked. 'Did you mention a treasure hunt?' he slurred.

Marge peered at him disdainfully over the top of her specs. 'Who are you?'

The man leant down to get a good look at her. 'The man of your dreams,' he grinned, toothless.

'I'm well out of your league,' Marge retorted. The man clutched his hand to his chest. His pint splashed. Marge sighed, 'If you know something about a treasure hunt then spit it out, otherwise kindly go back to pickling yourself.'

Giggles were bubbling close to Dolly's surface. Instinctively, she glanced over at Olive who was trying equally hard to suppress a smile.

'Come on,' said Marge, staring at the man with impatience. 'Chop chop.'

Dolly had to concentrate on staring at her beer mat so she didn't start laughing.

The sea dog leant hard on the table causing it to tip. A couple of empty glasses toppled.

Marge tutted.

The man had no idea what had happened. Instead, he just leant right over, stared at them one after the other and said, in a loud conspiratorial whisper, 'He hid something for you.'

Zadie bounced out of her seat with excitement.

Marge narrowed her eyes, suspicious.

The sea dog stood up straight, pleased with himself. 'Helped him do it,' he said. Then his face changed. 'Can't for the life of me think where though.'

Marge blew out an exasperated breath. 'Maybe somewhere in here? Come on, man, think!'

'Could be,' the old man said, as if it were Marge who was stumbling on the clue, not him trying to remember it.

This back and forth went on a while longer, until the man stumbled trying to sit down on a nearby stool, and in the process of trying to stop himself crashing to the floor said suddenly, 'I remember!'

And everyone round the table waited with breath bated as he gathered himself together, sat down on the stool and leaning forward said, 'It's in the old clock behind the bar.' He pointed up towards an old factory clocking-in clock that hung next to the optics with a glass-fronted case and pendulum, like a half-sized grandfather clock. 'It's in there,' he said with a dramatic whisper.

Everyone looked. Marge remained unconvinced. 'You're sure?'

'Would I lie to a goddess like you?' He grinned, toothless and proud of himself for remembering.

Marge tried to wave him away but the sea dog finished the rest of his beer, plonked it down on the table and said, 'Think that earns me a pint, don't you?'

'I'll get him a drink.' Dolly stood up. 'And I'll get the clue!'

'How?' It was Olive who questioned her.

'Don't know yet,' Dolly said, almost goading. 'But I'll get it.' She felt pumped. In control. She felt so much better about herself that she now wanted to prove to Olive that she was worthy. She wanted Olive, more than anyone else, to see her for who she was, to acknowledge who she had been and who she had become.

But Olive just nodded and said, 'OK. Fine.'

There was a queue at the bar and just one young guy serving.

Fox had propped himself up to wait. 'Your Ruben doesn't seem very happy,' he said, as Dolly came to stand next to him.

'He's not my Ruben,' she said, glancing back at their table where Ruben had returned and was scrolling on his phone while Zadie read a tourist leaflet for a theme park. With his head down, Dolly could see that Ruben was thinning slightly on top. She wanted to just stare at him and marvel at the differences like he was an exhibit in a museum, but she didn't want Fox observing her doing it. 'Anyway,' she said, getting back to the matter in hand, 'the clue's in the clock, according to that old guy.'

Before Fox could reply, the young, good-looking barman said, 'What'll it be?' his attention distracted by a couple of his mates on the fruit machine.

Dolly leant on the mahogany bar and said, 'I know it's a little out of the ordinary, but do you think I could pop round and have a quick look in that clock?'

The guy frowned, glancing away from his mates to Dolly. 'What?' he squinted as he spoke, like she was mad.

'The clock,' Dolly pointed, smiling sweetly. 'Could I have a look?'

'No,' the guy said, like she was nuts.

That wasn't what Dolly was expecting. 'Oh go on, just a quick look. It's just we think there might be a clue in there for us.'

'There's no clue,' the guy said with arrogant certainty. 'What can I get you, mate?' he said, directing the question to Fox now, Dolly forgotten.

Dolly felt her skin prickle. 'Erm, excuse me, you can't just ignore me.'

The guy huffed. 'Listen, lady, I didn't ignore you, I said you couldn't look in the clock. Different thing.'

Dolly ran her tongue along her lip. Had he just called her lady? She glanced in Fox's direction and saw him watching her. She rolled her shoulders back.

A young girl sauntered in wearing a bikini and iridescent cycling shorts sucking on a lollipop. She caught the barman's eye. To Dolly and Fox he said, 'Are either of you going to order any drinks because I've got stuff to do?' Over in the corner the girl was lounging against the wall watching him with a flirty grin, while his mates shouted over for him to come and check out how much they'd won on the fruit machine.

Dolly was seething. She looked at Fox again. He glanced between the cocky young barman, who was now laughing with his mates, and Dolly.

Dolly raised a brow. 'Can I?'

Fox said, 'You're asking for my permission?'

Dolly thought for a second. 'I'm asking for your collusion.'

The barman ambled back their way, his every move-ment exuding boredom. 'Right. Was it a yes or a no with the drinks?'

Fox looked from the barman to Dolly, who felt like a dog straining at a lead. 'No,' he said, 'It's not worth it. There'll be another way.'

Dolly frowned. 'What other way?'

'I don't know yet.'

'So what are we going to do?' she asked snidely. 'Wait for Buddha to give us inspiration?'

Fox opened his hands wide in a gesture of magnanimity. 'You do what you have to do, Dolly. It's not up to me what you do.'

Dolly ran her tongue along her top teeth, staring straight at Fox, her heart was racing. Then she reached into the pocket of her shorts and whipped out her police badge. Fox looked away like he couldn't believe the route she'd chosen.

Dolly took a step closer to the bar and said to the barman, 'Sir, if you don't mind, we have reason to believe the clock on the shelf behind you contains vital evidence in a case we're investigating.'

The barman scoffed. 'What is this? You just said it had a clue in it. How is it now suddenly evidence?' He folded his arms and smirked in challenge. 'I don't even think that's a real police badge.'

'Oh, it's a real police badge all right.' Dolly narrowed her eyes. She could feel her annoyance with this little brat rising, threatening to consume her.

'Prove it!' the guy sneered.

Dolly's breathing quickened. She was on the cusp of jump-ing the bar and reading the guy his rights when she felt Fox touch her arm. She glanced over and he did a tiny shake of his head. A warning that it wasn't worth it. Recognise, transcend, overcome. She said it in her head. It sounded ridiculous but to her surprise she felt the anger quell, felt it descend back to where it had come from like a beast retreating into a lair.

And that was when Fox leant forward, nodding towards the barman's friends who were now trying to sidle out sideways having seen the police badge, nervous expressions on their now very clearly underage faces, and said to the barman, 'Your friends are in a hurry, are they?'

The barman swallowed. It was the first time he'd looked marginally sheepish.

Dolly found that with her anger quelled, every other sense was on high alert. She saw the Lycra-shorts girl pass something to the fruit machine guy. 'Wait a sec!' she called to the group edging to the door. They all froze. Dolly took a step away from the bar and gave them the once up and down. The girl was hard as nails but the second fruit machine boy looked like he was about to cry. Dolly turned back to the barman, who was trying to regain his composure. 'I wonder,' she said, 'if I was to pat your friends down, what would I find?'

The barman rolled his shoulders. He was attempting defiant and unflinching but looked suddenly like a sulky schoolboy dragged to the headmaster.

Fox stood up straight, folded his big arms across his chest, watching and waiting like he had all the time in the world. The three frozen friends looked petrified.

Without saying anything, the young barman beckoned for Dolly to come round the bar and have a look in the clock.

Dolly stalked round and opened the glass case. Tucked right

at the back in the darkness behind the mechanism was a tiny green plastic box.

She took it and returned to stand next to Fox, who fixed the barman in his sights and said, 'See, that wasn't so hard, was it?'

'Can we go?' the girl in the Lycra shorts and bikini snapped.

'Yeah,' said Dolly, glancing briefly across, having forgotten all about them.

The barman watched with his hands in his pockets, expression thunderous.

Just then an older woman, the landlady, appeared from her break. 'Anyone waiting?'

Fox raised his hand.

She bustled over, looked at the barman apparently doing nothing. 'Not serving anyone, Danny?'

The barman mumbled something and, to his relief, another punter approached the bar so he scampered off to serve him.

The landlady rolled her eyes, then turned to Fox to ask, 'What can I get you, sir?'

Fox gave the order and the landlady went to pour the drinks.

'That's good, you got the clue,' he said.

Dolly turned round so she was leaning elbows against the bar. She felt like a fool for going in heavy-handed. 'Not if I'd had anything to do with it.'

Fox didn't say anything.

'You proved yourself right,' she said, irritated that she had done it so wrong.

Fox laughed. 'Don't take it out on me.'

'No, sorry.' Dolly turned, resting her head down on her clasped fists. 'God, why am I such a failure?'

Fox gave her a gentle nudge. 'You're not a failure. Listen,

you didn't pin the guy to the floor this time. That's a step in the right direction.'

She gave him a sidelong look. 'Is that your professional assessment?'

'If you want,' he grinned, dimple in his cheek. Then a little more softly added, 'Rome wasn't built in a day, Dolly.'

Dolly raised a brow. 'I don't think Buddha said that.'

Fox snorted a laugh.

The barwoman brought over the tray with their drinks. Dolly followed behind Fox to the table. Inside she berated herself for her lack of judgement. Her desperate desire to impress, to show she could get the clue by hook or by crook. The worst thing was that she was no longer just disappointed in herself; for the first time, she hadn't wanted Fox to be disappointed in her.

As she pulled up her stool at the table and handed Olive the little green plastic box with the clue inside, Olive said, 'Oh my God, well done, Dolly!'

Victory felt annoyingly hollow.

CHAPTER TWENTY

When they arrived back at the Big House, the sun was already dropping over the horizon. Great swathes of burnt orange and lipstick-pink lit the dusky sky.

Ruben gave Dolly, Fox and Marge the tour and showed them to various guest bedrooms, trying to sound as cheery as he could when Marge marvelled at the antiques and Fox blew out an impressed breath at the size of the ensuite bathroom. Really all Ruben wanted was to leave them all to themselves and go and lie face down on his bed in his pants. All the trip seemed to have done so far was make him feel middle-aged and unattractive. A far cry from his London life. What had become of him? Is this what fatherhood did to a person? Aged them ten years and forced them to invest in an unending supply of snacks and 4G while chucking in a lobotomy for good measure? He had spent most of the walk back to the house having to listen to Zadie's inane waffle about Animal Crossing, for which, incidentally, she seemed to have racked up a bill for £15.99 of in-app purchases.

And why didn't Dolly fancy him? He glanced at himself in one of the big gold hallway mirrors. He wasn't that bad, was he? Not that many wrinkles. He turned his head this way and that, skin still quite taut – what was the bloody point of the extortionate microdermabrasion if not?

'Mate, you've got a fire pit!' said Fox, staring out of one of the large windows on the landing. Most things on this level were still draped in dust sheets, but the first thing Ruben had done was throw open the curtains and keep them open. His parents always had them shut to protect the paintings from sun damage.

Ruben went to look out of the window too. 'Yeah, there's wood in the shed if you want to get it started.'

Fox didn't need telling twice, he was down the stairs and out into the garden before Ruben had allocated Marge a guest bedroom. Ruben felt like he'd been gazumped by He-Man. How could he compete?

Outside, the fire-starting was underway. Dolly had gathered kindling and was scrunching up an old newspaper to act as a starter. Fox was hefting some larger logs.

Olive sat on one of the patio chairs mulling over the new clue. 'It's almost impossible: *I am not gas but I have the power to burn. I am not liquid but I glisten like water. I am not solid but I crack under pressure. Find me and strike gold!*'

Fox paused, considered the words again and said, 'It doesn't get any easier the more you read it.' Then to Dolly he said, 'You'll need more newspaper, Dolly, it'll never catch with just that.'

Ruben stood in the doorway watching Dolly; from what he'd gleaned of her so far he expected her to bristle at the order but instead she said, 'You don't think? OK, I'll add some more.' He saw Olive glance up, surprised by her acquiescence. Then Marge sauntered outside, eyes glued to her phone in its diamanté case, seemingly satisfied now she'd found a hotspot of 4G and checked all her social media. She was tapping furiously on the screen with the tips of her acrylic nails. Laughing occasionally. Gasping, zooming in close to examine a picture of someone's grandchild and muttering, 'Little princess, my arse – looks like a pain in the neck to me.'

Ruben took orders for drinks. He went inside and raided the wine cellar for more of his father's precious vintage, enjoying the feeling of youthful rebellion. He picked out even better bottles than he had before. The really top-notch stuff, so good his father was happy to die before drinking it. For Zadie he got a lemonade from the fridge. The black cat was asleep on the kitchen chair. This time Ruben tipped the chair up completely so it had no chance of staying put, slumping to the floor somewhat dazed. 'Yeah, that's right. Bugger off. No messing with the boss,' he sneered.

By the time Ruben rejoined the group the fire was in full force. Flames licked their destruction on the new wood, a mesmeric distraction. Olive was gazing at it, hypnotised.

Zadie was stroking the bloody cat.

'Don't encourage that thing,' said Ruben. 'He doesn't live here.'

Zadie threw her arms round its neck. 'He's lovely. Like a panther. I love him. I always wanted a cat, can't we keep him?'

'No,' snapped Ruben.

Fox glanced up at his tone from where he was whittling a piece of wood into something with a penknife. Of course, he was a whittler. Was there anything the guy couldn't do? Who whittled anyway?

Olive asked, 'What are you making?'

Fox looked up, his brown eyes black in the darkness. 'I have no idea,' he said with a wry smile.

It made Olive smile too. He was one of those people who instantly put people at ease. 'Maybe a spoon?' she offered.

Fox tipped his head. 'Maybe a spoon.'

Bloody spoon. Surely there were enough spoons in the world without having to whittle another. Ruben wanted to make Olive smile.

He poured the wine. Filled his own glass up almost to the brim and handed round the others.

Sitting back in one of the large Adirondack chairs, Ruben closed his eyes and let the smooth melody of the wine play on his tongue. It was like heaven in a glass.

'I think it's corked,' said Marge, holding up her wine without looking up from her phone.

Ruben had to blow out a breath of frustration. 'It's not corked. I assure you. It's a rare 1988 Burgundy. This is how it's meant to taste.'

Marge made a face. 'I'm more of a Chardonnay woman, myself.'

Ruben couldn't deign that with an answer.

From the lawn, where she was still playing with the cat, Zadie said, 'I can hear the sea. Can you hear the sea? I love it when I can hear the sea.'

Ruben pretended not to have heard.

Fox paused his whittling and tipped his head to listen, endlessly patient. 'I can,' he said with a smile. Then his eye caught something in the sky and he said, 'Look, a bat,' and pointed into the darkness.

Zadie jumped up. 'Oh, I love bats! They're one of my favourite animals. Did you know that in French they're called *chauve souris*, which translates as bald mouse? Don't you think that's funny, Dad?'

'For God's sake. Can you just be quiet? For one second, just be quiet?' Ruben finally snapped. Standing up, his hands raised in the air.

Olive flinched.

Zadie stopped, mouth open.

'Just …' Ruben paused, took a breath; he felt Marge next to him pause her tapping on her phone. He pushed his hair back with both hands. 'Just give me a break.' Then he held a hand up as if holding Zadie back and said, 'And, please, don't call me Dad.'

He saw Olive close her eyes in disappointment. Dolly put her head down and focused on the fire. Ruben felt ashamed but he didn't care, a primal self-protective instinct had taken hold.

Zadie swallowed, eyes wide and round. 'But you are,' she said softly.

'No,' Ruben shook his head. 'I'm not. Not really. I don't want this,' he pointed between them. 'I didn't ask for this. I was perfectly happy before you came along. I don't want to be anyone's dad. All right?'

Silence in the garden.

Fox was watching them intently. Ruben wanted to tell him to bugger off, instead he sighed. Then he kicked an ornamental stone urn and really hurt his foot but couldn't acknowledge it. 'Just leave me be,' he said, hand raised in finality, picking up his wine ready to stalk off into the darkened garden and nurse his throbbing toes.

Zadie however had other ideas. Head held high, she said into the silence, 'No. You don't get to have the last word.'

Ruben thought of the time she said she'd been taunted quoting Shakespeare. She was stronger than she looked.

He paused, the pain in his foot was excruciating, as were all the disappointed adult eyes looking at him – or feigning not looking at him. 'Just leave it, please.'

Zadie carried on regardless, chin wobbling a touch but stoic in her delivery. 'My mum warned me not to have anything to do with you—'

'Yes, I know that,' said Ruben, putting his wine back down on the table. 'Because I'm a terrible person. You should have listened to her.'

'No, I shouldn't,' said Zadie, 'because I would have never believed her if I hadn't seen it for myself. Sometimes, like right now, you *are* a terrible person. But you shouldn't give up, you should try and do better!' she said with the dramatic urgency of a Head Girl. 'You can't be happy being a disappointment.'

Ruben put his hands in his pockets and nodded. 'I am, I'm afraid,' he said, as if he'd made his peace with it. The whole fatherhood thing was a weight around his neck that he was now determined to shake off. He did not need this complication in his life. She was better off without him.

Zadie was aghast. 'No!' she shouted, stamping her foot. 'This is not the way it's meant to be.' Her voice caught then.

'Zadie, I'm sorry,' said Ruben, refusing to look at anyone else round the fire. This was for the best. A clean break. Harsh but fair, as his father would say. 'But this isn't *Love Island* or whatever. You can't force a relationship. It's just not going to happen.'

'But we had fun, in the sea. Didn't we?'

Ruben stood with both hands in his pockets looking down at the ground. He felt like a real asshole.

Zadie didn't know what to do now. She looked confused. Couldn't formulate the next part of her argument.

After a moment's pause, Olive stood up and said, 'Zadie, shall we go in the house. Get a glass of water?' while shooting daggers at Ruben.

But Zadie shook her head, wiped away a tear with the palm of her hand, and said, 'Barry asked me why I wanted to meet you when I already had him as a dad, and do you know what I said? I said because you can never have too many people love you.'

Ruben's face went even more rigid than before.

'Well, I'll tell you something, *Ruben*, I don't think you're a terrible person, I think you're a scared person. Shall I tell you why I think that? Because we *did* have fun together and for some reason you're afraid to admit it. You're no better than the boys from my school on the pier when I was doing my Shakespeare. They're bullies. And bullies are weak. My mum's told me so many times that they're weak because they're scared. And it's just like you. You're nothing but a scared old man. I don't know why but you're scared of being my dad. Maybe you're scared of having too many people love you. Or just one person love you!' Ruben could see her little chest rising and falling as she got more wound up. 'And I'll tell you one more thing,' she went on, tears in her eyes now, 'if you did know your Shakespeare, you'd know this – *to thine own self be true*, Ruben. That's what Barry always says.' She stared him right in the eyes, her voice catching slightly as she said it again, '*To thine own self be true.*' Then she stomped past him into the house.

'Bravo!' Marge's voice cut in from behind him as she clapped wildly.

Ruben couldn't look at anyone. He could feel his jaw so rigid it might snap. He could feel Olive glaring at him in disgust.

This was unfair. He hadn't asked for any of this. Why did he feel like such a callow, pathetic bastard?

Through gritted teeth, Olive said, 'I'll go in and check she's OK.'

Ruben's fists were clenched tight by his side.

Marge folded her arms tight over her chest, bracelets all clacking together into the silence. 'Deary me, Ruben. Deary me.'

Fox and Dolly didn't say anything.

The black cat stalked its way smugly into the sitting room.

Then after a couple of minutes' silence, Olive suddenly burst outside in a rush of panic. 'She's gone, Ruben! She's not in the house!'

And Ruben felt a lurch of fear in his chest like nothing he'd ever felt before.

CHAPTER TWENTY-ONE

They organised themselves into various search parties to look for Zadie.

Fox was to go alone because he had the best tracking skills. Dolly and Olive would go together – while reluctant, they would pair up for the sake of Zadie. Marge would stay at the house in case Zadie came back. Ruben would also go alone because he refused to go with anyone and no one seemed particularly keen to pair up with him.

Dolly walked at such a pace that Olive struggled to keep up. Not that she'd admit it. Together they took the path that led through the woods in the direction of the cottage. Neither of them discussed a route, it just seemed to be where their bodies took them.

Olive said, 'Have you seen the cottage since you've been back?'

Dolly said, 'No.'

They walked on in silence. Feet crunching over forest leaves. The woods were spooky in the dark. Dolly used the torch on her phone to light the way. Olive followed behind, flinching at animal noises, thinking how the tables had turned. Now Dolly was the strong, brave one. Hiking into the darkness,

Dolly didn't show an iota of fear, just boldly marched on shouting Zadie's name every few steps. Olive almost found herself missing the little girl who had clung to her hand.

'So,' Olive said to Dolly's back, 'what's the story with you and Fox?'

'There's no story,' Dolly said, voice expressionless, like she was determined to remain robotically neutral. 'We work together. He's my boss. Kind of.'

Olive said, 'Oh right,' leaving it at that.

But Dolly immediately stopped and turned, so Olive nearly walked into her. 'He's completely not my type.'

Olive thought of big, burly, gorgeous Fox with his almost shaved head and tattoo. Surely he was everyone's type? 'I didn't say anything!' she said, almost laughing because Dolly's reaction was so uncalled for.

'You thought it though,' said Dolly, turning to walk back through the forest, faster now so Olive really had to trot to keep up and not be left behind to the wolves or whatever lived in the dark shadows. 'You have no idea what I was thinking,' said Olive, defending herself even though it had been exactly what she had been thinking.

Dolly paused again. 'Olive, I know exactly what you're thinking all of the time.'

Olive just raised her hands like she couldn't argue with such reasoning.

They crunched along the path some more. Shouted for Zadie. The sound of the sea got louder. The noises of the forest made Olive hurry.

'What about you?' said Dolly. 'How's "The God of Science"?'

Dolly had met Mark once. At a disastrous birthday dinner

for Aunt Marge where Dolly had shown up an hour late fresh from some terrifying shoot-out, her adrenaline was so high she proceeded to talk really fast and loud for the entire meal, drank too much and then when the come-down hit she fell asleep in her chair. Mark had found her brash and obnoxious. Olive wasn't sure what Dolly had thought of Mark but the fact she fell asleep at the point he managed to get a word in edgeways suggested boring might be one of her adjectives.

'We split up,' said Olive. 'Just the other day actually.'

Dolly paused walking, as if she knew at this point she should say something sympathetic, but then she carried on. 'Sorry,' she said a couple of steps later.

Olive said, 'It's fine. It's just a bit weird.'

Dolly said, 'Yeah.'

The cottage looked different in the darkness. More menacing. More eerie.

Dolly stopped short when she saw the state of it, the graffiti and the metal hoarding round the edge. 'Oh my God.' She glanced at Olive, who nodded sadly, wanting somehow to shield her sister from the heartbreak of seeing the derelict house.

Dolly took a shaky breath. 'What's happened to it?' Then she marched forward, yanking open the metal barrier just as Ruben had done. She shouted Zadie's name.

Olive didn't want to go in again, she took a few steps towards the beach and called for Zadie but the darkness was too unnerving and she ended up following Dolly inside.

The smell was engulfing. Mouldy and wet. There was no end to the weirdness of being back in what had once been their hallway. So hauntingly familiar underneath all the destruction. Olive looked for Dolly in the kitchen and living room, but when she heard creaking of the floorboards above, realised she had headed straight upstairs for their bedroom.

Olive could feel her own reluctance holding her back on every step. An old picture of their mother's hung at an angle on the landing. Olive found herself straightening it. When she got to their bedroom, she took a moment, trying to reorient her senses before poking her head round the door. Dolly was sitting on the edge of her twin bed, reaching behind to trace the outline of a popstar on a poster ripped from a magazine on the wall. She caught Olive's eye and said, 'I don't even know who this is, but I remember loving him!'

Olive could barely breathe, the room was packed full of so many memories. The notches on the doorframe that charted their height. The Blu Tack where other posters had been. The wallpaper with the little blue flowers. She went further in and saw on her own bed one of the two matching quilts their mother had made still draped over the mattress. She reached out a hand to touch it. The material was nibbled with moth holes and coated in a sheen of dust. The quilts had been on their beds forever. They wrapped themselves in them on Christmas morning when they opened their stockings and lay snuggled underneath them on the couch if they were ill.

Dolly's eyes widened when she saw it. 'You left yours here?'

Olive said, 'I didn't mean to.'

Dolly was incredulous. 'I can't believe you could leave it. I have mine on my sofa still now.'

'I think I was just too busy packing everything else up,' Olive said, conscious that this wasn't totally true, that part of her had left it out of sheer annoyance and whenever she'd seen Dolly's she'd felt a little stab of regret.

Dolly pursed her lips, 'Of course you were.'

Olive tipped her head, narrowed her eyes as she looked at her sister. 'What's that supposed to mean? Who do you think packed this place up? Who do you think packed your suitcase and made sure you had your quilt? Who do you think left her things behind so that you could have your things because they wouldn't all fit in Marge's car?'

'OK fine,' snapped Dolly. 'You. Perfect you! Saint Olive. Honestly, if I could go back and not be who I was then, I would do it in a heartbeat. Do you know how shit it is being the weak, pathetic one and being blamed for it for the rest of your life?'

Olive swallowed. Dolly had never said anything like that before. As Olive sat down on the bed opposite, she found her instinct was to protect her. 'You weren't weak and pathetic, Dolly, you were just young.'

'I wasn't young though,' said Dolly. 'I just wasn't tough. I was "the emotional one".' She rolled her eyes up to the ceiling. 'God, you know when you and Dad went off on your adventures, I would stay at home and practise not crying. And I couldn't do it. I can sure as hell do it now though, I'll tell you that.' Dolly laughed, hollow and bitter.

Olive felt a pang for the fact what she was saying was true. They had consciously left her, she was a burden. She watched Dolly stand up, walk round the little room opening cupboard drawers that had long since been emptied, and the ancient wardrobe door that fell off its hinges. Inside were a couple of old shirts and then Dolly laughed, reaching to the back to pull something out on a hanger. An old pair of flowery dungarees.

'Oh my God. I can't believe these are still here! See, people won't even steal them.' Dolly held them up against her. The colours faded, the fabric moth-eaten. She glanced up at Olive. 'I mean they are awful, aren't they?'

Olive smiled. 'They were sweet.'

Dolly sat down on the bed again. 'You would never have worn them!' She sighed, pushing a stray hair back from her face. 'Christ, I wore shit like this while you were having a deep life-changing love affair with Ruben!' She chucked the dungarees on the bed.

Olive frowned. 'You were just a kid.'

'I wasn't that young Olive. I was just stupid, forgotten Dolly. I spent my whole time wanting what you had.'

'Oh rubbish, you had a great life.' Olive couldn't believe what she was hearing. 'I made sure you had a great life. Everything I did was to protect you. I was the one who sat up with Mum when she was puking her guts out on booze. I was the one paying the bloody bills. I made sure you had a child-hood.'

'Well maybe if you'd let me carry some of it then I could be a martyr about it now, too,' Dolly snapped.

Olive narrowed her eyes. 'That's unfair.'

But Dolly carried on, 'And then I would have never done stupid things like try and kiss Ruben or tell Dad to go to the orangery so he found out about Mum's affair. And you wouldn't have blamed me!'

'I didn't blame you!' Olive's voice rose in frustration.

'You *did* blame me!' Dolly hit the dusty bed with her hand.

There was silence in the room. The waves rolled on the shore outside.

Olive expected Dolly to carry on shouting, to hurl another couple of insults, but instead she just stared at her, held her gaze with sudden calm, unwavering eyes. She saw her take a breath in through her nose and out through her mouth, she could almost see her brain thinking, forcing herself back from the brink, then after maybe three or four seconds, she stood up and came and sat next to Olive on her bed.

Dolly reached out and took Olive's hand. A gesture that had never happened before. Her fingers were long and thin. Her skin cool where Olive thought her own palms were hot and sweaty from the stress of the situation. Dolly took another deep breath and looking Olive straight in the eye said, 'You did blame me for Dad ending up at the orangery and seeing Mum and Lord de Lacy together. I know you did because I saw it in your eyes.'

'I didn't!' Olive denied it vehemently.

Dolly looked at her, eyes knowing and kind. 'You're really going to tell me you didn't?'

Olive had to look away, press her tongue against the roof of her mouth to stop the emotion. She felt suddenly like the roles had reversed. That she was the naughty child and Dolly the grown-up. She wanted to keep lying. To maintain the pretence but she couldn't, not under Dolly's serene, all-knowing gaze. She closed her eyes. Then she nodded. 'OK. I did blame you. I did and I shouldn't have done.'

'No, you shouldn't have done,' said Dolly calmly. 'Because from that point on you hated me, and you also mothered me, which is a tough combination. As well as losing everything we had, I also lost you. You were so angry with me and I know I didn't cope well at Marge's but,' Dolly swallowed, 'I don't think it was all my fault …'

Olive pressed the heel of her hand to her forehead. She thought of how angry she got when they were living at Aunt

Marge's house. Picking everything up, washing, ironing, making the packed lunches. All of it tainted with a mist of injustice; a vehemence aimed at her sister that if she'd just kept her mouth shut, none of this would have happened. Olive had been so full of anger, at everyone. Not least herself for not having clocked her mum's affair earlier.

Dolly carried on, 'The time we spent at Aunt Marge's together was pretty bad, Olive. You were always telling me what to do, always cross with me, but at the same time you could barely look at me.'

Olive replied, defensive, 'I was trying to talk you into going to school, to stop hanging out with those idiots! Of course I looked at you.' But she knew she hadn't. She remembered sighing a lot. While Dolly had physically spiralled out of control when they'd lived with Aunt Marge, Olive had always prided herself on maintaining a taut control. Of carefully refusing to think of the alternatives – the ones that Dolly would sob about. Sometimes she caught herself wondering how different life might have been had she run away with Ruben, how they might have been living in a cosy flat somewhere blissfully in love, but she swiftly quashed those daydreams, never admitting them to anyone – even herself when Ruben asked her just the other night.

Dolly was watching her.

Olive looked down at the bare damp floorboards, she thought about her chat with Aunt Marge in the shed, when she'd said that her parents' faults were their own responsibility. It made Olive wonder if, perhaps with the absence of anyone else to blame, she had blamed Dolly, taken all her frustration out on her. It was an uncomfortable realisation. She shifted in her seat as she looked back at her sister, at their touching hands. She saw their different skin tones. Recognised the shape of her sister's nails. Remembered the little scar on the back of her hand. And she said, 'I'm sorry I was a bitch to you at Aunt Marge's. I'm sorry I blamed you. I shouldn't have done.'

Dolly said, 'No.'

Olive closed her eyes for a second, unable to look at her. 'I feel like I really let you down.'

Dolly shrugged. 'I survived, I think I just wanted to say it. And now I've said it, all I can think about is how nice you were to me when I was little! How much you looked after me.' Then, fiddling with the quilt on the bed, she added, 'I was wrong about what I said earlier about being a martyr. I know you tried really hard.' Dolly kept her eyes averted, focusing on the fabric she was pleating between thin fingers. 'I think I was just jealous of everything you had. Of who you were. I felt like I lived in your shadow. Or,' she glanced up, big blue eyes on Olive's, 'it was like Mum always said, I just felt things more.'

Olive felt a swell of emotion inside herself. Thinking of all the effort she went to. How tired she'd been, how wrung out by life when still so young. 'I felt things too, Dolly,' she said.

'I know,' Dolly agreed, insistent, then she pressed her lips together and after a moment she laughed, 'but you always seemed to get what you wanted.'

Olive shook her head at the preposterousness of the idea.

Dolly shrugged. 'Well, that's what it felt like from the outside.'

Olive was going to go in for a counter-argument, to defend herself properly, but instead she took a moment, as she'd watched Dolly do, to take a few breaths, to sit with what had been said. From Dolly's point of view maybe it had seemed like Olive got everything she wanted. Whether that was true or not wasn't necessarily the point to be arguing right now, because like it or not, it had been Dolly's truth and Olive couldn't deny her that. In the end she said simply, 'I think we both lost.'

And Dolly nodded. 'Yes.'

It felt so much nicer than launching into another row. Especially when Dolly then said, 'I'm sorry I was such a pain at Aunt Marge's.'

And Olive replied, 'I'm sorry *I* was such a pain at Aunt Marge's!'

Dolly said, 'Shall we get Marge in here and she can apologise for being completely insane?'

Olive laughed.

Dolly grinned.

Olive wanted to capture the moment and keep it in her pocket.

Then Dolly looked across and said, 'I think all I've ever wanted, Olive, is for you to see me as a person. A real-life person. Rather than someone to take care of or an annoyance.'

Olive said, 'I don't see you as an annoyance.'

'You do!' Dolly countered. 'And I know I can be annoying sometimes. But I'm trying not to be; although I know everything I've just said is probably annoying. I am grateful, Olive.'

Olive looked across at Dolly. Adjusted her eyes slightly to see someone new. She saw the vague lines on her face where wrinkles would one day be. She saw the mascara on her lashes. Saw the seriousness of her expression. The sinewy muscles in her arms. She looked for her younger sister but she wasn't there. Instead, there was a woman with glorious blonde hair and interesting eyes. A contemporary. An equal. A person.

What was it Aunt Marge had said? We're all just human. Maybe that applied to them too.

Dolly went on, 'Perhaps we could start again from now – you not seeing me as annoying, and I won't be annoying. How does that sound?'

Olive said, 'Well I won't be annoying, either. I know I tell you what to do, it's just I worry about you.'

'You don't need to, I'm fine,' said Dolly.

'Except you've been suspended from work—'

'Olive,' Dolly cut her off. 'That's being annoying.'

'Sorry. Sorry.' Olive made a show of buttoning her lip.

Dolly nodded, satisfied she'd got her point across, then she stood up, the mattress lifting under them, and picked up the dungarees. 'So let's burn these and go and find Zadie!'

Olive felt like a parent must feel when their child flies the nest. 'I really did think you looked sweet in those dungarees.'

'Yes, and therein lies the problem,' Dolly replied, perfect brows arched. 'Come on, let's get out of here. This place gives me the creeps.'

Olive took one last look around her childhood bedroom before following Dolly's fast clip down the corridor. But at the front door she paused; behind her she could hear things for the first time. Like her memory was returning. She sensed the parties and the laughter. The Saturday morning TV, the clink of the cereal spoon. She saw her dad with his dark green adventure hat on his head, weaving stories like magic. She felt the hugs. The blankets. The weight of the dog's head on her thigh. The bedtime kisses. The autumn tides. The games. The shells washed up on the shore. The first tomato of the season. She clutched for the sadness but felt it drifting away. Suddenly Olive found herself dashing back, returning to the familiar darkness of her old bedroom to grab the dusty handmade quilt off the bed. She had left it behind on purpose once before, she wasn't going to make that same mistake again. As Marge had said, and she finally understood, none of them were perfect, least of all Olive. And sometimes, she realised, it was just as necessary to remember the good as it was to forgive the bad.

CHAPTER TWENTY-TWO

When Ruben fell down the ravine he'd been thinking about his ex-girlfriend's rabbit of all things. A great fluffy thing called Boo-Boo. Ruben hated the rabbit and he hated the name of the rabbit. It lolloped around his lovely flat, leaving little round rabbit presents all over his rug. It was disgusting. It did nothing. It smelt. Eventually he had to split up with Kylie – no Kelly – because of the damn rabbit.

'See, I can't even have a pet,' he exclaimed to the heavens, 'how in God's name can I have a daughter?' And then whoosh, he fell. Straight down. No messing. The rock was all jagged and sharp, slicing his back, his chest and his thighs as he slipped, eventually wedged by his small but not unnoticeable middle-aged belly, his legs dangling above waves sluicing into the crevice. The dark sky was far above him. It was like being stuck down a well.

'Shit,' he snapped.

He tried to push himself up but there was nothing to hold on to. Were he one of those agile free climbers he marvelled at in documentaries from the comfort of his sofa, then he'd be out in a jiffy. But no. Ruben had been seduced by the Peloton advert and was only good for cycling stationary in his living room.

He did a desperate, futile pat of the pockets of his shorts for his phone. Most of the time it lived in the right-hand back pocket but sometimes, if he'd been on it recently, he slipped it into the front pockets, which was exactly where it was now because he'd been desperately trying to call Zadie. But alas there was, as there had been when he was trying to reach his missing daughter, no signal.

He blew out a breath. He didn't realise he could feel any more wretched. Her words had gone round and round in his head, plaguing him. And that final, teary 'to thine own self be true' ending, he closed his eyes, that had been like a punch in the gut. He wasn't 100 per cent sure what it meant but he was going with: being honest with himself.

A tiny camouflaged crab scuttled across the rock in front of him. Then stopped still. Ruben moved his head back. He didn't want a crab on his face.

He checked what he could move. His hands and arms were free. One leg was free, the other was caught at an uncomfortable angle below him and if he moved it something sharp sliced against his ankle, but he couldn't see because of the rock wedging his belly.

He could hear the sea. Below him was just darkness. What if he was dangling above an underwater cave? Could the tide rise this high? He touched the rock below him to see if it was damp. He couldn't tell.

On instinct he looked up at the sky and said, 'Alexa, get me out of here.'

A seagull circled overhead and then nothing.

Ruben wriggled and writhed to no avail. He shouted but the sound just echoed around him in the ravine. He rested his head against the rock and shut his eyes. The waves out to sea crashed.

'Shit, shit, shit.'

The crab scuttled past his nose and he jerked his head back. He watched it, translucent green with little eyes like olives. Oh Olive. Would she ever look at him kindly again?

Ruben closed his eyes and said, 'Shit!'

Right, come on, pull yourself together, man. He tried again to free himself but it was no good. He looked up at the navy sky. OK, so, if he was honest with himself, what did he feel now?

Pain in his stomach. Annoyed that he was stuck here and not on the search. Guilty for what he'd said to Zadie. Foolish for saying it in front of everyone – but that had been him being honest. That was him telling the truth about how he felt about fatherhood. About responsibility. He didn't want it. He didn't want to be burdened with it. She drove him up the wall.

He remembered her crumpled face when she was shouting at him and the flutter it provoked in his chest.

He had to admit that when she'd stormed off, he hadn't felt good. It wasn't like when he shook off a bad date and was rolling his shoulders with relief by the time he got round the corner of the restaurant.

Zadie was quite sweet sometimes. Quite funny. Making her cry was like jabbing pins in his own heart.

But he didn't want to feel that.

Why not, Ruben? Because you're afraid of being loved?

'No, that's not why,' he said out loud.

Then he steeled himself. 'Come on then, Ruben,' he said. 'Be truly honest with yourself. What are you feeling right now?'

He thought for a moment. Squeezed his eyes shut and burrowed deep into himself. Unhappiness. Shame maybe. Annoyance.

Fear.

He opened his eyes. Fear that he had lost Zadie.

Fear that he would have to tell her mother that he'd lost her. But mainly fear that she was alone somewhere in the dark and in danger. For a split-second he saw her tumbling down into the waves below and realised he would risk his life to reach out and grab her hand, do whatever he could to haul her back up.

He put his hand over his mouth and let out a small sob.

'Oh Zadie,' he cried.

And then as if summoned from his imagination, there she was. Huge wide eyes staring down at him. 'Ruben? What are you doing down there?'

'Oh Zadie! Zadie! You're here. You're alive. Oh my God, I'm so pleased.' He exhaled with relief. 'I'm so sorry for upsetting you. Oh thank God I'm not going to have to tell your mother I lost you.'

Zadie was crouching over the ravine, puzzled. 'Are you stuck down there?'

Ruben nodded. 'Yes, yes I am. Where did you go? I was so worried.'

Zadie settled into a more comfortable position, lying down on her stomach so she could talk to him better. 'I went to call my mum. There's no signal unless you're practically on top of the hill.'

'But you could have got lost.'

'I'm really good at orienteering.'

'Oh.' Ruben looked up at her. Her messy hair, crazy long eyelashes, cherubic face. 'I didn't know that about you.'

'There's lots you don't know about me,' she said.

He nodded. 'I know.'

In front of him, the crab was wedging itself into a tiny overlap in the rock face. Snuggling in tight, legs underneath it.

'Do you know what my middle name is?' Zadie asked.

Ruben shook his head. 'No, I'm afraid I don't.' It was in his mind to ask her to run back to the house and alert Marge so someone could come and rescue him but just the sheer fact she was talking to him and not leaving him there to die alone, which was what he deserved, kept him from saying anything about rescue.

'It's Ruby,' she said. 'After you.'

'Get out of here! It's not.' Ruben couldn't believe it.

Zadie nodded. 'It is. I promise.'

'Well, blow me down.' Ruben half laughed. He was chuffed. 'Good old Penny,' he said, wondering, were the situation reversed, whether he'd have incorporated Penny's name into his child's. No, he knew.

'Do you know if I had named you, you'd be called Arlette?'

'Really? Arlette? Why?' Zadie scrunched up her nose with distaste. Her hair was all wild from the sea salt. He could just make out the freckles across her nose from the sun. Ruben remembered how much fun he had with her in the surf. Shackles of convention thrown to the wind. Just him and the water and this odd, excitable girl.

Arlette.

He couldn't picture it. Arlette was tall and blonde and a little haughty. She probably carried a skateboard but never rode it. She wouldn't have got in the water today, she wouldn't have wanted to get her hair wet. She would have been the one stretched out lithe on the towel with the swanky new phone and the withering gaze, beating the boys off like flies.

That would have been Arlette de Lacy.

And Ruben would have been proud. He realised to his shame.

'Because you are a de Lacy,' said Ruben, thinking how many times he had heard this told to him by various ancestors. 'And the de Lacys originate from Calvados, which is in the North of France – you may have been there,'

Zadie shook her head. 'No, I've never been to France.'

'Never been to France!' He imagined his grandparents' horror. 'Well Arlette was my grandmother's name. I would have had to call you Arlette. It's a family tradition. And if I had had a son he would have been called Montgomery after his grandfather.'

Zadie made a face. 'Montgomery? Yuck.'

Ruben frowned. He thought about his doddering grandfather Montgomery who would get so wound up about politics that spit flew out of his mouth and his liver-spotted hands shook. Would he really have called his son Montgomery? Montgomery de Lacy. Would he have subjected the poor kid to that? Monty? 'Yes, I suppose it is a bit yuck,' he agreed. 'But that's the way it's done. And has been done for generations.'

'But they're all dead, aren't they?' Zadie said. 'How would they know?'

'They wouldn't,' he said, 'but it's tradition. History.'

Zadie plucked some grass and let it fall next to her. 'Did you know that Barry says that history only repeats itself through lack of imagination?'

Ruben tipped his head. He was about to say something facetious about Barry and how conversation with him must just be one bad Instagram slogan after another, but in an attempt to rein himself in from offending Zadie he paused, which made him consider the sentiment. All those old de Lacys *were* all dead, he thought to himself. None of them know what's going on. And why would you try and please them when you didn't like them anyway? He swallowed. He thought of Olive saying that she bet he spent his life thinking if he'd passed his exams his dad wouldn't have whipped him and kicked him out. Had he? Of course, he bloody had. It's bullshit, you idiot. Of course, you don't have to do what they say. His eyes widened at the notion.

Zadie was watching him like a little owl.

Ruben cleared his throat and said, 'Your Barry sounds like a very wise man.' And for the first time, he didn't begrudge the perfect stepdad. He wasn't the enemy, Ruben realised, if anything that role had so far fallen to Ruben. He should be in awe of Barry because Barry had managed it – Barry hadn't shied away from parental responsibility, he had taken Zadie on and taught her stuff that she'd listened to and could quote at meaningful moments. What could be more flattering than that – being worthy of being listened to and looked up to.

'He is pretty clever,' said Zadie.

Ruben felt a fluttering of jealousy but tamped it down. Determining to do better.

He rested his head back against the jagged rocks and looked up at Zadie's little face in front of the blackening sky. He licked his dry lips. 'I am sorry about what I said earlier. It was unforgivable.'

Zadie nodded.

Ruben said, 'If you'll take me, I'd really like to go surfing with you again.'

'Yeah?' she said, hesitant.

'Yeah,' he said.

She did a small smile.

Ruben thought how he'd like to take her for dinner and show her some of the places he loved in London. How he wanted to see her Shakespearean monologue on the Hove promenade and stand by her side ready to do open-hand combat with any nasty, spotty little teenagers. Ruben had dabbled in karate in his time. And if he could get out of this bloody ravine, he would even, if it was absolutely demanded of him, sample a plant-based meat substitute. And he would read – the classics if he must – so they could have meaningful conversations, and she could quote him as often as she quoted Shakespeare and Barry. He would let the stupid black cat sleep in the house. He would do better with recycling because that was what her generation was obsessed with. And air travel. And those tiny beads that fish eat in the ocean. Perhaps they could plant a tree or two together to offset his gallons of carbon. The world was opening up before his eyes. He was a de Lacy but it didn't mean he had to be that kind of de Lacy. He didn't have to perpetuate what went before. History repeats only through a lack of imagination. And who did he know with imagination? *Zadie*.

'Shall I go and get some help?' Zadie asked, starting to stand up.

'No! I don't want you to get lost again,' Ruben said, feeling the creep of parental selflessness.

But Zadie just laughed. 'I didn't get lost. I was on the phone. It's a straight path from here back to the house.'

Embarrassingly Ruben wasn't quite sure where he was, he'd stormed off in such a huff. 'Are you sure you'll be all right?'

Zadie nodded. 'Yes, Ruben, I'll be fine.'

'OK then,' he said.

As Ruben watched her go, it was on the tip of his tongue to say, you can call me Dad.

The sky got darker and darker. The moon a thin white slice above him. Ruben rested his forehead on the rock above where the little crab was wedged, waiting for Zadie to come back with a rescue team.

He stared at the crab's tiny claws hugged tightly to its body. 'What a fool your Uncle Ruben is.' He thought how he would like to curl up tight. Wedge himself in a rock and disappear. Then he realised that was exactly what had happened – bar the curling up bit – and it was bloody awful.

Just don't think about the tide, he told himself, don't think about it. He should have asked Zadie whether the sea was close enough to swell up under him in an underground cave. Was it his imagination or was the sound of the waves getting louder?

Think about something else, he told himself. But what could he think about? He thought about Olive. Her smile. Her laugh. There was no doubt about it, Ruben surrounded himself with yes women. The more they giggled at his jokes, the more he kept them in his life. But he was beginning to realise the value of a real, proper laugh. When earned from someone like Olive, it was worth ten thousand little giggles.

He thought about her face. The sharp angles of it. The statuesque beauty. You wouldn't call Olive pretty. You'd call her striking. But actually, he didn't really care. She could look like the back end of a bus and he'd still enjoy her company.

Would he?

He tried to imagine Olive really ugly.

No. He'd have to be marginally attracted to her.

He imagined her really old with no teeth and moles with hairs sticking out of them, and black hairs on her chin that she was too short-sighted to pluck. He'd pluck them for her, happily. *'Give me the tweezers, darling Olive, and let me pluck your chin hairs.'* That must be a sign of love.

Ruben grimaced. Love.

Interesting.

He looked up at the sky.

Not all black but dotted with a trillion tiny pinpricks of light.

He presumed Zadie and Marge were waiting for the others before launching a rescue plan. Were Dolly and Olive still out searching or had they given up, choosing instead to laugh at how old and bald and ugly he'd become? He was loath to admit it but he had the first sprouting of back hair. Imagine if Dolly had got a glimpse of that, how much worse her impression of him would have been?

Ruben frowned. Who would pluck his back hair when he was too decrepit to contort himself and the tweezers into position? Maybe he wouldn't need anyone to because he would be old and alone, having tried too hard to be young and single. Because, as Zadie had said, he *was* just a scared old – well, approaching middle-aged – man.

Oh Ruben. What would Stormzy think of you now? Dangling between two rocks, wedged by your thickening belly. He'd demand those tickets back.

'Shit!' he shouted.

The crab woke up and scuttled off.

'Don't go!' he called, reaching out to try and stop the little crab and inadvertently knocking it off the rock down into the black sea. 'Oh my God, I've killed it!' Ruben could hardly breathe for shock. Was it dead? He'd never know. And to his surprise and horror, he felt tears well up in his eyes. Warm and hot, the moisture unable to be repressed as it spilled over onto his cheeks. He wiped it away but it kept coming. More and more. Big, heaving sobs.

And, of course, he wasn't crying for the crab. But he was seeing himself shivering on a garden bench, still reeling from the shock of being exiled from his own home. He was wincing from the good hard slap round the face when he'd tried to stand tall at the orangery and defend his love for Olive, questioning how it was any different from the fresh revelation of his father's affair with Olive's mother. The collective shame when Lord de Lacy had sneered, 'She's nothing. Just a common slag.' The strength of his father's hand on his collar as he'd frogmarched him away like a prisoner. Watching, helpless, the vicious punch-up with Olive's father on the steps of the Big House when he'd demanded Lord de Lacy face him like a man. The doomed reunion with Olive at the cottage, 'I can't leave them now, Ruben.' Her mother catatonic. Dolly desperate. It was all so muddied with hysteria. 'I think it's probably for the best, anyway,' Olive had said, unable to quite meet his eye, his shocked pleading turning curt from battered pride. He saw himself waving goodbye to Geraldine, the de Lacy housekeeper, who made him shepherd's pie and had been the one to hug him tight when he'd cried as a little boy. His mother sat next to him in the Bentley as they drove away. Didn't even turn to look at the house. Staunch. No one mentioned the affair, brushed it under the carpet and set sail for new shores. He remembered looking at her thin, tanned arms and wondering if they had ever hugged anyone.

Ruben stared at the cold, grey rock. Tears streaming of their own accord down his cheeks. He saw his father in his suit on a bed of satin, the cold grey face of a stranger who somehow managed still to be disappointed even in death.

'Shit!' he shouted again. He really needed to broaden his swear words. What was it Tatiana from the spa always said? Holy moly. Ruben laughed. Then a sob. There was snot everywhere and tears. He didn't have a tissue. He used his hand. It was gross. He didn't care. He put his head back, looked up at the starry sky and wept quietly, bottom lip trembling like he was a six-year-old boy alone in his boarding school bedroom.

And what was it Zadie had said? That he was scared of being loved? No, he thought of all the cool stares of disdain, the sighs of irritation, it wasn't being loved he was afraid of – Christ, to be loved felt like the pinnacle. What he was afraid of, he realised, dangling alone in a ravine, was the crushing disappointment of wishing to be loved in return.

He was snapped out of his weeping reverie by icy water suddenly splashing at his ankles.

'Shit!' he cried. Then, 'Holy moly!' Then 'HELP!' at the top of his voice.

The tide was most definitely coming in and it was coming in fast. His feet were soaked.

Ruben was going to die.

He was going to drown slowly like they do in the movies, head tipped back as water slowly rose around his frantic pleas. They would find him when the tide receded, dangling like a fool and somehow prise his limp body out. How would they do it? Especially if rigor mortis set in. Would they pull him out with a crane? Or a crowbar. Oh, it was so depressingly mortifying. He imagined all the villagers coming out to look.

Jesus. This was no time for daydreaming about a humiliating death. This was real. It was dangerous. He didn't want to die. He was a man in his prime. He had a young daughter. He was a new father. How would the headlines refer to him? Successful businessman and father of one – it had a nice ring to it. Would he make the headlines? Focus!

'HELP!' he bellowed again. He had living still to do. He'd only just got the Aston Martin for Christ's sake.

The water was rising.

'Please, I don't want to die.'

He wanted to see Olive again, if only for her to berate him for his unfeeling behaviour.

Then he heard Zadie's little voice bellow, 'He's this way!' as she led the charge for the rescue. 'He's stuck down here!'

'Oh thank God!' Ruben cried, hands together in prayer at the sound of his daughter. 'Please, come quickly, the tide's coming in! I don't want to drown.' Ruben swiped at his tears with his hands. The water splashed against his legs. His overwrought brain almost delirious, expecting the end but fighting the finality. *To thine own self be true.* He didn't want to die. He wanted to be loved. He wanted to be a father. He wanted to see Olive again.

'Oh, for goodness sake!' The voice was distinctly lacking in emotion. Ruben opened one eye. There was Olive. 'What are you doing down there? You complete idiot. You could have died.' She was staring down the gap in the rocks, her hands on her hips.

'I could still die!' Ruben pleaded.

Olive rolled her eyes. 'You're not going to die.'

'But the tide!'

'Ruben, you're nowhere near the tide. You're stuck in a gap in the cliff.'

'But the water. I can feel it.'

'The water is from an overflow pipe off the fields.'

'Oh.' Ruben paused, he wiggled his leg; now she mentioned it, the water did seem to be coming from one particular source.

'Yes,' said Olive. 'Oh,' she sighed, 'how the hell are we going to get you out?'

Half an hour later, Ruben had a rope tied under his armpits. The rope had been sourced by Marge from one of the sheds, who was currently staring down at him with unconcealed amusement. Fox had tied a bowline before chucking the looped rope down for Ruben to pass over his head and arms. Just the simple fact Ruben didn't know how to tie such a knot himself added to his sense of humiliation and failure. Marge's chuckling further exacerbated the feeling.

'OK,' said Fox. 'The rope is secure, so you're not going anywhere, Ruben. I'm going to abseil round' – 'course he was, Ruben sighed – 'and free your stuck foot, then we're going to try and lift you out. That OK?'

Ruben nodded. 'Fine, mate.'

Fox winked and chucked him a thumbs-up.

Everyone seemed to be finding it all a jolly good laugh.

He could hear Dolly saying, 'You sure you're OK doing this?'

'It's what I'm trained for,' Fox replied gleefully. There was lots of clicking and unravelling and whatnot. Ruben imagined him knotting himself some expert climbing gear. Everyone would be very impressed.

He heard Olive say, 'Maybe we should just leave him there. Best place for him.'

Ruben's mouth fell open. He felt thoroughly sorry for himself. His shoulders sagged. Maybe they *should* just leave him there. Zadie hadn't even really looked at him, just focused on the rescue attempt. Ruben stared dejectedly at the craggy rock face when suddenly a familiar little shape scuttled past. 'Crab!' Ruben gasped.

There was the tiny green translucent crab, happily nestling itself into the crack in the rock. By all accounts it could be a completely different crustacean but Ruben wanted to – needed to – believe that this was his friend, returned in his hour of need. He could feel the tears again.

'Pull yourself together, Ruben! Can't keep blubbing like a baby,' he said to himself. But Crab ...

And then he heard a voice from above, Zadie's voice, cut through the melee, 'Don't say that, Olive.'

Ruben strained to hear over all the talking and shouting and general abseiling noise.

'You don't have to defend him, Zadie,' said Olive. 'He's been dreadful to you.'

'OK! Stand back!' he heard Dolly shout.

Be quiet, be quiet, he urged. Trying to hear Zadie's reply.

'... and my mum said, "Zadie! I told you Ruben's a prat. But you wanted him as a father and you can't pick and choose a parent," and when I said, "But he said he didn't want to be my dad," she said, "Zadie, I've never known you to give up so easily. I'm sure even Ruben has some good points. We all have our faults," and then she said some other things that I can't really remember. But she said, "You can't expect too much of people." Which is something that I know that I do. And she said, "Zadie, you know that's something you do." And she said, "Did you go in all guns blazing? I warned you this isn't a Disney film! You've got to give people a chance to change. You've waited all these years, are you really going to write him off this quickly? You're cleverer than that, Zadie, surely!" And I *am* cleverer than that and, I mean, I've had time to adjust to this. He's had like, no time at all.'

Ruben basked in the melody of her non-stop explanation. The irrational rationality of her reasoning. Her lyrical defence of his character. He allowed himself a small smile. He gave a nod of thanks to her mother, who he was going to have to work on getting onside asap.

Zadie was still talking. 'And then on the way here, Fox said there was this Tibetan proverb that went, "Nine times fail, nine times try again." And I kinda liked that. You know, however hard it gets, don't give up. I'd like to go to Tibet. Have you ever been to Tibet?'

Praise be to Fox.

Speak of the devil. 'All right, mate?' came Fox's dulcet tones from below him.

'Just dandy,' Ruben drawled wryly. He'd never say a bad word about this guy ever again. He was true hero.

Fox laughed. 'Hell of mess you've got yourself into.'

'Tell me about it,' said Ruben, closing his eyes with unmitigated relief as he felt Fox's big hands free his stuck foot. And above him he heard Zadie asking, 'Where even is Tibet?'

CHAPTER TWENTY-THREE

Olive had to admit she had drifted off a couple of times during Zadie's explanation as to why she'd forgiven Ruben. But it was heartening to see them now, Ruben all scratched and bruised – both in ego and body – with his arm wrapped tight around Zadie, her salty hair tickling his cheek as he rested it on her head, closed his tired eyes and said, 'I thought I was going to drown before being able to tell you properly how sorry I am.' Zadie's arms gripped tight around his waist like a toddler refusing to let go, so when they walked they walked as one, a three-legged race back to the Big House. Her grin as wide as anything Olive had ever seen. Victorious in her relentless campaign.

Later, when most people were in their rooms and Zadie was fast asleep, Olive went to sit in the garden on her own. She couldn't sleep, there was too much whirring in her brain. The dying embers of the fire pit glowed in front of her. She gazed, hypnotised, feeling strangely hollow. The feeling one gets from having wasted time.

She could tell by the tread of the footsteps behind her that it was Ruben coming to join her outside. She turned her head.

He was standing in the doorway with a tumbler of whisky in hand. 'Want one?' he asked.

She shrugged. 'OK.'

He poured her a glass and came and sat down. He smelt of lavender bubble bath. His hair was still damp. He was dressed in tracksuit bottoms and a T-shirt. More casual than she'd so far seen him.

She thanked him for the drink. Their eyes caught. Just for a fraction of a second in the glow of the sitting-room lights. Olive immediately looked away. Neither of them spoke. The silence became so entrenched it felt impossible to break. Olive didn't know what she wanted to say anyway.

Ruben chucked a handful of kindling on the fire pit and gave it a blow. Tiny flames started to lick. 'She's a good one to have in your corner – Zadie,' he said, coaxing the fire back to life.

'Yeah!' Olive laughed, surprised by the opener. 'You're damn lucky.'

He caught her eye and smiled, broad and cocky and perfect white teeth. Immediately Ruben. 'Forgiveness is a valuable trait, Olive.'

Olive arched a brow but didn't say anything.

Ruben looked down at the floor like a naughty schoolboy. 'I am sorry, you know. That I was such a prat with Zadie. It was unforgivable.' He looked up from under dark lashes, almost testing the water. 'Do you think it's unforgivable?'

Olive looked at him, face softening. She shook her head. 'Who am I to judge?' she said, 'especially in the face of Zadie's all-encompassing compassion.'

Ruben smiled, sat back in his chair. 'As I said, great one to have in one's corner.'

When Olive studied him closer, he looked tired. Bruised and scratched. His eyes were lined. He looked suddenly like he was stripped back to the Ruben of yore. He shifted position, wincing from the pain of various cuts and bruises. Having to move his leg with his hands because of the vicious wound on his ankle. In the end, he sat with one leg outstretched, the other bent and supporting his elbow. His chin resting on his palm. Like injury scaffolding. 'I think I got my punishment,' he said, glancing with wry amusement at all his ailments.

Olive laughed.

Ruben grinned like he'd scored a goal. Then he said, 'So what happened with you and Dolly?'

Olive looked down at her drink. 'She just showed me how much I did wrong. You know, back then.'

Without missing a beat, Ruben said, 'I thought you did amazingly.'

Olive glanced up. 'You did?'

'Hell yeah!' he laughed. 'Our families were a nightmare. Looking back, I don't know what world they lived in.'

Olive leant forward with her elbows on her knees and looked out at the dusky parkland ahead of them. 'This world,' she said. An owl hooted as if on cue. 'It wasn't real.'

Olive could just picture her mother and father walking arm in arm through their secret paths in the grounds. Happily oblivious to the hierarchy of the place. When they were together, when he was home, blissful in their bubble.

'I wouldn't have wanted to deal with your mum the way you did,' Ruben said. He looked at Olive, more serious now. 'It was like you got one side of her and all the rest of us got the other.'

Olive blew out a breath. 'I don't know, I don't think I was very patient. I really remember wanting to hit her more than once. One time specifically when she was moaning about her life, about my dad never being there. And now I just feel guilty because I know she was struggling. But living with her, it was like you're a rubbish truck and someone comes and empties all their rubbish in you and goes away happy, and there you are left with all the rubbish. Just churning it all up inside. That's what it was like. All the time here.' Olive glanced across at Ruben to check if he was judging her but he was just listening. She had a sudden memory of similar outpourings. Her pacing, him listening. 'God, this is what we used to do, isn't it? Me ranting on about my mother. No wonder we wanted to get away.'

Ruben laughed, eyes sparkling. 'Remember all those hours spent working out where we could go. Which countries we'd visit. Because stay here and we'd end up like them.'

She remembered the planning. Lying on a blanket in the orangery, his fingers toying with her hair, and she'd say something like, 'How about Greece?' And he'd say, 'Yep, Greece is good. Hot. Great food. Blue sea.' And she'd say, 'And me.' And he'd say, 'That's all I need.' She remembered the certainty of his voice, the smell of his skin, the security of him next to her. She remembered how talking to him was like talking to an exact equal – the very best friend she could have – who made her laugh, made her feel better. Made her feel worthy of her own emotions.

Olive glanced surreptitiously across at him now. His face relaxed, lacking in bravado. And she suddenly kicked herself for ever letting him go.

Ruben leant forward, swirled the whisky in his glass. 'I'm sad that I lost you as a friend,' he said.

Olive felt her whole body tense. 'Yeah?'

'Yeah,' he said. 'When I'm here, now, I don't only see the bad times.'

Olive pressed her lips together. She took a sip of her drink and it burnt her throat, made her wince. When she glanced up, he was still looking at her.

'I'm starting to see other stuff,' he said. 'I'm seeing everything I'd forgotten. My life here wasn't just about my hideous parents, it was … I don't know. I see myself with you—'

Olive felt a flicker in her chest. 'I see myself with you, too.'

Ruben kept looking at her. 'I really loved you, Olive.'

She felt her breath catch. She looked at him and remembered what it was like to really feel. To be in a place where someone could reach in and take your heart and wring it out. To be that vulnerable. She thought of all the years she'd spent with Mark and knew in that moment she had never been madly in love with him. She had sedately, safely, cared for him but they had called it love because that was the next logical relationship step.

She smiled a little shyly across at Ruben. 'I loved you, too.'

He said, 'You're right you know, we never could have made it.'

Olive felt her mouth open in surprise. 'Now who's being the pessimist!' she said, stupidly disappointed by his change of heart.

'It's not that.' He sat back in his chair, seemingly surveying her. 'It's because – whatever Dolly's saying now about things you did wrong – you were never the kind of person who would have left her. That's what I loved about you. Olive, nearly everything you did was to make sure they were all OK. If you'd left with me, you wouldn't have been you.'

Olive felt her whole body tingle. It was possibly the nicest thing anyone had said to her. 'Thanks, Ruben,' she said.

His eyes creased with a smile. 'You're welcome.'

Neither of them said anything. The dark sky encroached.

'So go on then,' he said, 'tell me about the clothes I'm going to buy that don't crease.'

She rolled her eyes, unable not to smile. 'You don't have to buy them because of me.'

'Of course I do.' Then he grinned. 'Actually, I'll let you into a secret. I already have the cashmere jumper.'

'You don't!' Olive couldn't believe how much the fact pleased her.

'I do.'

'And you like it?'

'It's a favourite,' he said.

She felt a bubble of pride join her unexpected pleasure. 'I actually think it might be time for me to move on from them. Do something new.'

'Sounds good,' he said, like it was as easy as that. She thought how with Mark the comment would have elicited a sucked-in breath, an expression of concern. 'Like what?' Ruben asked.

'Have you heard of eco nylon?'

Ruben laughed. 'Does that sound like something I would have heard of?'

'No.' She shook her head. 'It's fabric made of ocean plastic. It's generally turned into technical sportswear. I've got an idea for a range of athleisure and swimsuits and stuff. All ethical, all recycled.'

'Sounds amazing,' he said. 'I've got some contacts actually in the athleisure market.'

'I wouldn't want to sell my idea this time, though,' she said quickly.

Ruben made a face; she expected him to retaliate with the practicalities of big corporate investment. But instead he said, 'Absolutely not. You're the brand, Olive. You're the brains. You don't give that away. You need to learn your value.'

The words stopped her short. Her brain falling over itself at something so simple as someone's confidence in her. She found herself staring. Remembering what it was like to have a cheer-leader in life.

His mouth tipped up in a smile of recognition. Then he drained his glass and said, 'Do you think we'll ever have our time again, Olive?'

Olive was taken aback; he said it so casually that she felt confused as to what he was proposing – a quick fling or picking up where they left off, which in itself felt impossible. 'I have no idea,' she said, a little wary.

He nodded, then seemingly confirming asked, 'You don't think it's now though?'

She laughed at the prospect, imagining him quite happy with a quick shag for old time's sake. 'I don't think so, Ruben,' she said, serious Olive back in place, 'now you have to get to know your daughter and I have to sort my life out.'

'Yes.' He nodded, cocky, cool Ruben back in place. 'I completely agree.'

There was silence. Out in the far distance the sea glistened. The black cat stalked over and to its pleasure, Ruben reached down and gave it a scratch under its chin. When he glanced up at Olive, he was grinning. 'It wasn't a no, though.'

Olive rolled her eyes.

'That look, you see, that look has haunted me my whole life,' he laughed, gesturing to Olive's expression. The awkward, bittersweet tension broken. 'That look has guided most of my decisions, did you know that? It's why I bought the Aston Martin rather than a Porsche. Because of what you'd think.'

'I think they're both dreadful,' Olive replied.

Ruben laughed, loud and hearty. 'Yeah, I thought you might say that. Bit of artistic licence on that one. But admit that you'd think the Porsche was worse?'

'Without a shadow of a doubt,' she said, lips twitching into a grin.

Ruben sat back in his chair, pleased with himself. The cat stretched out by his feet. Olive sat back too, looking out at the dark silhouettes of the trees, still smiling.

She could sense Ruben glancing over occasionally to check she was still amused. It felt like old times. And with it came the forgotten feeling of never wanting something to end.

CHAPTER TWENTY-FOUR

Fox cooked scrambled eggs for breakfast. They all sat round the large wooden table in the kitchen and drank coffee and orange juice, the sun streaming in through unpolished windows. The journey felt like it was reaching its end and none of them really wanted to leave. All of them united suddenly as a team. Knowing that when the hunt ended, this would end. They would be closer but never this close. Never all eating together in this big house, searching for something, bonded by their exposed vulnerabilities.

Marge put her knife and fork together, dabbed her mouth with her napkin and said, 'Fabulous eggs, Badger.'

'Fox.'

'Of course it is, sorry, darling!' Marge laid a ring-clad hand on his in apology.

Fox gestured it was nothing. 'What's a mammal between friends?'

Marge guffawed. 'Oh Dolly, you have done well with this one!'

To which everyone round the table paused their eating and Dolly felt herself go all-over crimson. 'Marge!' she hissed, like she was a teenager.

'What?' Marge asked, unable to see what she could have possibly done wrong.

Fox chuckled.

Dolly refused to look at him. Instead she went, 'So come on, this clue? *"I am not gas but I have the power to burn. I am not liquid but I glisten like water. I am not solid but I crack under pressure. Find me and strike gold!"* What do we think? What's not a liquid, solid or a gas?' The subject hadn't been broached, almost because of its finality.

Ruben put down his coffee. 'I've got an idea what it is.'

Across the table, Olive frowned. 'What is it? Why haven't you said anything?'

He paused, seemed to think before going ahead. 'Glass is neither a liquid nor a solid. It remains part liquid even when cooled. I remember having to draw the molecules in physics.' He shrugged. 'I suppose boarding school was good for something.'

Dolly felt her face mirror Olive's. 'Glass,' she said quietly. 'A greenhouse. The orangery.' The one place they'd all avoided. Dolly shuddered internally. The vast, echoing orangery and all its snaking vines and secret hideaways encroached on her memory. The idea of her mother and Lord de Lacy somewhere entwined in the dark recesses. The scrambled eggs rose in her belly. She wondered if she might be sick.

But then Marge looked at them all, rolled up her sleeves and said sternly, 'Well, that's it then. What are we waiting for? Face it head-on. That's what we need to do. That's what they do in the military, isn't it, Fox? None of us here are afraid of ghosts, are we?'

Zadie said, 'I am a bit.'

'Nonsense,' said Marge. 'En masse we'll be fine. We're a team. We've got gold to find.'

Brambles and bindweed tangled round their ankles. Midges circled in clouds. The sun scorched as they traipsed through undergrowth in the direction of the now derelict hothouse.

They were all sweating. The heat was intensifying, the sun fierce overhead. Zadie trod in poo. Ruben got stung by something. Marge ruined her pristine pumps. A beetle got caught in Olive's hair. Dolly just felt her heart rate rise as they got closer to the looming glass structure.

Closer and closer they got. Ruben directing them to the shade of the trees. The undergrowth thick beneath their feet. And then as the sun sparkled like stars through the thick canopy, she saw it. There standing broken and dejected, much smaller than she had remembered, the ruined glasshouse. Tangled with creepers and ivy, reclaimed, barely recognisable.

Dolly was the first to walk into the space. The glass all smashed to the ground, the shelves for pots rotten and collapsed, the floor littered with kernels left by mice.

She turned to look at Olive and Ruben, who seemed equally lost for words. She could feel Fox watching her.

Olive said, 'It's nothing like I remember.'

Dolly shook her head. 'Me neither.' She almost wanted to laugh as the fear that had clutched at her loosened its grip.

Fox stood next to her and said under his breath, '*The more honest and open you are the less fear you'll have.*'

To his surprise, Dolly thwacked him in the belly. 'You are so smug! Can you give me this one thing without some bloody quote?'

Fox doubled over at the unexpected hit, laughing now. 'It's true though, isn't it?'

She mimicked him childishly, '*It's true though, isn't it?*'

'Dolly, you really need to move on from that kind of insult,' he said, but Dolly didn't reply. She found she had to walk away. Stalk off in mock rebuke to hide the fact her cheeks were pinking because when she'd punched Fox, her brain, for the first time, had noted the rock-hardness of his stomach, the dimple in his left cheek when he smiled and the unexpected pleasure she'd felt having him whisper insights so on point they nailed her emotions in one fell swoop.

Zadie, who was balancing on a low wall held together with moss and vine, said, 'It's fine here. I can't feel any ghosts.'

'No,' said Ruben, 'maybe they've all been put to rest.'

And Marge said, 'About bloody time.' Then turning away went to sit on the fallen log under the shade of a nearby oak tree. 'I need a little rest.'

Fox said, 'So shall we start looking?'

Dolly nodded, 'Let's go round the back.'

Olive and Ruben investigated the further reaches inside the building. Glass crunched underfoot. Ruben tried to jimmy up a flagstone with an old spade.

'Be careful,' Zadie called, balancing along the wall, then clearly got spooked and ran after them not wanting to be left alone.

Dolly and Fox circled the perimeter of the stone ruins. Vines matted like hair over the walls. A buzzing inferno of wasps fed off the rotting grapes.

They ripped down creepers, searching the ground for any clues or trap doors, anything where another clue or the treasure might be hidden. Dolly scratched in some disturbed earth but came away with nothing.

From over the wall Olive shouted, 'Have you found anything?'

'No!' Dolly called back. 'Have you?'

'Nothing.'

Dolly kicked a bit of old wood in frustration. Then she froze with the sharp shock of pain. 'I've been stung!' She winced, clutching her ankle.

Fox looked where she'd kicked. 'Bloody Hell, Dolly, it's a wasps' nest!' He dragged her away round the corner of the orangery while she tried to breathe through the burning sensation in her leg.

Fox bent down to have a proper look. 'Ouch.' Then he said, 'I've got some stuff for stings in the van.'

''Course you have,' said Dolly drily.

Fox said, 'If you don't want it, you don't have to have—'

'No, no, I want it,' said Dolly.

He started to walk away down the stony incline towards the house. Dolly limped behind, calling to Marge that they'd be back in a second.

'What are you doing?' Fox asked as he noticed her behind him.

'Coming with you,' she said.

'Why?' he asked.

'I don't know. I suppose I didn't want you to get lost or something to happen to you.'

Fox frowned. 'Really?'

'I know. Weird, huh.' They carried on a bit. 'I think it's because we're a team, you know? Aren't we? We've done everything together.'

'Dolly, you don't have to justify wanting to hang out with me,' Fox laughed, brazenly self-assured.

'You're the one who asked.'

'Yeah, but I didn't need an essay.'

Dolly bashed him on the back.

'Ow!' he laughed again.

Dolly laughed. She realised that somewhere along the line they had passed a point into the ease of friendship. She wondered if, had it not been this specific journey, whether she would ever have allowed it. How many people did she feel at ease with? Her mum. Marge. A couple of her friends. Maybe Olive after all this.

She paused to get her balance when some stones rolled under her feet. 'What do you think it will be like back at work?' she asked.

'If they take you back,' Fox replied.

'Oh thanks!'

He looked over his shoulder and winked. 'I'll put in a good word for you.'

Dolly rolled her eyes.

Fox saw. 'You can *not* deny that being with me has helped you.'

'I can deny it,' said Dolly as she shimmied down a slope of rubble, catching a frond of ivy to steady herself. Fox reached out to offer her a hand. She waved it away.

It was his turn to roll his eyes.

Then he stopped and turned so he was facing her. Hands on his hips, he said, 'Look me in the eye and say that your altercation with Olive yesterday wasn't better because of the time you've spent with me.'

Dolly looked him in the eye and said, 'My altercation with Olive wasn't better because of the time I've spent with you.' She tried not to smile. She'd told him about it when she'd got back to the house mainly because she'd wanted to prove to him that she could get control over her temper.

Fox sighed. 'You're so annoying. Without my influence, you'd have gone headlong into that argument and never calmed down for a second.'

Dolly tipped her head from side to side considering the fact. She knew he was right, she would never have paused. She would never have listened. But he was far too smug for her to admit it.

He was still watching her.

Dolly winced. 'I'm torn between not wanting to boost your ego and being grateful.'

'I'll take that as a thank you,' said Fox and carried on across the grass to where the van was parked up ahead.

Dolly followed on behind him. 'There's probably a Buddhist proverb for it. *"Pride be the enemy of gratitude."'* Dolly paused. 'Or *"Shame on the person who is too proud to see the truth"*. Hey, I'm quite good at this.'

'You're terrible at it,' said Fox without turning round.

Dolly snorted the ugliest laugh through her nose.

'What was that laugh?'

She shook her head, refusing to let her smile out. 'Nothing.'

He made a face, very dubious.

She had that same weightlessness she'd had when they'd returned from the waterfall. She felt like when she was a kid. Her laughs came easier. Her limbs – the ones that weren't recovering from dislocation – swung freer. When she prodded her mind for her anger she couldn't remember what it was for.

They reached the van. Fox opened the door and reached into one of his rucksack pockets for some sting relief cream.

'You don't carry that in your rucksack all the time, do you?'

Dolly leant against the side of the hot metal van, thinking how she hadn't thought about the sting on her ankle once.

'Always be prepared, Dolly,' he said, very pleased with himself as he also had some natty little tool with a sharp knife and scissors that could cut through the orangery vines.

Dolly watched him gathering his survival bits together as she rubbed the cream into her leg, his big hands unzipping various pockets in his rucksack, rooting around for other items of use, and she felt a sudden, uncontrollable urge to throw her arms around him. To hug him tight to herself and claim him as her own. She didn't want anyone else to have this special, kind, funny person who carried After Bite and a snazzy souped-up penknife with him everywhere he went. She wanted to box him up and keep him for herself.

'What?' asked Fox.

Dolly stood up straight, handing him the tube of cream. 'Nothing,' she said, and they walked back across the park to the orangery.

There was a haze in the air. A midmorning light that felt it would never dim. That evening would never come. The heather was alive with bees. The cerulean sky echoed the sea. The luminescent clouds drifted like grazing sheep.

Dolly distracted herself with the task of yanking down vines.

Don't think about him, she warned herself, hauling a matted section away from one corner of the property to reveal even more densely criss-crossed roots and tendrils. Fox was up at the entrance working on a mass of ivy. Across from her, Ruben and Zadie were lifting flagstones, one after the other, finding ants' nests and fat worms.

'Found anything?' Dolly asked.

'Nothing,' Ruben replied. Then he straightened up, rubbing his back like all the lifting was strenuous work. 'You're the policewoman, shouldn't you be able to detect things like this?'

'Well, I'm not a very good one,' said Dolly, practically hanging off the matted vines.

Zadie was quick to disagree. 'Fox said you were a great policewoman.'

Dolly paused. She felt herself blushing. 'Did Fox say that?'

She saw Ruben clock her expression with interest. She remembered how desperate she had been to prove herself to him. For him to fall at her feet in awe of her adult self. And he had done just that when she'd arrived. Yet far more significant was this tiny scrap of compliment that Fox had paid off the cuff about her ability to do her job.

'He said you were unique,' said Zadie. 'A maverick.'

Dolly felt herself deflate. 'I'm not sure they're compliments, Zadie. I think they might just be polite ways of saying I'm not so great.'

'Oh no.' Zadie shook her head. 'No, they absolutely weren't. He was using you as an example to me about the power of being yourself. They were totally compliments,' she added. 'Well to me they were. I'd love someone to call me unique.' She grinned, stretching out her arms. '*Zadie, you are unique* …' she said in the over-the-top theatrical tones of a potential stage suitor. Then back to her normal self she added, 'Who wouldn't want to be unique?' as if anything but was preposterous. 'Come on, Dad – I mean, Ruben – we should try lifting the ones over there.'

Ruben followed behind her, bewildered by the little

firecracker now ruling his life. 'I completely agree,' he said to Dolly over his shoulder as he was dragged away.

Dolly stayed where she was, holding her bundle of vines, not sure what to do next. She could hear Zadie in the distance saying, 'Is it too soon still for me to call you Dad?' And Ruben's voice, 'No, no, I'd like it if you called me Dad ...'

Alone, she replayed the chat about Fox in her head. She could feel her blood rise from her toes up through her body. Her fingers start to tingle. Her cheeks blush with excitement.

He thought she was unique.

Zadie was right. There could be nothing better. She *was* a great policewoman – if a little hot-headed. She was a maverick. She was strong and tough and could box like a champ – although not as well as Fox but there was still time. She could keep pot plants alive. She could coax a confession out of her sister. She could, if Fox hadn't done it for her, pop her own shoulder back into its socket. And if she could do all those things, she could damn well admit to herself how she felt about Fox.

Whether she could admit it to him was another matter.

She started to walk a little faster to where he was at the front of the orangery. 'I like you,' she tried. 'I really like you.' She screwed up her face. 'I think I like you more than I thought I liked you.' She was getting closer. *'The woman who doesn't confess her feelings is alone forever.'* She bit her lip. Come on, Dolly, you can do this. Her heart was beating so fast she worried it might burst out of her chest.

But as she neared the front doorway something was happening. Olive and Fox were prising open a small manhole next to the entrance. Fox was holding the heavy lid, laughing as Olive reached inside, grimacing at the smell and the grime. Dolly watched as she fumbled around. 'Anything?' Fox asked.

Olive said, 'No,' pulling back so Fox could drop the heavy manhole cover with a thump. Olive put her hand on his arm. 'Nice try,' she said.

Fox's eyes were alight. 'I really thought we had something there.' He brushed some dirt off Olive's T-shirt.

Dolly found herself watching in horror. She could feel her confidence wane as she watched the easy camaraderie between them. It wasn't so much a jealous fear that something might happen between the two of them – but then, who wasn't charmed by Olive? – it was the foolish feeling that she, Dolly, was something special. When he was like this with everyone. That was why everyone liked him! He was the great Fox Mason. Her boss. Her mantra-prone mentor. He'd be all, *Love exists boundless within us and can not be confined* or some other mumbo jumbo to let her down gently. She had fallen for it – believed herself, in his eyes, to be different, when he was all about the job. Oh, it was so embarrassing. The idea of them going back to work an item was laughable. She blew out a breath, *Lucky save, Dolly*. She felt foolish for even thinking she could march up and tell him how she felt.

Fox glanced over and noticed her standing there. 'Find anything?' he asked.

Dolly shook her head. 'No,' she said, unable to work out what else to say, where else to go. Standing like a lemon when she should have sauntered away. She felt upended by disappointment.

Fox's forehead furrowed as he studied her.

Next to him, Olive said, 'I'm going to go and look over there.'

'OK,' he replied, 'I'll be over in a sec.' Then he ambled cautiously over to where Dolly still hadn't moved, her brain pulling her in one direction, her body in another, the result locking her into place.

When he got level with her, Fox said, 'What's the matter?'

'Nothing,' Dolly replied flatly.

Fox laughed. 'Yes there is.'

'No there's not.'

Fox frowned at her, trying to decipher her expression. She felt like he was trying to say something to her with a look. Like his eyes were speaking. But then suddenly she was fourteen again, watching Ruben putting baby birds into a nest, misreading signals, wondering if the look in his eyes matched the look in her own. So she looked away.

Fox sighed.

Dolly glanced back. Did he just sigh? In annoyance or disappointment? She tried to think like him. All his negotiator stuff. Fox wasn't a sigher. Only when things got really bad. As he said himself, he was controlled. He didn't look controlled now. His brow creased, his eyes dark with what looked definitely like annoyance. His eyes were normally wide and welcoming.

He was looking around, surveying the area. 'I don't think there's any treasure here,' he said with none of his usual verve.

Dolly tipped her head, taking in the downturn of his mouth, the defeat in the drop of his shoulders. How do you know when something's not right? Compare it to how they are normally. 'You don't think there's any treasure here?'

He turned to look at her with a shrug. 'Not gold anyway.'

Dolly didn't know if he was talking in some secret code

or not, but the way he said it made her fingers start to tingle and her heart thump hard in her chest. She stared as hard as she could into his eyes, looking for something, some real, concrete sign, but she couldn't tell. She couldn't be certain. But then she figured, maybe the fact he wasn't looking away was the sign, and she knew it was now or never. Nothing would ever be concrete. Without allowing herself to think of the consequences, she reached up, put her hand on the back of his neck so she could pull him towards her and she kissed him with every breath she had in her being. Her bad arm pressed between them, her shoulder screaming, but she didn't let him go. His mouth, his smell, his skin, all locked with hers. Like everything her teenage-self had hoped for in a kiss. And even if he pushed her away, she didn't care, because she had done what she thought she would never do again. Acted on instinct, taken the first step. She didn't breathe. She had her eyes squeezed tight. If this was it, it was enough. She had tried. She had shown herself to care.

She felt his surprise. The momentary instinct to jerk back. But then she felt his hand as it touched softly to her waist. His fingers spread, warm and solid against the fabric of her T-shirt. And then his other hand moved to the other side of her waist and still she feared that now he would set her away. But instead he moved her slightly to the side so there was no pressure on her dislocated arm, then he reached a hand to her hair and stroked it through his fingers like he'd wanted to for weeks. And she felt herself relax a fraction, loosened her grip on the back of his neck. He was free, if he wanted to go.

But he stayed.

And finally she breathed.

Then she heard Zadie's voice say, 'Ooooh, look, Dolly and Fox are snogging!'

And she felt his mouth smile on hers. She moved away so her forehead pressed against his collarbone and she breathed again. Inhaling the calm safety of him. And he stroked her hair.

Then she looked up into his dark black smiling eyes. And he looked down into her beaming blue ones and said, 'Christ, it's about time. I've wanted that to happen since I first met you.'

'You have?' Dolly pulled away with surprise. 'Why didn't you say anything?'

'Because I had to let you realise it for yourself.'

Dolly closed her eyes and leant her forehead to his chest. 'How can you manage to get the upper hand even now?'

Fox laughed. 'Because I'm Fox Mason. That's what I do.'

Dolly looked up at him, eyes narrowed. 'Except I saw the nametag in your backpack, Mason. I know that's not your real name.'

For the first time Fox looked a little caught off-guard. His grip loosening slightly on her waist.

Dolly licked her lips, smugly satisfied. 'You're a big fat liar, *Algernon* Mason.'

'Sssh!' Fox tried to silence her. 'No one calls me Algernon.'

'I'm not surprised!' Dolly laughed.

Fox blushed, it was his turn to hide his face on her shoulder.

'Yes,' Dolly whooped with a snigger. 'Finally, I have the upper hand!'

To shut her up, Fox kissed her. Hard and powerful, engulfing her smugness.

When Dolly pulled away, almost giddy with glee and

endorphins, she said, 'You can't silence someone by kissing them. What would Buddha think?'

Fox thought for a second. 'I don't think he'd mind. He was a fan of seizing the moment: "*For who can say for sure that one will live to see tomorrow?*"'

Dolly groaned. 'You could use that about anything! I think you pull any old proverb out to justify the means.'

Fox just kissed her again by way of response.

Dolly pulled back a third time. 'So where did you get Fox from?'

'An accidental drunken tattoo.'

Dolly snorted. 'So you do make mistakes!' she said, unable to hide her pleasure at the fact.

'Yes, Dolly, I make mistakes. Can we get on with the kissing now?'

'Certainly.'

CHAPTER TWENTY-FIVE

Olive watched Dolly and Fox with a little tear in her eye.

'That's sweet,' said Ruben.

'Yes,' she replied, unable to believe quite how emotional she was becoming. She supposed once you opened the gates a touch, it all came flooding in.

The fight with the vines and the ivy was becoming more half-hearted. Everyone was tired and hungry and the sun was only getting hotter. Even the previously indefatigable Zadie sat slumped on a fallen column and said, 'It's hopeless.'

Olive couldn't deny it. She was about to suggest they give up and go back to the house when her phone rang.

Marge perked up. 'How have you got reception? I didn't know there was reception here. Oh goodness, I have reception too. How fun.'

Olive looked at her screen. Mark.

She moved away from the others. 'Hello.'

Mark didn't say hello, instead he just said, 'Olive, I think I made a mistake.'

Olive frowned. 'What do you mean a mistake?'

'I mean what we had was good and solid and I've ruined it.'

Olive found she didn't even need to think about it before

replying. 'No Mark, you didn't make a mistake. What we had was lovely but it was holding us back.'

'No, no I don't think it was. It's different with Barbara. Olive, I'm a mess, I don't know if I'm coming or going.'

Olive smiled into the phone. 'I think that's how it's meant to be, Mark.' She felt so completely removed from him that it was hard to believe how long they had been together. She felt so platonically about him that it was like she was giving her brother or an old friend relationship advice. 'You've got something good now with Barbara.'

'I don't know, Olive. We argue more and she doesn't think the same as I do.'

As Olive listened, the warm sun on her face, she said, 'Mark, I didn't think the same way as you either. And we didn't argue because neither of us were saying what we really wanted. What you've got now, I don't know, it might not work, but at least it's real.'

He started to speak again but Olive realised they were completely wasted words. 'Mark,' she said, 'we're not going to be together again.'

He stopped talking.

There was an awkward silence.

Olive looked around at the derelict orangery then she said, 'Mark, can anything be a liquid, gas and solid at the same time?'

And Mark said, 'Well not many things. In thermodynamics it's called the triple point.' This was his favourite kind of conversation. 'So there's a liquid called cyclohexane that can be all three states of matter but under very specific conditions. Do you know, actually Barbara was working on something …'

Olive listened to what Barbara was working on. She said

that all sounded very interesting. Mark said that yes it was. And Olive said, 'I think you and Barbara sound like a very good match.' And Mark said, 'I'm not sure you're meant to be the one persuading me into my relationship.'

And Olive said, 'I want you to be happy.'

'But not with you,' Mark said.

'You wouldn't be happy with me,' Olive replied, and when she hung up she looked at the blank phone screen for a second and felt the slightly terrifying feeling of freedom.

Ruben was waiting by the orangery entrance. 'All OK?' he asked.

Olive nodded. 'Yes,' she said. 'Yeah, good actually.'

He tipped his head like he was happy for her.

She found she wanted to tell him all about it but instead she focused on the search. 'OK. We need to think about this differently,' she said.

Ruben said, 'We need to think about it like your dad.'

'Yes!' said Olive. 'Yes, we need to think about him. What he was thinking. He'd just come back and he'd supposedly hit the jackpot. He'd be what? Feeling jolly?'

'Cheeky?' proffered Ruben.

'I don't think he was ever cheeky.'

'No.'

Olive suddenly had the image of her dad with his gold, hiding it somewhere, waiting expectantly for the big reveal. Adrenaline high. Excited. And then crash, the hideous disappointment and horror that followed.

'Don't think about it,' said Ruben, like he could read her mind. 'Stick to the bit before that.'

Olive glanced up with surprise. He winked. She smiled down at the dusty floor.

'Come on,' said Ruben, 'he's found treasure, what's he thinking?'

'He's thinking, there's no such thing as buried treasure. You want something in life, you have to go looking for it. X never marks the spot.'

Ruben nodded, remembering the stories himself. 'Yet he'd already done the hard work.'

'So X *could* mark the spot,' said Olive.

Ruben spun around. 'OK everyone, we're looking for an X!'

Dolly and Fox appeared. 'What do you mean an X?' Dolly asked, her hand wrapped tight in Fox's.

'X marks the spot,' said Olive. 'Some kind of cross.'

'OK,' said Fox. This was his kind of thing. 'Let's get to it.'

Even Marge got involved.

Everyone ripping down vines, sweeping paving stones, lifting fallen benches to spot any kind of marking.

Olive and Ruben worked in a frenzy side by side, clearing and hauling away debris. Like finding the X meant more than just treasure. It proved a point, somehow. Maybe of how well they worked together.

But it was Zadie who found it. Having climbed up onto a high windowsill she shouted, 'Look, look, it's there. The sun on the back wall!'

They all stopped what they were doing to look. Like some pagan trick of the light, when the sun refracted through the panel of glass in the top section of the building it made a shimmering X on the brickwork at the back.

Ruben frowned. 'It's bloody lucky that bit of glass is still there!'

Olive said, 'We haven't found it yet.'

'True.'

They walked towards the back wall. Just before they got there, Ruben said, 'I wasn't being flippant, you know, last night. I may have come across as flippant but I assure you I wasn't.'

Olive swallowed. 'I didn't think you were flippant.'

Ruben's mouth spread into a grin, 'Yes you did.'

She couldn't reply because Dolly and Fox had jogged to join them, followed by Marge and Zadie.

Olive ran her hand over the bricks touched by the shimmering light, then moved to others that she knew would be lit at different times of the day until she found one that was loose. She looked back at the others. 'I think it's this one.'

'Take it out then,' Dolly urged.

Olive gently pulled out the brick, slightly concerned the whole remaining structure might topple. Then she reached into the dark space left behind. When she withdrew her hand, in it she was holding a gleaming nugget of gold, about the size of her palm.

'Holy moly,' said Ruben.

Dolly laughed.

Marge whistled.

Olive turned the gold over in her palm. She had an urge to drop it. It felt gaudy and grotesque. She wondered how something so small in the scheme of things had caused so much trouble. Set so much in motion. While the others watched in gleeful astonishment, all Olive could think of was the bittersweetness of the victory; if only they had found it twenty years ago. If only it had never been hidden in the first place. All the alternative pasts offered by this lump of shiny metal.

But then Ruben caught her eye and said, 'Reckon your dad would tell you a chunk of that would be enough to start a new business with.'

Olive frowned back at the mottled gold. She imagined her dad watching them find it. Chuffed with his final hiding place. It occurred to her then that he would be as gutted as she was by the way things turned out. But, she realised, how proud – maybe even relieved – he would be that he had left them with this glinting treasure and all its possibilities.

Dolly plucked the gold from her hand, weighing it up with giddy excitement.

Olive looked at Ruben, 'Thanks,' she said, and he said, 'You're welcome,' knowing her too well, even after all this time, to have to say, 'What for?'

CHAPTER TWENTY-SIX

The various cars were all packed. Everyone had said their goodbyes. Ruben and Zadie were staying on till Zadie's mum came to pick her up. Fox and Dolly were entrusted with the gold and were heading off on a road trip to get it valued and sold.

Aunt Marge and Olive were about to head off in their respective vehicles when Aunt Marge said, 'How about one last turn of the estate?' And Olive said, 'All right.'

It was a clear, bright day. Not too hot, not too cold. Marge was dressed in leopard-print Gucci leggings and a red diamanté T-shirt. 'I think I'll spend my cut of the gold on a cruise. What do you think?'

Olive said, 'I think you'd get bored on a cruise.'

Aunt Marge thought for a second, her arm linked through Olive's. 'Yes, you might be right. Maybe I'll go to Vegas. Blow it all on slot machines and bag myself a beefcake, like Dolly.' She guffawed.

The lawn was almost emerald in the sunlight. The sea in the distance a swathe of turquoise.

Marge said, 'So what about you and Ruben, then?'

Olive could feel her aunt's beady, gossipy gaze. 'Oh nothing,' she said. 'I think we've got enough to deal with at the moment.'

Marge blew out a breath like a horse. 'Fiddlesticks.'

'I'm serious.'

They paused together at the top of the slope that led down to the potting shed and the polytunnels. Terence, the groundsman, was cleaning his Land Rover. He looked up when he saw someone watching and waved. Marge waved back. 'At last,' she said under her breath. 'That's who I'm here for.'

'What do you mean?' said Olive. 'I thought you came for us?'

Marge said, 'Well I did. But he's always been such a dish – and ever since his widower status came up on Facebook a couple of years ago, I've been dying to get back here. Got to take it when you can get it, don't you?' she sniggered. Then she shouted down at Terence, 'Terence! How are you? Marge King, remember me? Do you want to make me a cup of tea?'

He seemed a little taken aback, then did a thumbs-up.

Marge clapped gleefully. 'Excellent. Put the kettle on, I'll be right there!'

Olive looked across at her aunt, her satisfied grin and her red hair glowing in the sunlight. 'Thank you, by the way,' she said.

Marge's forehead creased. 'Whatever for?'

'For everything. For the chat the other day. For taking us in. For putting up with us. For shopping Dolly to the police.' Marge rolled her eyes at that memory. 'You had a life of your own and you didn't have to take us in. And we didn't make it easy for you, I know that. So thank you.'

'Oh, tush,' Marge gave her a little bash on the arm, 'Seriously, don't think too highly of me, I *am* only here for the hunky gardener.' She tried to make light of it, but Olive could see the flush of pride on her face at the unexpected recognition.

'Well thanks anyway,' Olive said, reaching over to give her a hug round the shoulders.

Marge gripped tight to Olive's hand and gave it a squeeze. Then before she went to get her cup of tea with Terence, she turned and, holding Olive's cheeks between her hands, said, 'You can't control life, Olive darling. You just have to live it. No one knows what the future holds so you must grasp every opportunity. Look at me, I live every day as if it's my last and I'm fabulous.' She spread her arms wide and declared, 'The world is chaos. Olive King is not going to change that.' Then she trotted off down the hill, a massive grin on her face.

Olive left Marge and started to walk back to her car. The fox darted across her path into the undergrowth. A hawk hovered in the distance. She strolled without thinking, her mind on autopilot, aware of every twist and turn like muscle memory. But obviously her memory wasn't quite as good as she thought because she took a wrong turn somewhere and ended up by the lake and the Diana fountain. Ahead of her was the Big House. She walked on, past the statue, in the direction of the house, then stopped abruptly.

She took a step back so she could see Diana's face and suddenly saw herself clinging onto the statue, dripping wet in just her underwear.

She stood for what seemed like hours. Time morphing around her. She felt Marge's hand on her cheek. She saw Dolly throwing her arms round Fox. She saw Zadie calling down to Ruben in the crevice of the rock. She saw her dad gleefully planting clues with an old sea dog in the Hope and Anchor. She saw her mother in the living room, dancing to Christmas music with a crown of ivy in her hair and a wide white-toothed grin on her face.

She remembered the feeling inside her when Ruben said, 'I did love you.' The free-falling terror of excitement.

She leant on the edge of the lake and looked down at her reflection – her hair loose from its ponytail, her face a little freckled from the sun, her shoulders lightly tanned.

'I thought you'd gone?'

She looked up to see Ruben walking towards her, wearing blue jeans and a T-shirt, hair still wet from the shower.

'No,' she said.

He paused at the other side of the water. 'What are you doing?' he asked, dark brows drawn together, inquiring.

'Thinking,' she said, standing up, tucking her hair behind her ear, looking across at him over the water. Feeling sixteen. Gauche and faux-confident.

She saw his eyes narrow slightly, thick, dark lashes. She saw his expression change ever so slightly as if something might be dawning on him. Something that may or may not be true. 'What are you thinking about?' he asked, almost wary, possibly allowing himself to hope as he started to walk towards her round the lake.

Olive felt herself trying but failing to hold in a smile as she skirted the stone wall to close the gap. When she got within touching distance of him, her heart thrumming with possibility, she said, 'I'm thinking that maybe now might be exactly our time.'

ACKNOWLEDGEMENTS

Thanks go, as always, to my editor Kate Mills for her brilliant ability and determination to ensure books are always the best they can be. Thanks also to Melanie Hayes who worked on *One Lucky Summer* with such enthusiasm and a fantastic editorial eye. The whole team at HQ – Editorial, Design, Production, Marketing & PR, Sales – have worked so hard through a really difficult year and I thank and admire them for it. And of course, thanks go to my fab agent, Rebecca Ritchie. Lastly, thank you to all the readers who will hopefully take a well-earned break and enjoy a book in the sunshine.

ONE PLACE. MANY STORIES

Bold, Innovative and
empowering publishing.

FOLLOW US ON:

@HQStories